Jury Rig

a novel by Jason Phillip Reeser

First Edition, Feb 2012

Cover Illustration and Design by Kathryn Reeser

ISBN:978-0615593289

Rocket Fire Books
Westlake, Louisiana
editor@rocketfirebooks.com

Dramatis Personae

The Passengers:

Barry Alum—A street-smart business man who, by his own efforts, is both wealthy and a bore.

Ida Claire—A woman who never married a man she didn't bury. She is traveling with her sister.

Mrs. Kaufman—Ida's sister, who's never quite sure of what's going on in her life, but then again, do any of us?

Fanny Odston—A tough cookie that is hell-bent on taking her husband on a vacation, even if it kills him.

Wavel Odston—A retiree who can neither afford this vacation nor talk Fanny out of taking it.

George Sherman—A gentleman from Atlanta who knows how to treat a lady, her husband, and the world at large.

Martin Vale—As the owner of *The Jenny*, he fervently hopes the trip will be a success and that just maybe, his wife will enjoy it enough to leave him alone.

Cora Vale—The stay-at-home alcoholic who can't, for the life of her, remember why she married her husband or the vows she once made to him.

The Crew of *The Jenny*:

Captain Sloe—An amiable father to his crew, as

well as the childish passengers under his care.

Never Gamble—The steward who just wants to see that everything is done right with as little pain and injury as possible.

Tom—The porter, who just wants to do his job and help everyone, but most especially the girl of his dreams.

Alice—A pleasant, quiet girl who just happens to clean up after everyone.

Melvin—*The Jenny's* elderly pilot who minds his own business as well as he handles a boat.

Bob—A cook we know very little about. And he'd like to keep it that way.

<u>The Pirates:</u>

Captain Robert Montane—A man who understands just how unforgiving the world of pirates can be, but knows the world at large can be even more so.

David Wayne—Montane's Priest, whose radical ideas may just be the death his acolyte.

Hamlet and **Matvie**—Two pirates who are willing to sacrifice everything for their Captain.

Lear, Macbeth, and **Othello**—A trio of unstable pirates who not only scare the passengers, but anyone else who's ever met them.

Castle, Kit, and **The Old Man**—Men who are just trying to keep their heads above water in a trade that doesn't have the greatest job security.

TABLE OF CONTENTS

It is a very delicate job to forgive a man,
without lowering him in his estimation,
and yours too.
--- *Josh Billings*

It is very easy to forgive others their mistakes.
It takes more gut and gumption to forgive them
for having witnessed your own.
--- *Jessamyn West*

If I die, I forgive you;
if I recover, we shall see.
--- *Spanish Proverb*

This novel is for my children:
Alex, John, Kathryn, Maxwell, and Simon.
Forgive me this farce

Chapter One

The Jenny Goes to Sea

Fanny Odston snapped shut her pink, shell-shaped makeup mirror and cursed her husband.

"I said you'd make us late, Wavel." She placed the mirror in her purse and withdrew a cigarette in an ebony holder like a magician pulling a rabbit out of a hat. At the same time, she paced crisply along the paved quayside in her three-inch heels, stopping every so often to spin back in the direction of her husband. "I said, 'Take me to Europe", that's all I said. A simple request. Nothing complicated. What could be simpler? How could you foul this up?"

"You changed your mind and said you wanted a cruise," came his even reply.

"Wavel, if I had changed my mind, I would have known about it. Where are we anyway? This place smells like fish."

"A quay. A boat dock, Love."

"That has nothing to do with anything. Don't try to change the subject. I don't just walk around changing my mind. I wanted to go to Europe."

"I've arranged something better than that, I told you. We're taking a semi-private yacht. You were well aware of this, and you agreed to the whole idea. You're just nervous, and a bit upset. You will be fine."

Their banter went on like this for several more minutes. They were an older couple; he in his sixties, she in her fifties. As a rule, she never stopped talking. He never passed up a gentle retort.

Fanny Odston had a square jaw and high cheekbones. Thinly-drawn lips and deep-set eyes gave her a dried-out look. Her scarlet hair sat atop her head in a bobbed cut that would have been more appropriate on a school girl. She was wearing a high-collared, white blouse with lace on the front and a gray polyester jacket that matched her knee length skirt. A wide black belt, held tightly with a white plastic buckle, wrapped her nearly-nonexistent waist.

Her husband Wavel wore a soft yellow cabana shirt with pearl white buttons and a pair of khaki pants. He had the look of a man dressed for vacation who would have been more comfortable in a business suit, absentmindedly attempting to brush back his missing suit coat in order to stick his hands in his pants pockets.

Wavel was a good ten years older than Fanny. He was not a round man, but he had been slowly gaining on that label for some time. His hair had long ago turned white, and it now formed only a soft ring around the back of his head. He had kind eyes and wore wire-rimmed glasses, the better to see his lovely Fanny by.

"At any rate, Wavel, we've missed the ship. It won't be fine."

"We haven't missed the *yacht*. She's just coming in. That's her now, just passing the outer buoy."

Wavel and Fanny Odston were loaded, along with their luggage, within the hour. They were aboard *The Jenny*, a fine old sloop dating back to the carefree travel era of the early 20th century. Golden brown teakwood decks lay across a gleaming white hull. She had recently been beautifully restored. The restoration had included the large, single funnel for her steam engine, although the boat's propulsion had been converted to diesel years ago. The jet black funnel maintained its distinguished silhouette of that bygone era. To the funnel's great dismay, those in charge of the restoration had decided to turn it into a top deck storage closet.

Her captain, a short man with an open, cheerful face, welcomed the Odstons aboard.

"Are all your things aboard?" he asked. It seemed a superfluous question, considering the large amount of trunks and bags piled about the Odston's feet, but he felt it necessary.

"Yes, thank you Captain..." Wavel paused, waiting for the Captain to supply his name by way of introduction.

"Captain Sloe. And I want only to make certain you receive the best service possible from my crew. My steward, Mr. Gamble, will show you to your stateroom. If there is anything else we can do...well, enjoy yourselves."

Mr. Gamble did indeed show them to their stateroom. He was most helpful.

"You should know that although the rooms are a bit small, you will find plenty of space for... clothes, articles of clothing—all manner of garments will fit, you know. The closets—two of them at both ends of the room. That sounds as if I mean there are four of them. There are two closets, *one* at each end of the room. Plenty of drawers, well anyway. As you can see," Mr. Gamble stopped mid-sentence and cocked his head, exclaiming "Excuse me, just a moment," and left the room.

"What was that?" Fanny stared at the doorway, now empty.

"The steward, Fanny."

"I'm not an idiot, Wavel. What was *that* all about? *All manner of garments*? He seemed completely unbalanced."

"Nervous—not unbalanced."

The steward stepped back into the room.

"I'm sorry. Now, there's really nothing more, unless you have questions."

"Young man, will our cell phones work on this ship?"

"They won't work on the yacht, not once we are out to sea, ma'am. There is a satellite phone reserved for extreme emergencies." Fanny cast an irritated look at her husband. The steward smiled, and then frowned. "Yes, I forgot to say... well we have a safe—a hidden safe. If you have any valuables; jewelry, currency, anything... valuable, you are encouraged to place them in our keeping. The safe is well hidden, I assure you."

"Whatever for?" Fanny asked incredulously. "Why would you hide a safe on this ship?"

"Yacht, Ma'am. And you can't be too careful."

"About what? Just what types of passengers are traveling with us?"

"I wasn't speaking of the passengers. There are only eight of them, and with the crew and captain there are a total of 16 souls, all of reputable character. I only meant there are always dangers."

"Like what, Mr. Gamble?" Wavel asked pointedly. "What dangers did you have in mind?"

"I didn't... only, I was merely—theoretically—speaking of... dangers."

"That's broad, isn't it?" Fanny scoffed. "Name one danger for which I would need to lock up my jewelry in a hidden safe."

The steward stood silent, weighing his answer with care. He pulled at his ear, then ran his hand over his upper lip. Taking a deep breath, he finally spoke.

"Pirates?" he suggested.

Wavel eyed the steward silently as Fanny's face set like concrete.

"I will look after my own valuables, Mr. Gamble."

"Very well, ma'am."

Mr. Gamble hurried along the cabin passage speaking to himself just above a whisper.

"Pirates! Why did I say *Pirates*? I'm certain I looked like an idiot. Not that I should care, really. I don't give a nit what the Odston's think of me. Why should I? It's no good worrying what passengers think of me—anyone, for that matter. Everyone's always taken me for a fool. I'm not a fool. I'm not!"

The steward ascended a short staircase at the end of the passage and pushed open a door that opened onto the deck of *The Jenny*. He continued to jabber aloud to himself as he passed a small group of passengers consisting of three men and two ladies.

"Who is that?" asked one of the ladies, an unremarkable woman with a face no one ever remembered.

"That is the steward, Mrs. Kaufmann." Martin Vale, majority owner of *The Jenny's* operating company, knew the details of every member of the crew. "He's a good steward, no matter that he's a fool."

"What's his name?"

"Never Gamble."

The remaining two men laughed appreciatively.

"What do you mean, Mr. Vale?" The second lady, Mrs. Kaufmann's sister, Ida Claire, wrinkled her already lined face as she tried to understand what was being said.

"That's his name—Never Gamble."

"Oh, God forgive those people. I can't abide when people try to be cute with their children's names. Does anyone ever think of the poor child?"

"Ida, your parents weren't thinking of you, I suppose?" Vale smiled mischievously.

"Claire is my married name." Ida stiffened at the slight jest, "besides, Ida is a perfectly acceptable Christian name. Who ever thought of naming someone 'Never'?"

"*I'da never* thought of it," said a man whose accent placed him due south of the Mason-Dixon Line. He winked at Mrs. Kaufmann as he spoke.

"*I'da never*! Dang, that's funny!" the third man nearly shouted.

"Mr. Alum, watch your language, and don't shout," Ida scolded. "Really, Mr. Sherman, a southern gentleman such as you ought to know better than to make a joke at my expense. It's not nearly as funny as Mr. Alum makes it out to be."

"I've never understood why people are so quick to accuse another of being a gentleman, Ida. I would caution you in that respect. Keep in mind the more men upon whom you bestow the title *Gentlemen*, the more Gentlemen are apt to act like *men*. And men can be a rather ungentlemanly lot. But as for myself, I always accept the title. And I do regret the joke made at your expense."

"You are forgiven, Mr. Sherman. Of course you are right about men. If only there could be Gentlemen who weren't men. That would be worth something."

"Those are called husbands," Barry Alum scoffed.

"We haven't all lost our manhood, Alum." Vale shoved his hands into the front pockets of his suit pants. "But unfortunately for many husbands, what you say is true. And most unfortunately for them, they are instantly recognizable. And here comes Mr. Odston with his lovely wife even as we speak."

A twitter of snickers passed among the group as Fanny and Wavel climbed the stairs and came on deck.

"You must be the Odston's," Ida Claire floated towards them, both hands outstretched as if her bulk were carried in that direction by the ocean breeze. "Mr. Vale told us all about you."

"I wasn't aware he knew anything about us," Wavel said with a raised brow.

"Oh, don't be grouchy, Wavel." Fanny allowed Mr. Sherman and Mr. Vale to kiss her extended hand, beaming at the attention. "I just can't believe I'm on a cruise. You can't know how it makes me feel."

"I can," Wavel said without being heard.

"May you enjoy every moment you spend on *The Jenny*," Vale nodded somewhat stiffly. "Is everyone here a first-timer? Have any of you been on a cruise before?"

"I've been cruising before." Barry leered at Fanny Odston for effect. "I was a few years younger then, but I certainly enjoyed every moment of it."

"Really?" The word was more of a judgment from Ida than a question.

"Have we been on a cruise before?" Mrs. Kaufman asked her sister.

"Not as a vacation, dear, though I have traveled by ocean liner on several occasions. My second husband was disinclined to travel by airplane."

"Disinclined—"Barry repeated the word in mockery, "That's what we simple people call *chicken*."

"Don't speak of my late husband so."

"Speaking of chicken," Vale pulled a pocket watch from his vest, "I do believe dinner will be served shortly."

The Jenny moved further out to sea.

It took several days for the passengers to become familiar with each other. They learned the superficial things one learns about shallow acquaintances: occupations, hometown, basic familial outlines, and social characteristics. These were simple facts that, laid out for all to see, did not depend upon perspective or opinion.

Martin Vale was the majority owner of Ardeco Travel. He was a native of Long Island, married, had one son, and was a serious, money-minded man. *The Jenny* was the premier yacht in their fleet of craft that had been designed to resurrect the magic of the travel industry that had once sailed the seas of the early 20th century.

Cora Vale, Martin's wife, was a stay-at-home alcoholic who was also native to Long Island. Her square face projected nobility and social graces with a shot of bourbon.

Mrs. Kaufmann was the widow of a banker, and had been pleased to fulfill said role for the past thirty-five years. She was from Chicago, childless, and a quiet woman in a room full of strangers, where she only spoke in order to ask a question.

Ida Claire spoke as often as her sister Mrs. Kaufmann kept silent. Ida had two children about whom she didn't care to think, and had been married to three men about whom she always thought bitterly. From her perspective, she had never been in a room full of strangers; from her perspective, as soon as she entered a room she was everyone's friend and embroiled herself in everyone's affairs.

George Sherman was a Georgian native who never let the fact be forgotten. His accent was exactly as any proper gentleman's accent from Atlanta ought to have been. He traveled in all of the proper circles. He never let you forget that, either.

No one could forget that there was nothing proper about Barry Alum. He was coarse, nomadic, and never lacked for money. His coarseness could be forgiven, his nomadic background overlooked, but with men such as Barry Alum, other men found his wealth inexcusable.

Fanny and Wavel Odston had no social background, though they came from adequate St. Louis families. They were not poor, yet they were in the midst of spending the only money they had ever saved in their twenty-five years of marriage and children. Fanny boasted it was sort of a "coming out" trip for them. Wavel said it was more like "going under."

On the morning of the third day, George Sherman and Barry Alum were standing at the rail of the stern holding shotguns. A porter in a white jacket stood next to a skeet launcher, a cord wrapped around his hand.

"The Devil!" Barry exclaimed, turning dangerously and inadvertently pointing his 12 gauge at the porter. "Did you see that? I'd call it luck, but this prancing fancy just can't miss! Did you see that?"

"I did, sir, very skillful shooting." The porter raised the cord with his hand. His eyes never left the open end of the shotgun's barrel. "Ready?"

"To miss again? Why the heck not... pull!"

The porter pulled and Barry fired.

"Now Mr. Alum, what we have here is a simple problem. I believe you would like to hit the clay pigeon, correct?"

"Yeah George, I'm trying to hit the pigeon. I may not have been raised at the country club, but I know as much as you about skeet." He slid another shell into the shotgun.

"Apparently. However, I did want to suggest—" "Don't bother. Pull!" Barry yanked the shotgun to his shoulder and fired three shells. "There George, I killed it. Think I'll quit while I'm ahead."

"I'd like to shoot a bit more. But Barry," George stared out at the rolling horizon, "would you ask Mr. Gamble to come see me if you run into him below deck?"

"Never!" Barry laughed at his own joke and handed his shotgun to the porter. He walked off laughing, repeatedly shouting out the steward's name.

Only a few minutes passed before the steward appeared on deck and approached George with a questioning look.

"Mr. Gamble—I wonder if you might take a look to the west and tell me what you see."

"Is there a problem, Mr. Sherman?" The steward stood facing the wake of *The Jenny,* scanning wake, horizon, and sky. He drew in his lips, then puckered, and sucked in again: a nervous habit he had long ago ceased to notice. "I'm sure there is something I'm supposed to see, though I can't see it."

"Dead astern, Mr. Gamble. Surely you see something?" Mr. Sherman grew impatient.

"Terribly sorry, Sir. What was it I should have seen?"

"Never mind, Mr. Never Gamble." The Georgian handed his shotgun to the porter. "Did you happen to see anything, young man?"

"Nope. I was reloading the kitty. Didn't see a thing." The young blond porter, known as Tom to his co-workers and 'you, there' by the passengers, showed no sign of regret for his inability to confirm whatever it was the man with the fancy manners thought he had seen.

The three men stood staring into the morning sea, its gently heaving waters winking at them now and again as the rising sun at their backs found sharp facets on the surface. The sky was deep blue, the western horizon not quite fully lit, though it was clearly defined. Nothing moved about that rolling surface; *The Jenny* was alone.

"Well, I do not see it now. Thank you, Mr. Gamble." Mr. Sherman pulled at the hem of his shirt and adjusted his collar. A puzzled expression appeared briefly as he turned and left. The porter began to break down his machine.

"You'd better wait a bit, Tom. Others might want to shoot this morning."

"Alright," Tom grudgingly acknowledged. "You know, we didn't load enough discs for this trip. I tried to order the usual amount of cases, but could I?" He waited just long enough for the steward's silence to confirm he did not know if Tom had been allowed to order the customary number of cases. "No. I'm told that half of the usual amount will do. I don't understand that. We'll run out. Sure to run out."

"A cut in the budget." Mr. Gamble spoke with disinterest. Tom could not tell whether the comment was an indictment or an endorsement. Mr. Gamble's attention was on the water. The gray blue surface just off the port side was becoming disturbed. Long rings of frothy white bubbles broke the surface and slithered back alongside the yacht. He watched this, staring while the white rings shifted and changed shape as if some giant child were stirring the water with a stick.

"Tom—fetch the Captain; Mr. Vale too."

"Is it—?"

"Just get them," Mr. Gamble snapped. As Tom ran forward to find the captain, the steward watched a conning tower rise from the sea. In a very short time, a submarine, easily doubling the length of the yacht, rose to the surface and lay menacingly alongside.

Chapter Two

Boarded!

Fanny Odston had just reached the deck in search of a chaise lounge when the vessel heaved into sight. She dropped her towel and paperback and stood speechless. Barry Alum was just a few steps behind her and turned his attention to the sub.

"Mr. Alum, what in the world is that?" a startled Fanny demanded.

"It's sweet, that's what it is. I'd say that's gotta be over fifty years old. And what condition!" Barry moved to the side and gazed with admiration. "Oh man, I'd call this a replica, but it looks like the real deal. Doesn't look new, doesn't look like a wreck; it just looks like it's been in service for a long, long time, and well taken care of to boot."

Fanny shouted in surprise, tightly grabbing Barry's arm at the sound of metal scraping on metal. A hatch close to the bow of the boat opened; it rose up and fell back slightly against its stops. The two passengers watched as a large man in black climbed to the deck and gave them a stare. After a moment of this, he took even steps towards a gun mounted upon a swivel-hinged post. With large muscled arms providing the strength required to make the big gun appear as a mere toy, he seized the handle of the gun and spun it towards *The Jenny*, training it on Mr. Gamble, Fanny Odston, and Barry Alum.

"I would guess that cannon is in good working order." Barry's comment was unusually droll; his thoughts more on the situation at hand than on cracking jokes.

"Mr. Alum, what is that man doing?" Fanny asked in alarm.

"For now, I'd say he has the drop on us. But my money is on him being part of the trip." To the best of his ability, Barry Alum had worked out the situation. "I'd say it's sort of like *live* entertainment. You ought to scream. Why don't you? That'll sure get this gag going."

Fanny did nothing.

"You're no fun, old girl," Barry taunted, nudging her with an elbow.

At the same moment, a hatch on the small conning tower yawned open and a second man emerged. He was not as tall or as muscular as the fellow stationed at the gun, but his demeanor suggested command. He climbed lithely down the tower ladder and planted his feet on the deck of the boat.

"Prepare to be boarded!" The man spoke loudly enough to be heard, though he did not shout.

Mr. Gamble stopped staring long enough to rush to the steps and yell: "Captain Sloe! Tom! Get the Captain!"

"I'm here, Mr. Gamble." The Captain's head bobbed into view as he pulled himself up the stair and stepped up on the deck. "What in the world is going on? What are they doing there?"

The Captain's remarks were in reference to two more men who, having emerged from the sub, were tossing lines onto the yacht and setting up a metal gangway between the two vessels. This was being done with the utmost speed and skill, so that nearly as soon as the captain's question had been asked, the deed was done and the apparent commander of the sub walked across the plank and jumped lightly down onto the deck of *The Jenny*.

"Captain," the man presented himself rigidly and with respect. "Though I don't ask permission to come aboard, I do ask that we can conduct business with a minimum of conflict. I'm Captain Robert Montane." He nodded and allowed Captain Sloe a moment to think.

"Bedeviled tempest! I don't know what to say." It was true. Sloe remained standing with his mouth slightly open; speechless.

By now most of the passengers and crew had made their

way to some portion of the deck in which they could observe the goings-on. Mr. Sherman and Mrs. Claire stood off a ways, weighing and measuring the situation coldly. Wavel had joined his wife, and now stood just an arm's length from the intruder. Barry Alum flanked the Captain, obviously enjoying the show. Mrs. Kaufman and Mrs. Vale were still below, although they stood in the passageway listening to everything being said. Martin Vale, who until now had not appeared, shortly came pushing past the two ladies, bursting onto deck as only an owner can.

"Captain, I want—"no one ever found out what it was he so vehemently wanted. At the sight of the Submarine's captain, he snapped his mouth shut in astonishment. "Montane!" he finally hissed.

"Martin Vale, I should be so lucky." Montane transformed before the others, his controlled façade slipping into an expression of disgust and bitterness. "You're in the way again."

"And you keep terrorizing my vessels!" Vale pumped both fists in a tantrum.

"*Terrorize* is a strong word, but we'll argue semantics at dinner. Matvie!" He called to the man at the swivel gun. "I don't see any armed resistance. Why don't you stand down? Captain, please tell me right off what weapons are on board so we can be sure there'll be no violence."

"Now you wait just one minute! This is my yacht, and you will not just come aboard like this. Captain Sloe, tell the men to resist. Stop them!"

Everyone stood silently while Martin Vale tried to rally his crew to the defense of *The Jenny*. Like a cuckoo popping from a clock, he jumped in the face of Captain Sloe, then the steward Mr. Gamble, and from there, ranted at nearly everyone, demanding action. Matvie had ignored Montane's suggestion to step away from the gun, and all who listened to the desperate owner were well aware of it; their silence and stillness giving testimony to that awareness.

Montane stood silently as well, watching Vale with irritation and a hint of amusement. The breeze from the morning sea ruffled the onlookers. A tarp over the starboard lifeboat flapped. Martin Vale's protest drifted into silence in the same manner his protests drifted off over the water. In that moment, Montane cleared his throat and faced Captain Sloe.

"Mr. Gamble!" Captain Sloe called sharply. "Please bring the pistol from my quarters. And *The Jenny's* rifle. You will find my pistol in the bottom drawer of my desk."

"Certainly, Captain. Tom!" Never Gamble called sharply although Tom stood right beside him. "Retrieve the Captain's pistol and *The Jenny's* rifle."

"You want the skeet gun too? It's still at the stern. I hadn't put it up yet."

Mr. Gamble stared icily at Tom.

"That's very honest of you, Tom," Montane intervened. "I like to think you can be trusted. Shame on you, Captain."

"You know, I had to try something." Captain Sloe was neither embarrassed nor proud of the brief effort to subvert his captor.

"Yes, you did. No, really; it was appropriate." Montane agreed heartily, and dropped his voice as if he were Sloe's partner in the deception. "The pistol would have been a better choice. I bet Tom knew nothing of your private pistol, am I right?"

"Yes, you're right. The steward knew, but he wouldn't have said anything about it. Only, it's merely a .32 caliber, hardly able to sustain a revolt. I had to take the chance on the shotgun, you understand. And the rifle, well, you would have assumed we had something for sharks and the like. So like I said; the shotgun was worth a shot."

Montane nodded, appreciating the Captain's logic. "That makes sense. But I still think the pistol would have done it. You might have found I was quite the coward with a pistol pointed at me." He winked at the Captain.

"You a coward? I doubt that, Captain Montane." Captain Sloe allowed himself a rumble of laughter.

"Maybe you're right." Montane poked the bearded Captain good-naturedly and laughed with him.

"Conspiracy! Do you people see this?" Martin Vale regained his voice. "You see? My own Captain conspiring with pirates!"

"I bet you won't be sorry about this," Montane said under his breath to Captain Sloe. In a louder voice he called to the men who had laid down the gangway. "Hamlet, Othello! Lock that man in his cabin. Vale, you're making too much noise. I have a little speech to make and I'll never get through it with you yapping like this."

Hamlet and Othello crossed the gangway and grabbed the still yammering owner, pushing him roughly below deck. Those topside could hear his protestations long after he had disappeared from sight.

"Can everyone hear me? Come in a little closer, I have a few words to say."

No one moved.

"Gather 'round." Montane motioned at them as if they were his pupils. "Matvie's not going to shoot you, okay? Come on."

One by one, they began to close about him, until they stood in a semi-circle. Mrs. Vale and Mrs. Kaufman came from below and joined the group as well.

"Now," Montane sighed, rubbing his palms. "This won't take very long. Let me first assure you that everyone's safety is at the top of my list."

"But Mr. Vale called you a pirate, didn't he?" Mrs. Kaufman asked in trepidation.

"Now, hold on. Questions at the end. But yes, he did call me a pirate, and that is what we are."

"Oh, for Pete's sake," Ida Claire spat contemptuously. Mr. Sherman touched her shoulder and hushed her with due propriety.

"Stop!" Montane's informal manner vanished, replaced with coldness. "I'm talking right now. You're listening." Ida Claire recognized the menace in his voice and cringed. "I will start over, and no one will speak."

He stared at them all, making eye contact with each. Hamlet and Othello could be heard tromping up the stairs and onto the deck, but no one turned to watch.

"Let me assure you," Montane's manner lightened again, though with a reservation it had not kept previously, "that everyone's safety is at the top of my list. We are pirates. And we are boarding you forcefully. Let's not forget that, okay? I am in charge.

"Now, there are a few rules I must enforce during our visit with you. First, there will be no calls to the authorities. That's more of a fact than a rule, come to think of it. I can jam anything you try to send, so don't bother. Technology is on my side in this so just forget it. Now, the second rule—"

"First," corrected Mr. Sherman. "You said that first one was only a fact, not a rule."

"*First* rule; if you don't interfere with us, we will generally leave you to yourself."

"That's more like advice." Montane's deadly gaze cut Mr. Sherman's interruption short.

"And advice that should be heeded, Mister—?"

"Sherman. George Sherman." Mr. Sherman nodded to the pirate leader.

"If you'll allow me to continue," Montane wanted to be angry, but knew immediately he liked the stately gentleman who dared to correct him, "I will move on. The next rule we come to…the *first* rule, as it were, is that while I can be a reasonable pirate, I will…what is it now?" Mr. Sherman was obviously holding back a comment.

"Simply; that's an opinion, isn't it? Reasonable is a relative term."

"Let him finish, George." Barry Alum insisted. "I want to hear these rules."

"There hasn't been a rule mentioned yet, Mr. Alum." George Sherman defended his position, unwilling to back down.

"Is there a rule against drinking?" Cora Vale broke into the conversation abruptly. "I want a drink."

"Wasn't Prohibition repealed?" came Mrs. Kaufman's ever-ready question.

"I could get you a drink, Mrs. Vale." The steward offered quickly, heading for the open stairway, eager to be out of range of Matvie's gun. Othello moved two steps to his right and blocked Mr. Gamble's way. The nervous steward stopped inches from the beefy pirate and swallowed with difficulty as he tried to say *excuse me*; his lips moved but no sound came from his fear-parched throat.

"I think you're losing them," Barry Alum offered Montane his bemused assessment, encouraging him with a gesture of his arm, "crack the whip on their fannies. Give 'em what for. Tighten 'em up."

"Whose side are you on?" Ida Claire bristled at the suggestive language. "For shame! You white trash—"

"Don't go there, blue blood!"

The whole group dissolved into something resembling a wild debate in the House of Commons. Ida Claire swung a parasol at Barry Alum but was held in check by the gentleman from Georgia. Cora Vale began verbally abusing Othello for blocking the steward's attempts to bring her gin. Mrs. Kaufman stood alone asking no one in particular what was going on. From the growing din, one voice began to dominate the atmosphere.

"Curse you, Wavel Odston. You had to do it, didn't you? I should have known; you pathetic, selfish pig." Everyone stopped speaking and stared at the unfortunate man under attack. "What was it? The money? You just couldn't stand to spend the money, could you? So to spite me, you booked us on this disaster; a lousy ship."

"I keep telling her it's a yacht," Never Gamble mumbled out loud to no one in particular. He had done so just a little too loudly.

"Who cares, you little freak!" Fanny shrieked. "Ship, yacht, boat, blimp—"

"Blimps don't go in the water," someone had the nerve to correct her.

"Whatever! You just wanted to humiliate me, Wavel. You can't help but do it. Just like the whole affair over Ted Warner. You just can't let me be happy. I've seen IRS agents with more pity in their hearts than you. You cold son—"

Othello reached around her waist with one arm and

snatched her up like a bratty child. Wavel's protest was cut off by a gesture from Montane. As Fanny began to shriek louder, the solid black man descended below deck with her struggling form.

"Steady, sir." Montane cautioned Wavel. "She'll not be harmed."

"All the same," Wavel said after a moment's thought, "I do protest that man's handling of my wife. And at the same time—thank you."

"No, no. Your thanks are hardly necessary; had to be done, that's all. How many years of marriage?"

"Twenty-five. This past March."

"I have the greatest respect for you, Mr. Odston. Something I lack regarding the rest of you." He raised his voice and turned to look over the group. "Everybody feel better? Finished blowing off some steam? Nerves gone? Yes? No? Any of you want to join Marty and the delightful Mrs. Odston?

"Let's forget the speech. Hamlet, you and Othello search the ship, be sure we have everyone up on deck besides the two mouthy ones. Matvie! Call Lear up here, and tell him to bring his brother. Once they're aboard, cast off but stay close by. Everyone else, sit down and shut up."

"Should we sit here, on the deck?" Mrs. Kaufman couldn't help herself. The question just came too easily.

"I will not sit on the deck!" Ida Claire insisted.

"Mr. Gamble, get drinks for anyone who asks. And put me at the top of the list; a double," demanded Cora Vale.

"Captain Montane—that is your proper title, isn't it?" Mr. Sherman approached the angry pirate. "Could we move to the other side of the yacht? There are deck chairs there and the ladies would be more comfortable and less trouble, I believe."

"Who are you calling trouble, you puffed up peacock?" Ida Claire cast a hard glare at Mr. Sherman.

"God help me," Montane shook his head. "This is never going to work. Matvie! Summon the Priest."

Chapter Three

The Priest

A hush fell on the bickering mob, as if a live hand grenade had been thrown into the midst of them.

"Ladies," Mr. Sherman spoke with soft yet urgent authority, "please move to the port side and sit down on the deck chairs. *Go on, please.*" Mr. Sherman's smile fooled no one. He was suddenly worried.

Montane said nothing to contradict the new order and so the women, all now aware something important was happening, followed the order quickly and silently.

"This ought to be good," Barry Alum nudged Wavel Odston mischievously.

"Sounds ominous," Wavel pronounced glumly. "The only Priests I ever saw presided over funerals."

"Weddings, too," added Never Gamble.

"Same thing."

Matvie had slipped back into the submarine. The men on deck stared apprehensively at the sleek vessel of war; each man contemplating what this new development might bring.

Several minutes after the large man had vanished, a blond man appeared at the same hatch. He rose into view wearing a black sweater and matching black pants. He was thin and gangly, though no taller than average. But the most memorable aspect about the man was his sallow, triangular face. It had the look of madness upon it; madness with a smile. Hanging about his neck was a large black cross on a silver chain.

"Geez," Tom spoke aloud what everyone was thinking, "that guy's creepy."

"That's a scary Priest." Wavel was still thinking of funerals and weddings.

Montane began to laugh as though enjoying their nervous fear. "That's no Priest. It's worse; that's Lear."

Lear stepped to the gangway and called to Montane.

"Come on over, Lear. Where's your brother?"

"He's bringing the Priest. Captain, I would rather stay with the Sub, if you don't mind." Lear's voice was raspy, with a high pitch. Those listening had no idea if he was hoarse or if he always sounded that way.

"Nonsense, Lear. I need you aboard with me; at my right side." Montane and Lear watched each other with equal wariness. The men of *The Jenny* could sense the merest whisper of friction.

"Right you are, and right side I'll be." Lear took two steps then leapt forward onto the deck of the yacht. All wariness had evaporated from his manner. He shook Montane's hand as his gaze swept the length of the yacht. "Congratulations, Captain. She's a fine catch. Pretty little thing, hmm? What's the deal with these guys? No women on board?"

"No, we weren't so lucky; there are women. They went to find chairs." Montane said petulantly.

"Chairs? Whatever. Shall we begin to strip her down?" Lear was amused to see several of the men begin to raise a protest. "Settle down there, boys. I meant the yacht, not your women. But, it's a thought. How do they look, Captain?"

"Knock it off, Lear. And no, we don't strip the yacht."

As they spoke, two men appeared from the belly of the submarine. The first was an ordinary looking man dressed in jeans and a loose fitting pullover. He looked young, somewhere in his twenties, with dishwater hair and a lean frame. After him came a man who was very obviously Lear's brother. Physically they were identical. But where Lear had the look of madness, his brother had the look of death; identical twins who could be easily identified separately. As the two men crossed to *The Jenny*, Matvie reappeared at his post.

"Ah, Macbeth. You've brought him. I was just telling your brother we won't be stripping the yacht."

Macbeth said nothing. He just stared at his brother Lear, as if waiting for something.

"And I was just going to tell the Captain I think it's a great idea," Lear announced.

"Father David, welcome aboard." Montane addressed the man in the pullover shirt. "Gentleman, may I introduce you to my Priest, Father David."

"Hello. I'm not really a Priest. Call me David." His manner was friendly enough that they all might have shaken hands and poured drinks until the men of *The Jenny* remembered he was part of a pirate crew.

A sigh of relief ran through the men, though no one was sure who this Father David really was. They stood waiting for some kind of explanation.

Hamlet came back on deck and reported they had found two crew members hiding in the galley. Othello was still with them, awaiting orders on what to do with them.

"That's just Bob and Alice," Tom explained, trying to mollify the pirates. "Bob's our cook, and Alice cleans the staterooms. I'm sure they weren't hiding. They generally keep to themselves. They barely talk to me, let alone the bosses and the passengers."

"That big fellow might cause trouble," Hamlet noted. "But as long as he stays in the galley, Othello or I can keep an eye on him. One of us just needs to stay in the passageway."

"Big fellow?" Montane looked at Tom. "Bob?"

"Oh, he grumbles a lot. But no trouble for you."

"And Alice?"

"Mousy thing," Hamlet answered quickly. "Nothing to worry about there."

"Anyone else we should know about?"

"My pilot," Captain Sloe readily admitted. "I don't want your men startled when they find him in the wheelhouse. I don't want him hurt. His name's Melvin. He'll give you no trouble. He's been pilot of *The Jenny* longer than I've been Captain."

"Alright, have Othello stay down in the passage. Hamlet, you go collect the old timer at the helm and bring him below.

Lear, get these men to the dining room. Macbeth, get the ladies to join them. I want everyone together. After I talk with Matvie, I'll help Othello gather the others. Come with me, Father David."

These commands were given quickly, without pause, and each man turned to follow them immediately. Montane was accustomed to giving orders, and his men were accustomed to following them.

"May I be allowed to check on my cook and chambermaid?" Captain Sloe dared to ask.

"You may. Hamlet, see to it Othello lets him in the galley. He may join the others when I return."

He led David across to the sub and conversed with Matvie for several minutes. Matvie said very little, nodding a few times. As was his usual way, he used very little visible response to anything said to him. When they were finished, Montane and David crossed over the plank and Matvie quickly withdrew it and stowed it out of sight. The submarine's engines backed down just enough for her to fall slightly behind *The Jenny*. Once just a shade off her port stern, she picked up speed and kept pace with the yacht.

For a moment, Montane and David were alone. Montane watched his sub fall back into position and leaned on the bulward rail; it was still morning and he was already tired.

"This is never gonna work, Father." Montane blew out a breath in order to calm his nerves. David, having long ago given up on correcting Montane when he called him Father, ignored the title.

"Give it a chance, Robbie."

"I can't get used to you calling me that," Montane grunted at the familiar usage of his Christian name. "At least you don't call me that in front of anyone else. I'd have to—"

"—kill me." David finished the oft repeated threat. "I know, but I don't do that in front of anyone."

"You fear for your life. Yes, a wise move."

"Well, not really. I just don't want to embarrass you. And I know it makes you uncomfortable."

"So why is this going to work? If you were a betting man

I would take you for everything in your wallet. You haven't really met all these people yet. You'll see. What a bunch of puddin' heads. I've a mind to leave right now."

"But you won't."

"What makes you so sure?" Montane turned and searched David's face.

"You're arrogant. You can't fathom anyone more worthwhile than yourself. You know this deep down, and so you know you'll never find people you'll deem worthy of this venture. So you'll stay."

"Man, I love you." Montane reached out a hand and mussed David's hair. "What a Priest. You're gonna make this work. I can't see how, but you…you'll find a way."

"I can't do it, Robbie. You can take the steps you need. The rest will be up to God."

"So let me go introduce you to these yahoos."

Chapter Four

Suspicions and a Request

"What's happening?" Mrs. Kaufman spoke as soon as the women joined the men in the dining room.

"It's too early for lunch; I refuse to eat this early." Ida Claire looked for a pirate to aim her comment at, but there were none in the room. Discovering this emboldened her and she raised her level of ire. "Who is going to do something about all of this? Why are you men sitting around drinking coffee?" She peered at Mr. Sherman disapprovingly.

"May I get you a cup? It's fresh."

"Fresh?" Mr. Sherman nodded at her. "Well, yes thank you. I'll take a cup. But only a little sugar. I don't like it too sweet."

"What did you want us to do, Ida?" Barry Alum sat sprawled upon a dining room chair with his feet up on another. He alone was enjoying the show. "I was just advocating we all wait till nightfall, take the dory boat, and try and overrun the sub. I'll bet they'll never expect that. I'll bet it's never been done. We'll win."

"Have you gone out of your mind?" Never Gamble approached the mad plotter and leaned into his face. "If it's ever been done, the last people to try it are probably at the bottom of the ocean right now. Our only hope is to appeal for mercy and hope they at least leave us alive. There's nothing to win here. Do you think it's a game?"

"Well, it's very well done and all, but a little far fetched in this day and age."

"It's ridiculous, that's what it is." Ida accepted the cup of coffee from Mr. Sherman and managed to thank him while simultaneously whining to the rest of the room. "If I were a man, I'd never—"

"*Ida Never* surrendered!" Barry Alum blurted out the play on names, laughing while he pounded the table. "That gets me every time."

Mr. Sherman hushed Barry and tried to speak loud enough to arrest everyone's attention.

"Now we have to keep our heads. There can be no attempts to recapture *The Jenny* unless everyone is agreeable to the plan. Otherwise, we put at risk those who are unwilling to be at risk. But action is not what we should be about at this time. We need information. We need to know this Montane's intentions. What do we know about him? Is anyone familiar with him?"

"That steward knows something," Wavel said evenly. All eyes swiveled to Wavel, then centered on Mr. Gamble.

"Me?" The steward bit his lip.

"Why do you say that, Mr. Odston?" asked Mrs. Kaufman.

"He tried to tell us about these pirates yesterday; while showing us our stateroom. Now come on, Mr. Gamble. What do you know?"

Never Gamble mumbled a few words, too nervous to say anything of value. He was stalling for time.

"Come on, spit it out." Ida Claire demanded.

"Never!" Barry Alum alone laughed at his joke.

"A shakedown, that's what this is!" Ida Claire said with finality, as if she knew anything about shakedowns. "This steward is running a shakedown on us; he's in league with them. Didn't he see to the stowing of our gear? He knows where everything is. He may even be their leader." She set her cup down hard on its saucer to indicate her judgment had been passed and the man had been found guilty. She could not have been more pleased with herself.

"That's not a shakedown, baby." Barry Alum couldn't help himself. "What you're suggesting is an inside job. A shakedown is when someone—"

"I don't care what you call it, the steward's in on it."

"That's crazy!" Never Gamble finally found his tongue.

"I'll tell you what I know, alright? Just shut the old woman up. I'm no pirate!"

"Old woman?" The gauntlet had been thrown down and Ida eagerly snatched it up. "You listen to me, you little snit. I may not be as young as you, but I was never as stupid at your age as you so obviously are."

"Now Ida," Mr. Sherman quickly poured more coffee into her cup from a silver decanter and made eye contact with her, "Mr. Gamble may need to have his eyesight checked, because everyone else can see you are still in your prime, my good lady. You've nothing to worry about."

"Oh, Mr. Sherman."

"Call me George."

"Really…George. You needn't flatter me. You're so very sweet. Are you any relation to the Shermans of Peach Hill?"

"There were more than a few times my father would have denied such a heritage, but after all, doesn't everyone have a few Uncle Johnny's in their family?"

Ida Claire laughed discreetly and leaned towards George. "I had no intention of mentioning Jonathon Sherman, I assure you. No offense was intended—"

"None taken, Ida. May I call you Ida? I never shrink from bringing Uncle Johnny into a conversation. He's the flavor every good family needs, though they never care to admit it."

"Mr. Gamble," Wavel cleared his throat and cut in, "ignore them please, and go ahead. I want to hear what you know."

"Well, first of all, it's Vale's fault. Don't blame me."

"For what?" Wavel cocked his head to the side, willing the steward to continue.

"This isn't the first time one of Mr. Vale's yachts has been captured by this Montane. He's been hitting ships in this corridor for a while now. Mr. Vale is too afraid of what the news will do to shares of Ardeco to report what's been happening. I'm not supposed to be saying any of this. You are all putting my job at stake."

"Your job?" Ida Claire snorted. "Who gives a whit about

your job right now? Our lives are at stake."

"Now, Ida, that's not been proven yet." Mr. Sherman tried to calm her down, though he was as unclear of their safety as she. "No one's been harmed, and this Montane fellow assured us he wants no violence. I think it's only right to take the man at his word. We have no reason to do otherwise."

"You're kidding." Wavel sat looking at the dandy, an open look of exasperation on his face. "The man had my wife dragged below decks to lord knows what."

"You thanked him," countered Barry Alum.

"I wasn't thinking clearly at the time. Look, I'm not saying one thing or the other. These guys may really mean us no harm. I only think it is foolhardy to dismiss the threat they may represent. Now Mr. Gamble, tell us more."

Never Gamble never got the chance to tell them more. At that moment, Montane entered the dining room. David, Captain Sloe, Martin Vale, Melvin the Pilot and Fanny Odston followed after him with Hamlet bringing up the rear. Fanny did not exactly run into her husband's arms, but she did make straight for him and seemed less angry with him as he stood and took her hand.

"I'm fine," she whispered to him, whether he cared or not. They both sat down.

Melvin was a thin man in his seventies. He was wearing a dark blue blazer and white turtleneck sweater. Seemingly unimpressed by the presence of pirates, he stalked slowly to a corner of the room where he dropped into a chair and rested his head against the wall.

Martin Vale strode across the dining room and sat in a corner. He was every bit a scolded schoolboy who has finally decided to give in to the rules, sitting with his mouth closed tight and his gaze fixed solidly on the table in front of him. Cora Vale watched him from another table but said nothing and made no move to join him.

"What have you done with Bob and Alice?" Tom managed to speak up on behalf of his co-workers.

"I had them thrown overboard after they spoke before

being spoken to." Montane answered dryly. David frowned at him and shook his head disapprovingly. "They've begun working on lunch in the galley. Now that I have you all together, is it possible for all of you to behave? I don't want to have to call Lear and Macbeth in here. You may have gathered those two are not so easy to control. If you haven't figured it out, I'm trying to be decent. I will limit their access to you if you simply stop all the noise.

"I need a moment alone with Captain Sloe. Keep it quiet in here."

Montane left with Captain Sloe. David slipped out the door with them.

Melvin was already asleep. His worn form hardly moved as he took shallow breaths and never moved a muscle.

"Are you sure you're alright, dear?" Wavel asked Fanny. The question was mere obligation. Her affirmative response was the same.

"You and your screwy cruise, Wavel; what an asinine idea."

"I'm so glad you're alright. It's a pleasure to have you back." Only Wavel could have said it with a straight face. He had twenty-five years of practice.

Montane walked the length of the passageway and led Captain Sloe and David Wayne up the aft stairs. The three men walked a short distance from it and stopped at the stern; the skeet machine was still standing where Tom had left it.

"Captain Sloe, I'm going to need your help with something." Montane was uncomfortable soliciting help. It showed.

"Do you mind? The salt gets to it so quickly." Captain Sloe indicated he meant to break down the skeet machine, and Montane nodded at him to continue. "You've commandeered my boat by force and now you need my help? That's intriguing. I suppose I should outright refuse."

"You could do that. I can't make you help."

"Would it help if I asked you to give him a chance?" asked David.

"Young man, I don't know you from Adam. You're in the company of pirates; not exactly a sterling reference, if you see what I mean. Of course, you hold all the cards, so I can't stop you from telling me whatever it is you want me to hear."

"But I need you to keep an open mind, Captain." Montane looked at David with a shrug. "I wish I'd learned how to negotiate. Dictating's more my style; a pirate's prerogative."

"The limitations of your trade," David added.

"Go on, then." Captain Sloe finished with the skeet machine and stood straight, crossing his arms. "What's this about?"

"I'll remember to let Tom up before lunch so he can stow that." Captain Sloe thanked him, and Montane proceeded to explain his reason for seizing *The Jenny*. They spoke at length; Montane presenting his case, Sloe responding with disbelief. David intervened at times, confirming Montane's sincerity. At times he had to step in to keep Montane from losing his temper.

As their conference continued, the sea flowed beneath *The Jenny* and ran out under her stern in a steady wake. Lear held the helm and steered their Prize on a course that slipped them out of the main shipping lanes. His orders were to hide her in the great vastness of the ocean.

"You believe me?" Montane measured the Captain's response, hoping to see a flicker of belief.

"I'll hold my final judgment on that until another time. But will I assist you? While I may have no choice, I also have very little to lose. I admit you've made me curious. I just wish I knew if you were sincere."

"There is the problem of bringing this to the others." Montane was certain they would not believe him. Not that herd of stubborn asses. "That's why I need you to tell them, Captain. You'll have to sell this to them. I won't be able to help much."

"I already understood that. It will be a challenge. But to start with; you've got to stop threatening everyone. Put away your weapons."

"Oh, of course. You'll go through with my plans just as

we discussed them, right? I'm a pirate. I'm not an idiot. Don't go about acting as if you'd do this of your own good will. As soon as I disarmed, you'd have me locked up—call in the marines. Now let's get this straightened out between us, Captain. I'm trusting Father David on this enterprise, and you're trusting me. Don't begin to believe I won't use force if Father David turns out to be wrong. You're looking for weakness in me, but it is a mistake to do so."

"I guess I was." Captain Sloe lowered his head; ashamed to admit the truth of the matter. "I do want to help you. I understand what you need. Only, there are certain obligations."

"Exactly, and until this is over, coercion must rule the day. There's something else you don't understand. You saw those two who came aboard last? The brothers? That's a dangerous pair. As far as they know, you're all simply plunder. You need me in a strong position until I can deal with them. Tell him I'm not lying, Father David."

"He is right about that, Captain. You—your people couldn't handle them."

"I'll do it." Captain Sloe shook his head. "I'm not sure I like it. Just understand that I agree only because there seems to be no alternative. I'm not volunteering. I will cooperate; but only so far."

"You're wrong again, Captain. Once you cooperate, and we start this affair, you and I will only be able to go the entire distance. There is a point of no return. Be certain of that."

The conversation had come to an uncertain resolution. In the silence that followed, Lear's voice could be heard coming from the wheelhouse. The words were mixed with a heavy laughter, and the three men at the stern turned their attention to the sound. They stared at the wheelhouse door, waiting, expecting to see movement there. No one appeared; they heard only the murmurings of the two pirates.

"Captain," David said softly, his gaze still concentrated on the door, "Take us completely at our word regarding those two. Stay away from them. Give Montane a chance to show you his sincerity. You won't be betrayed."

A loud vicious shout of curses shot from the wheelhouse. A window pane shattered. More laughter erupted.

"Let's get below." Montane took Captain Sloe by the arm and urged him to the stair.

Chapter Five

Montane's *Raison d'être*

It was no surprise to Montane, Sloe, and David when they returned and found the rest of the passengers arguing noisily. The din could be heard outside the dining room door. Montane rolled his eyes at his councilor, paused at the door, and tried to hold down his anger.

"Outright exaggerations!" Fanny Odston was barking again. "You're all wrong! Tell them, Wavel."

Wavel told them. What he lacked in sincerity he made up for with his willingness to assist his wife.

"You're right, dear. You did nothing to upset these men. You put no one at risk."

"Oh, be a man, for crying out loud." Ida spoke with disgust. "Don't defend her. For pity's sake, you even thanked the man for taking her away."

"He what? You what?" Fanny turned on her husband.

"Misinterpretation, Fanny dear. I thanked him for not harming you. He assured me you would not be harmed. It only seemed right to thank him." Everyone, including Ida, had to admire his quickness and sharp thinking.

"Of course it was, Wavel." Fanny stroked his head and flashed a cutting look at Ida.

"What's up with the Captain?" Barry Alum felt like playing devil's advocate. "Seems funny, his going off with those pirates. Something's up there, I'll bet. He was quick to tell them about that pilot. If they hadn't known about the pilot, he may have retaken the ship when they weren't expecting it."

Everyone in the room turned and looked at the frail and elderly Melvin sleeping in the corner. He did not appear to be breathing. Tom, the closest one to him, stepped over to him and felt for a pulse. After establishing a pulse, he gave a thumbs-up and a nod of affirmation to the group.

"Now hold on one minute!" Never Gamble jumped at the captain's defense. "You'll take that back. Captain Sloe is an honorable man."

"Of course, of course. But let's not forget you mentioned the pirates before they ever arrived." Ida stared defiantly at him. "Maybe you're in it with the Captain."

"Slanderous hag!" Never Gamble shook with indignation. "Mr. Vale, are you going to allow this?"

"Now," Martin Vale finally spoke up, "let's remember we're all under stress at the moment, and we should be careful not to say things we'll regret."

"I'm told you know something about this—" Wavel said with an even manner. Never looked at him with eyes wide, begging him to keep silent.

"What are you saying?" Martin Vale sat up straight and stuck out his chest.

"It was a simple statement, I should think. I was told you knew something about pirates in these waters."

"That's a lie!"

"No—I did hear that you knew about pirates. That's a fact."

"I don't know who you heard that from—"

"Now I'll accept that. I don't expect you to know who told me. But that's not the point. What did you know about pirates before we were boarded?" Wavel stared hard at the owner of *The Jenny*.

Everyone stared hard at him. The point was suddenly important to all of them, though none of them could have any idea what it would have mattered. It was simply a matter of needing a scapegoat.

Martin Vale took several ragged breaths and looked mournfully around the room. Not a friendly eye met his own. Even his wife Cora scowled at him. He picked up a napkin from the table and fumbled with it, twisting it around and then crumpling it roughly. There was no where he could go. The question could not be avoided.

"So there'd been reports of pirates. That's nothing new. There was no reason to change our plans."

"Jackass!" Cora Vale threw a glass at Martin. It missed him and shattered on the wall behind him. "I should have known you were bullheaded enough to do something like this." She jumped up from the table and reached over and grabbed another glass from an adjoining table. Mr. Sherman stood and tried to persuade her to desist. Fanny Odston cut in from of him, declaring Cora's right to hit the man with anything she might choose to throw. As Martin fell out of his chair in order to crouch behind his table, the door swung open and Montane stepped into the room.

"Everyone getting along?"

The passengers, so eager to chatter like chickens when left alone, now sat quiet in their seats. Cora stood still with hand cocked, preparing to throw a decanter she had just snatched up. Mr. Sherman and Fanny Odston were locked in what looked like the opening moves of a wrestling match. Martin Vale peered uneasily from under the table and could see Montane was angry.

"I thought I would leave you all together to give you some comfort; a sort of companionship in time of trouble. But it appears what I'll need to do is separate you all like a bunch of misbehaving children. I suddenly feel like my father—and what a miserable man he was."

For once, no one made a comment. Montane looked at them with a shudder. He paused, on the verge of a great decision. He had purposed to do just what he had explained to Captain Sloe, but standing there in front of these people, he was having trouble taking that final step. Could he do it? He knew David was right; there would never be a group of people that he deemed worthy of the task. So why not this group of buffoons? It was an odd yet tantalizing challenge.

"Well?" David cocked his head and sought an answer out of Montane. "Now or never?"

"Hang on," Montane stalled. He responded as if he were a kid being asked to hurry up and swallow his medicine. "You'd better be right."

"No guarantees; but there is a chance."

"Okay, then. Ladies and Gentlemen," Montane said with a trace of sarcasm, "Captain Sloe will explain why I have boarded *The Jenny*. I will leave it to him to answer any of your questions. I have things to attend to, and so I will leave you all alone. Do yourselves a favor and get along."

Montane cast a glance at David then retreated from the dining room. Everyone sat staring at Captain Sloe and David. It was a pivotal moment. There was a chance they would all break into an arguing mob once again. Yet, there was the slightest of chances that Captain Sloe could keep them under control. David saw this and seized the opportunity.

"Captain, go on. You have their attention."

"Here goes nothing," he muttered in return. "Okay people, listen up. I need to explain a few things. Don't ask any questions until I can get it all out, alright?" There was a long silence. The face of Captain Sloe, covered with a salt and pepper beard, twitched as he made several attempts to begin.

"Perhaps," David said softly, "I should do this? Maybe I could find a way to explain it all."

The captain accepted his offer with great relief. He sat at a table next to Martin Vale and waited.

"My name is David Wayne and I want to explain just what is happening aboard this boat. I'll try to be brief, but I want to be as clear as possible so there are no misunderstandings. Can we all agree that would be best?"

"Just who the dickens are you?" Wavel Odston questioned.

"That's a great place to start. I'm nothing more than a volunteer at a counseling hotline. I help talk people out of suicide, crimes of rage, depression, and simple insignificance."

"Why does this pirate call you his priest?" Mrs. Kaufman, a lifelong protestant, was certain this David was a representative of Rome.

"A matter of being the one who answered the phone. By Montane's upbringing in the Catholic Church, he felt the need to talk to a confessor. Only, he couldn't bring himself to actually call a Priest, so he called our hotline instead."

"About what? Just what is this about?" Ida Claire was losing the poor bit of patience she had to begin with.

"Robert Montane called the Cleveland Youth Center Hotline one night nearly six months ago. I took the call. He was depressed, suicidal; I really found it hard to keep him from going off the edge. He had been considering leaving his life of piracy, but had found an obstacle to such a path. He was certain that no matter what he did in the future, his life would be forfeit for his past. We talked a great deal that night. I told him that it was obvious he wanted more than redemption. He was seeking forgiveness. It was the only thing that would fulfill what he was craving."

"Boy," Cora Vale interrupted, reaching out to the steward with her glass, "this sounds like a long story. Refill this glass with whatever you can find."

"So the pirate's got a guilty conscience and wants to start anew, is that about it?" A glint of cruelty shone through Fanny Odston's eyes. "He's off to a bad start, don't you think?"

"Shut up, Fanny." Wavel wagged a finger at her.

"He should have just turned himself in." The suggestion came from Mr. Sherman.

"I said the same to him over the phone. He won't do that. That would only prove what he already knows; that he's guilty. He doesn't care about that. He wants forgiveness. I must say I was a little at a loss for what to say, so I told him the next time he captures a boat, to try and get forgiveness from those on the boat. I really did not think he was listening to me at that point."

"You told him what?" There was general astonishment and disbelief from the group as a whole. David waited for a chance to continue his tale. He had to wait for some time.

"I said I did not think he was listening to me. At any rate, all I know is that two weeks ago, three of his men broke into my apartment and kidnapped me at gunpoint."

"Good grief!" Ida Claire looked suspiciously at him. "You're not serious?"

"It was a great shock to me as well. I have no idea how he tracked me down. I had only given my first name on the hotline. Anyway, he seems to have taken me up on my suggestion."

"And just how is that?" asked Mr. Sherman.

"He asks… well more demands really, that we hold a trial."

"Who does he intend to try?" Wavel sat up straight at this turn of events.

"He intends for us to try him." David spoke slowly so he could not be misunderstood. "He has asked Captain Sloe to preside over the trial. He would like one of you to be chosen as the prosecutor."

"Does he seriously think that one of us will defend him?" Ida shook with indignity.

"I," David said deliberately, "I will be defending him."

"How absurd," Cora Vale announced as she drank down the martini Never Gamble had placed in front of her.

"Now that's funny." Barry Alum laid his head back on the headrest of his chair and stuck a cigarette into his mouth. "*Ida Never* guessed this."

"I do believe the man needs more than a Priest." Wavel pronounced to Fanny and anyone else who could hear him. "He needs a shrink. Maybe a shrink and a Priest."

"You are serious, aren't you Mr. Wayne?" George Sherman sat thinking over the scenario that had just been given to them. "This man thinks he's in need of a judge. Is that right?"

"That's a misunderstanding," David warned. "Robert Montane feels no need to be judged by anyone. As I said before, he knows he is guilty. He only wants to know if men could ever forgive him for what he's done."

"What has he done?" asked Mrs. Kaufman.

"A murdering, thieving pirate! That's what he is, and that's what he's done."

"Now hold on, Mr. Vale. That will all come out in the trial. Are you volunteering to be the Prosecutor?"

"Now you hold on, you Dial-a-Priest. This is my boat,

and I will not have it used for some silly sham trial." Martin Vale had been listening to the conversation in mute fury, but had finally found his voice. "No God-damned pirate is going to waste my cruise while he plays the conflicted soul of the sea."

"Oh that's bright, Marty." Cora lifted her face from her drink in order to disrupt her husband's rant. "I think the point being made is he knows where God stands on the issue—seems he's more interested in how we stand on his damnation. And as far as that goes, it's not your boat anymore, remember? You're not so very in charge around here. And a nice change it is. I say, hear ye, hear ye—bring on the defendant. Put me on the jury."

Half a dozen separate conversations began around the room as all those in attendance gave forth their individual opinions. David watched them intently, trying to single out the various comments being made. For one moment, his eyes locked with those of Captain Sloe's, and they stared softly at each other. As if by prearranged signal, the two men stepped to one side of the room and spoke quietly together.

"They seem to have given in to the idea, no matter how reluctantly." Captain Sloe was not sure just how it would all come out but was curious enough now to want to see it through to the end.

"I feel sorry for Montane," David admitted, "I'm not sure I would ever submit to the findings of this ship of fools. Excepting you, Captain."

"That's alright, David. I'm not thrilled at the realization that I'm their Captain. Just remember; not a ship of fools—a boat of fools."

"A fool requests permission to approach his Captain," George Sherman sidled up to David and the Captain with a drink in both hands. "Would one of you like one of these?"

David declined the glass, and watched the delicate Georgian pass it to the Captain.

"My apologies on the fools comment. You are?" David offered his hand.

"Sherman. Mr. George Sherman of Atlanta. I don't mind

the comment if you don't mind my elitism. It's not showing much right now, but you'll see more of it as you get to know me. Tell me, David Wayne of Cleveland, when you're not solving the world's problems over a telephone, just what do you do to pay the bills?"

"I'm a High School teacher." David admitted with a smile.

"Teaching what?"

"A little History, Comparative Religions, Civics and the like."

"An idealist, or pragmatist?" George Sherman smiled at his own question.

"The idealist in me says *both*."

"Well answered," Captain Sloe tipped his glass in salute.

"You know, this trial or yours, while interesting, will only be a waste of time."

"And so the man from Atlanta is a pragmatist." Captain Sloe drank to that as well.

"He may only be fatalistic," David countered.

"All and the same, Mr. Wayne; pragmatism and fatalism," answered Captain Sloe, a closet philosopher.

"No, Mr. Sherman is no fatalist." David changed his mind as he noticed the bemused expression on George Sherman. He was intrigued and wanted to know the Atlantan more. "Why a waste of time?"

"For the simple fact that the jury has a gun to its head. The outcome is decided. The defendant, in this case the man holding the gun, will get what he wants. The forgiveness is a hollow, yet foregone conclusion."

"That may be the initial thought process of those involved. But I suggest that there are just as many who would decide 'in for a penny, in for a pound'. If you've got a gun to my head, then I might as well tell you what I really think. A proud *go jump off a cliff* would not be a surprise. Such are the two extremes. Somewhere in the middle, the truth may be found."

"Could make for an interesting wager." Captain Sloe chuckled, "Of course as presiding judge, I really couldn't in good faith."

The room was interrupted by the entrance of Alice the chambermaid, who announced that lunch was about to be served. Despite being in the hands of pirates, the passengers were eager to grab a seat and be fed. Like children at a birthday party they vied for seats and watched the plates of food to see who got the largest portions.

Chapter Six

The Pirate Captain Sees to a Few Details

The man Montane called Hamlet sat on a stool in the doorway that separated the galley from the main passageway. From where he sat he could see Bob the cook and Alice the serving girl carrying trays of food through the swinging service door that led to the dining room. His feet were hooked on the lower bar of the stool. Montane was eating a sandwich while sitting at a stainless steel counter.

Hamlet was roughly the same age as his boss. He had rusty brown hair that curled in many different directions. A few of those curls headed down the side of his face and formed themselves into a light and disorganized beard. He was not large like Matvie, nor did he have the mad or deadly eyes of Lear and Macbeth. He was a good-sized man, however; though soft around the edges. With a gentle face and easy voice, he was often mistaken for being weak and overly kind. He was close to Montane; a smart, level-headed man who was loyal at all times.

"Should I give them a hand?" he asked.

"No, I want to talk to you. Othello's taking care of them."

Othello was in fact only watching the two crew members struggle with their loads. He was a tall man; silent like Matvie, yet more mysterious. Those who saw Othello were never sure if he was watching what went on around him or if his mind had wandered to some bleak, sand swept horizon in the depths of the Sahara. With half closed eyes he could stand for hours without moving. In this way he stood beside the service door and watched over the lunch preparations.

"All he's doing is standing there. Hey, Othello! Make

yourself useful. Don't make that little girl carry everything. Where's your manners?"

Othello turned his head slowly and stared hard at Hamlet. A hint of a smile curled at the edge of his lips, and he turned back to watch the work. Reaching towards Alice, whose arms were full with large platters, Othello snatched an orange slice and dropped it in his mouth. A tilt of his head and shift of his eyes told Hamlet the defiant act was designed to irritate him. He ignored Othello and gave his full attention to Montane.

"Why in the world did you bring Lear and Macbeth on board? We could do without those lunatics."

"What I can't do is abide them on board the sub without me. That's why Matvie took the sub back a short distance. I gave him clear orders to keep the sub out at a distance that no one can move from the boat to the sub. Those two are getting cocky."

"I just wish you'd given us a few more of the boys to keep at hand on this yacht. I'm not so sure Othello and I can watch over you."

"They'll behave themselves as long as Matvie is on the sub." Montane sounded sure of himself, though in reality he was just guessing.

"But what if they've got support back on the sub and they make their play now? Matvie could be taken by sheer numbers." Hamlet realized that the numbers required to take Matvie were large indeed, but it was possible.

"They weren't expecting me to bring them on board the prize. They had no time to arrange anything. And I don't think any of the other crew who might be lured into joining them will make that type of independent decision. No, for the most part, everyone will want to wait and see what I'm up to."

"Well," Hamlet snatched a piece of Montane's sandwich off his plate and held it up for inspection, "I'd sure like to know what you're up to."

Montane stood up and stretched his legs. He could hear muted voices coming from the dining room, and the constant hum of the engines. All else was quiet.

"You know what I'm up to, Hamlet. I went over everything." There was an air of uncertainty about Montane; a sudden indecision.

"I know what you want to do, Robert. But can you really go through with it? What if they don't find in your favor? And what of Lear and Macbeth? What of any of us?"

"None of that matters." Montane's tone changed. He was alert; there was no hint of concern or hesitation. "Remember—I want Lear and Macbeth kept away from the passengers. You and Othello just do your jobs. No one is to come aboard from the sub. Matvie has my instructions on that. If anyone should attempt to board, know that it is with hostile intentions. Even if the sub leaves her present position, I want to know about it. And please—I don't want any of the passengers harmed. Make sure Othello understands that."

It was as if a timer had been engaged. Montane was filled with energy. He left Hamlet and made his way quickly to the dining room. Once there, he pulled David into the passage and asked for an assessment.

"Better than I had hoped. There is no concerted effort to stop your plan. A few complaints, but there is more curiosity than anything else. Sloe's prepared to oversee things, and I would bet the boat's owner will take on the prosecutor's role."

"Vale? No, that won't do. Get someone else."

"Why? What's wrong with him?"

"I've had dealings with him before. He knows me too well. Has a hatred for me. It just won't work."

"You're nuts, Robbie. You think anyone here likes you? And besides, it doesn't matter what he thinks of you. The role is ceremonial. You're already admitting to your crimes. The mercy you're looking for will come with or without this man's condemnation."

"You recommend keeping him?" Montane saw the nod of David's head and relented. "You're the Priest. I've trusted you up to this point. I don't see any reason to stop now. So let's go pick out a jury."

"Wait a minute." David held Montane back with a hand to his shoulder. "You can't be involved in that. Find something else to do. We'll get this thing all worked out and call you when we're ready."

"I'm beginning to wonder who's in charge around here."

There was little left to say. David returned to the dining room while Montane headed topside. The sun was nearly overhead and cast a few rays through several breaks in the clouds. Montane walked to the stern and leaned on the bulward rail, running his gaze from *The Jenny's* wake to the sub that lingered back about two hundred yards.

She was the *Prowler*, a restored German U-boat. One of only a few that survived the war. Bought by a collector of dubious character, it had been carefully restored and refitted with modern communications and navigations systems. It had been stolen just months after it was finished, and over time, had been stolen so many times the original owner had given up trying to track it down. Montane was most likely the first man to ever acquire it without stealing it. It had been a present from an old friend. And now she lay in the water with a fresh coat of paint. She was sleek, deadly, and for the moment, under his command.

There was every possibility that she would cease to be under his command regardless of his intentions. Montane did not avoid acknowledging that fact. There were personalities and plots and activities that had been mixed and set in motion over the past few months that left the future highly uncertain. If being a pirate for over twenty years had taught Montane anything, it was that no matter how well one planned, there was no telling what the sea might throw at you.

But Montane was determined to allow what he had started to continue to its fruition, despite the uncertainties. And although he abhorred uncertainties, he believed the Priest. There was a way out for him. There had to be a shore on which he could set foot and leave his old life behind.

For a brief moment Montane felt a passing of danger like a spirit upon the deck. He spun around and stared down the empty stern. There was no one there. He waited. After a pause of five heart beats, Lear, the mad twin, came into view. He strolled along the deck with a relaxed gait. With pursed lips, whistling silently, he slid alongside Montane.

"The sun shining through this cloud cell spread, could never dispel our fear, pain, and dread."

"Lear, you should write greeting cards. You've got a real talent. So how's your situation at the helm?"

"Drives like a peach. On course, on time, and off the beaten path." Lear caressed the rail and took a deep breath. "She's a pretty little thing. I think I'm in love."

"Kind of risky; a pirate getting emotionally attached."

"I've always been able to get emotionally involved without the messy complications of getting emotionally attached."

"Are you forgetting Maria?" Montane picked out a name that he knew would draw a strong reaction from Lear.

"I was never attached to Maria. She latched onto me." He grasped at his own throat with both hands and made choking gestures.

"Never lie about an event when your listener was a witness. How bad a memory do you think I have? *Captain, please let me take a wife! I want to keep her! Make her stay!*"

Both men laughed freely at the memory. For a brief time, they were off their guard. As once they had been, they were good friends for that moment. Each of them felt this more than thought it. They both allowed it to linger, glad to be free of the tension and weight of their distrust. Montane missed the friendship he had once enjoyed with Lear. And although Lear now decried Montane's overbearing role as Captain, he recognized how he had at one time felt a love for the man who had filled a father's role in his and his brother's life.

"I should have married her. She was a good knot."

"She cursed you and ran off with Fennig."

"Well, I would love to skin Fennig alive. But Maria…" Lear smiled wickedly, "she was a good knot."

The wickedness in his smile moved on easily into his eyes. The two pirates retreated into their protective stances. Montane stiffened and eyed Lear with caution. Lear became agitated. Now that it had passed, they were unhappy they had allowed the genial moment to occur.

"Back to the bridge for me," Lear announced suddenly. "You just count on me and my old brother. Trust us to keep a good watch on this boat. Don't worry 'bout a thing Captain. I gotcha covered."

Lear slunk off in the same crooked manner he had appeared. Montane eyed his retreating figure carefully. It was evident Lear had been sniffing about to judge Montane's present state. Had he shown any signs of the stress he was under? Had Lear seen a crack in his armor? He's been on top a long time now, and he'd known enough men on top who had finally fallen. He was also very familiar with Lear's prowling ways. Montane had been in that same role once. This reversal of roles was no shock to him. He'd been expecting it. He only hoped the plan he had developed would spring him from the fate to which his predecessors had succumbed.

Chapter Seven

Ordering the Court

Lunch had calmed the passengers but Captain Sloe was not quite convinced they were ready to begin. David had prompted him to get things started on two separate occasions but he had been certain they were still too edgy and would only descend into more cacophonous anarchy. A minor delay before starting would be worth it if it held off a major delay or even postponement in the middle of the proceedings.

"Captain Sloe," David leaned over and spoke confidentially, "I'm in no hurry. But Montane may get a bit irritated if we don't begin."

"I have asked for your patience long enough, my new friend. And I now agree it is time to get this show on the road. Wish me luck."

No one paid attention to the Captain as he stood and walked to the middle of the room. He stood eyeing everyone in their seats. As his eyes met the steward's he nodded. Never Gamble nodded in response. It took him a few seconds to realize he was being signaled. Though slow to understand, he was quick to comply.

"Ladies and Gentlemen!" The steward leapt to his feet. "Your attention, please!"

There came no drilled military response; two of the passengers continued to talk, Ida Claire gave her attention just enough to stare at the steward's rudeness. Most of the others, however, stopped eating or talking and looked in his direction. The effect was enough for the Captain. He could now be heard by everyone in the room.

"Though we of course are being forced to perform this trial, we have decided as a group to cooperate as much as possible to ensure the safety of the ladies. With your permission, I shall assume the role of judge as ordered by our pirate invader Captain Montane."

"I don't see we have much choice," groused Martin Vale.

"Well on my position as judge that's true. But we do have a choice that we can make. We are to appoint a prosecutor. Does anyone volunteer to be the prosecutor?"

No one answered right away. Mr. Sherman whispered something to Barry Alum, who started laughing out loud and exclaimed "Oh, perfect!" quite boisterously. Ida Claire eyed them suspiciously, correctly assuming she was being mocked in some way.

"Where's all that bravado you had earlier?" Cora Vale asked her husband. "Did all the wind blow out of your bag?"

"Apparently not. You're still talking." Martin Vale felt petulant enough to risk his wife's anger.

"I nominate my powerful husband," Cora announced with an inebriated tone. "The man of money, power, and a recently pirated boat. Go get 'em Sheriff!"

"I won't do it." Martin Vale stared defiantly at his wife.

"My husband will do it," Fanny Odston said with pride. Wavel looked at her with a good bit of curiosity. "He's not afraid of a rogue like that. Are you, Wavel?"

"Bravo, Wavel." Ida Claire said approvingly.

"Isn't he brave?" asked Mrs. Kaufman.

"Just getting up every morning is an act of bravery for that man," observed Barry Alum.

"Are there any objections?" Captain Sloe reluctantly asked as he offered Wavel a sympathetic smile.

"I certainly object." Mr. Sherman stood and addressed the room. "While I applaud Mr. Odston's sense of duty, it is not his obligation to bring charges on this pirate. Presently, the only one here who has been a victim of this pirate is Mr. Vale. I think it is only appropriate that we move to make Mr. Vale defend his boat's honor wearing the mantle of the Prosecution."

"Long live Dixie!" Cora toasted Mr. Sherman's motion.

"Jeff Davis couldn't have said it better."

"Cora!" Martin Vale tried desperately to silence his wife. "Don't tell a black man 'Long live Dixie'. Are you that drunk already?"

"No offense taken, Mr. Vale," Mr. Sherman assured him.

"Don't change the subject, you little coward." Cora stood toe to toe with her husband and poked him just above the belt with a red painted fingernail. "I second his motion to make you take on the Pirate."

Captain Sloe rushed in to close out the discussion. "All those in favor?"

As near as it was possible, the group unanimously said "Aye."

Taking a deep breath, the owner of Ardeco Travel closed his eyes and stood straight. He lifted his chin and his eyes flashed open. "Fine. I'll do it. Let's just get this over with."

"I think there's a problem."

All eyes focused on Never Gamble. He was still standing up and shrugged his shoulders sheepishly.

"Well, speak up, boy!" Ida Claire barked impatiently.

"There's not twelve. Short, you see."

"Who's short?" Mrs. Kaufman, like those around her, had no idea what the nervous steward was saying.

"He's referring to the number of jurors, I think." Captain Sloe began counting names in his head. "I think I make out only nine, when you consider I can't be a juror. He's right. We'll be three short."

"I counted eleven," Never Gamble said.

"No, my boy. There's the Odston's, and the sisters Mrs. Kaufman and Claire—that makes four. Then there's Mr. Alum, Mr. Sherman, and Tom and you. That's four more to make eight, then add Mrs. Vale, and that's only nine."

"Yes, but I was adding Bob and Alice. That's only left us one short."

"I don't think that really matters," David offered in opinion.

"Doesn't matter?" Fanny Odston could not believe what she had heard. "You tell us he wants a proper hearing, but that the number of jurors doesn't matter? You can't short cut the law. A jury's a jury. If the Captain says we need three more and this little nut of a steward says there's eleven of us, then I say get it right. We need to have fourteen for a proper jury. Any idiot knows that."

"Twelve, my dear. I hate to contradict an idiot, but the right number is twelve." Wavel endured a hard look from his better half.

"I believe a Naval Review Board is made up of three admirals." This was Tom trying to be helpful.

"We haven't got three admirals," Ida Claire corrected him. "One captain. We've only got one captain."

"Wavel was a colonel in the army." Fanny smiled, expecting this news to make a big impression.

"Corporal, Fanny dear. I was a corporal." Wavel shook his head and made apologetic gestures to Mr. Sherman and the Captain.

"Marty was a coward, weren't you darling?" Cora ran her fingers through the ridge of hair on the back side of her husband's balding head.

"Will eleven be enough, David?" The Captain tried to get the conversation back on track.

"Is there an alternative? I think we'll have to just go with the eleven."

"It's not right." Barry Alum wanted to stir the pot for entertainment value. "Miss Fanny says it's gotta be right. I stand by her and say 'fight on, old gal'."

"Old gal?" Fanny arched her heavily penciled brows.

"There are twelve," Tom said with sudden certainty.

"Now, I went over this, Tom. The Odston's and the two sisters make four—"

"But you've all forgotten Melvin." Tom looked over at the old pilot and watched carefully to see if his chest was still moving. Seeing the faintest of movements and satisfied Melvin was still among the living, he turned back and smiled.

"You're right, young man. How could I have forgotten Melvin? Twelve it is." Captain Sloe was pleased to have the issue settled and looked at David for approbation. "

"I guess we have what we need. I'll go get Montane."

"Hold on just one minute." Fanny Odston jumped up. "We must take advantage of being left alone. I say let's plan to overpower these bullies."

"Isn't the Priest one of them?" Mrs. Kaufman cautioned.

"He's in the same boat that we all are." Ida Claire joined Fanny in her cause. "I say we organize and attack. Forget this silly trial."

"And just who were you expecting to lead the way?" Wavel knew well enough whom she expected. "The men, I suppose?"

"Do you think we women would do it?" Ida questioned incredulously.

"A crying shame there's no children," Cora blurted out derisively, "we coulda sent them out to battle."

"Is she serious?" Mrs. Kaufman asked Mr. Sherman.

"She's inebriated," he assured her.

"I'll lead the charge," Barry Alum bravely offered.

"There's no point in it, people." Captain Sloe shook his head. There wasn't one of them in the group that seemed able to think clearly. "Once the trial is conducted, this Pirate will either leave if we acquit him, or give himself up to be taken to the authorities. At any rate, *The Jenny* will be given back to us. There is no advantage to be gained by putting any of us in peril."

"I quite agree with your Captain." David offered his support. "The last thing he wants is to see anyone get hurt."

"Well why didn't he just ask to be tried?" Never Gamble was definitely in the non-thinking column of the group.

"The Captain would have had him arrested and taken to the nearest authorities without this trial." Mr. Sherman could see everything plainly and tried his best to help the others understand. "I think we should look at this reasonably. While we are helpless in regards to holding this trial, we have the option of conducting it with alacrity and finishing it as soon as humanly possible. Wringing our hands about it will only delay the final rap of the gavel."

"Does the Captain actually have a gavel?" Mrs. Kaufman

was surprised to hear such a thing.

"I was speaking symbolically. I did not mean an actual gavel."

"So there's no gavel?" Ida Claire griped. "How can we hold a trial with no gavel?"

Captain Sloe and David exchanged looks of dismay as the newly formed jury started yapping like a pack of lost hounds. These tangents upon which they constantly embarked drew a simple discussion out into a never ending debate.

"Forget the gavel," Barry Alum managed to make himself heard above the din. "I'll devise a plan and take this boat back. After all, isn't that the point?"

"People, we can't do this," intoned the Captain.

"I say we take a vote, at least," demanded Ida.

Captain Sloe looked helplessly at David and gave in to the defiant Ida Claire. In a further sign of his defeat, he sat down and allowed the others to conduct the vote.

"Those in favor of attempting to take back the ship say as much." Ida proudly raised her arm, as if she were Lady Liberty herself. Barry Alum and Fanny Odston raised their hands at the same time. Mrs. Kaufman raised a hand to ask for clarification on the vote but her gesture was taken in the affirmative and she was too timid to correct the mistake. After giving it a solid thought, Tom raised his hand, feeling game enough to do his part for *The Jenny*, though he felt guilty for voting against his Captain. After a long pause, when it seemed no one else would vote in favor of Ida's proposition, Cora Vale toasted a glass in the air with a "Damn the Torpedoes!" It was the sixth vote to retake *The Jenny.*

"Should we send for Bob and Alice in the galley?" Tom asked.

"By all means," Mr. Sherman said with a bemused look on his face, "just tell Montane we need them to come in and help vote on a proposition to retake *The Jenny* by force. He should send them right in."

"Six votes in favor." Ida Claire spoke with pride. "Your turn, Captain."

"Well, then, who is not in favor of Mrs. Claire's proposition?"

The Captain held up his hand and saw Wavel Odston, Martin Vale, and George Sherman take his side. Never Gamble made eye contact with Ida Claire and hesitantly raised his hand, preparing for the verbal attack from that truculent woman. When David raised a hand, Ida protested.

"He doesn't count! He's one of the pirates."

"You said he was in the same boat as us." Wavel had a way of reminding people about things they wished they had never said.

"Fine, I'll concede he's in the same boat, but his vote doesn't count. Six votes for, and only five votes against. We've won the day."

"You're all forgetting Melvin again," Tom pointed out. "Wake up, Mr. Melvin."

"What are you doing, young man?" Fanny tried to pull him away from the sleeping old man. "We won the vote, don't go messing around with it anymore."

"But that wouldn't be right," Tom was still young enough to care about integrity. "Mr. Melvin!" He shook the old man until his eyes began to open.

"What the devil do you want?" He growled at the group that stood staring at him.

"We want to know how you vote on whether or not we attack the pirates and take back *The Jenny*."

"Attack the pirates?" Melvin eyed the young man with severity.

"Yes. Do you feel we ought to?"

"Do I think we should attack the…? Glory no, boy! Are you out of your mind?" He looked at everyone as if he believed they were all out of their minds, then turned his head back to the wall and fell back asleep.

"Tied vote!" Never Gamble exclaimed.

"Overtime!" Cora called out festively.

"Then as Captain, I say David's vote counts, and we will not make any attempt to recapture *The Jenny*."

The Captain's tone was sufficient to settle the debate. No one else spoke, and David stood up and left the room in search of Montane.

Chapter Eight

Interruption to the Proceedings

"I can't believe you're not stuck in some chaotic debate." Montane was genuinely surprised when David showed up on deck to inform him Captain Sloe was ready to proceed. "This is a good sign, don't you think?"

"I can't say how things went, but I wouldn't say there were a bunch of great signs being erected. However, I think you'll get your trial as you wanted."

"Be optimistic, David. The very fact that Lear hasn't slid a knife between my ribs is a good enough sign for me."

"You've gotta get some new friends."

"That is what I was trying to say that night I called you on the phone." Montane reached out a hand and placed it easily on David's shoulder. "And I've got you now, right?"

Just before they entered the dining room, Hamlet caught up to them in the passageway. He was edgy, and a little out of breath.

"Captain, you'd better come back up on deck." Hamlet was in earnest and Montane could see it in his eyes.

"Lear?"

"No, the *Prowler*. She's pulling alongside."

A muttered curse sounded in the close quarters of the passage. Montane thought a moment, then turned his attention to David.

"I assume that roomful of nut cases is a bit wired out. Why not give them all a break? Hamlet and Othello will get them all to their staterooms for a little while. Hamlet, come first with me before giving Othello a hand."

Rapidly, Montane bounded up the steps and came onto deck determined to face what was coming. Hamlet was right behind him.

The *Prowler* was indeed back alongside *The Jenny*. Matvie was standing alone at the base of the conning tower. Montane stood warily across from his large crewman and tried to keep an eye on the deck around him in case Lear or Macbeth showed up. Hamlet stood back at the open hatch. He reached behind him and assured himself his 9mm automatic was ready to be pulled at the slightest sign of trouble. But even he realized that if Matvie had been swayed to join Lear and the others, then there was nothing much he could do for Montane.

Othello came up the steps behind him and stared at the Captain standing abreast of Matvie. He cast a blank look at Hamlet.

"I want you to go check on those two twins in the wheelhouse. Just make sure they're staying put." Hamlet hoped that if push came to shove, Othello could hold his own against Lear and Macbeth. "You be careful."

Othello turned and headed back towards the helm without saying a word. Hamlet returned his gaze to Montane. The gangway was back in place, and Montane crossed over to the sub. He stood extremely close to Matvie. Neither of the men moved. If they were talking, Hamlet could not hear them. They stood like that for a full two or three minutes. Montane crossed back to *The Jenny*, and Matvie stood rooted to the sub.

"The devil's at work." Montane approached Hamlet and shook his head. "There's an electrical problem."

"Sabotage?"

"Can't tell. Matvie said it'll take a while to fix. But as she stands, the *Prowler* is a sitting duck. She can't dive; wouldn't be able to go over to battery power. I need to see to this and make sure that if it wasn't sabotage, no one takes the opportunity to make it worse. I need you to come back with me to the sub. Matvie's going to come over here. He's picking two good men to bring with him. If he says they're solid, I'll trust him."

"You're leaving Lear and his brother over here? Now think that through."

"I have. They won't oppose Matvie if he has support. Besides, with me on the *Prowler*, they'll be in a sticky situation. They don't really need the yacht. They want the sub. You think you can watch my back?"

"I'd rather have Othello with us."

"He's gotta stay with Matvie."

The exchange was made quickly and without fuss. Montane and Hamlet were aboard the sub, pulling the gangway with them. Matvie and two loyal crewmembers stood beside Othello and watched their Captain enter the door at the base of the conning tower.

Othello dropped back down the steps and went to the dining room. Entering, he walked straight to David and spoke in a dark, rich voice.

"Tell them all to go to their rooms. Now."

David did not repeat the command since everyone in the room was able to hear his bass voice. They also read the urgency in his face and tone. With little small talk, everyone made their way to their rooms.

Never Gamble sat on the edge of his bed and tried to lose the nervous shakes he had acquired since the submarine had surfaced that morning. He was a round faced young man of twenty-six years. The last thing he had wanted to deal with on this voyage had been pirates. Pirates were a real fear of his, just as some people fear cancer. His uncle had been in the merchant marines for over forty years and he had always filled young Never with tales of butchering pirates and rogue privateers. Never was not one to search the skies and expect to be killed by a falling meteorite, but pirates had always been one of those things he just knew he would end up facing. And now he had been proved right.

"Tom, this is just crazy." Never was bunkmates with the younger man Tom, even though Never, as ship's steward, outranked Tom. "What were the odds we'd get taken by pirates? And what was all that about—voting to try and retake the ship. What were you thinking?"

"I think we could do it. We've got them greatly outnumbered."

"Are you forgetting that submarine out there? Good lord, that's not something you out run.'

"You know," Tom thought about it, "I really did forget about it. Holy smokes."

"Yes, well I don't think I like the alternative either. This whole trial thing. What's that all about?"

"That's a new one to me." Tom slipped up to the top bunk and lay flat on his back, tucking his hands under his head. "You suppose he's serious? About letting us go, I mean?"

"He doesn't act like it, with those big goons of his running around in charge of the poor *Jenny*. It hurts to see them commanding her."

"How odd it would seem, to go back to work after something like this. Just a simple, alright Tom, let's see that the deck chairs haven't any loose screws. Mr. Sherman will be shooting skeet at…oh my word," Tom leapt from the bunk and reached for his tennis shoes. "I left it out. I can't believe it."

"What's the matter? Left what?"

"The skeet machine. You told me to leave it out. It's still sitting at the stern."

"Tom, forget the skeet machine."

"I shouldn't. Especially if he really is going to turn this all back over to us. That salt spray is a booger on the release mechanism. I'll have to go over it with some lubricant to compensate for the extended exposure."

"They won't let you out," Never whined. "Don't open the door. They'll likely shoot you."

"I'm sure if I talk to them they'll understand." Tom stepped lightly to the door and cracked it open. He peered into the passageway and looked for any sign of the pirates. Never continued to whisper at him, demanding he shut the door. Tom could see no one immediately at the door, so he pulled the door open more and waited. No one appeared. The hall was silent. Leaning his head out into the passageway, he looked both ways and saw no one. The other stateroom doors stood silently shut, like soldiers at attention.

"There's no one there." Tom said softly to Never. "I'll bet they're guarding the steps leading topside. Do you think they know there's another set of steps at the rear end of the passage? I'll bet they don't."

"Tom! Get back in the room."

"All I'm going to do is slip down the passage and take the back steps up to the deck. I'll just grab the skeet machine and be back down in a few minutes." Tom flashed a smile at Never. "Never fear."

Tom closed the door in one swift and silent motion, and Never was left alone in the room.

With eyes closed, Captain Sloe lay on a soft leather, hush-puppy brown couch in *The Jenny's* day room listening to Barry Alum and George Sherman debate whether or not to make an attempt to retake *The Jenny*. It was more of an academic debate, from Mr. Sherman's point of view. As is often the case, Barry Alum, representing the losing vote, continued to debate as if the issue were still in question. Whatever happened to losing with dignity?

The three men had asked to be allowed to wait in the day room. It was a room as large as the dining room, yet furnished with couches and small tables. There was a billiard table with a tiffany lamp hanging over it done in rose and turquoise glass. A wet bar stood in one corner while in another corner a vintage jukebox that played 45 speed records sat waiting for nostalgia buffs to drop a nickel in its slot. The heads of springbok, impala, and bushbuck were staring placidly from the walls. On a pedestal in the center of the longest wall, opposite the entrance, stood a three foot tall Geisha . She coyly hid half of her white painted face behind a fan of bright greens and reds revealing a face that was melancholy yet beautiful.

"It makes no difference whether or not he's going to let us go." Barry was lining the billiard balls up and taking practice shots. He was still under the mistaken impression the whole pirate plot was a show put on for the entertainment of the passengers. "It's our obligation to work together and throw them off the ship."

"Mr. Alum," Captain Sloe spoke without opening his eyes, "would you kindly not refer to *The Jenny* as a ship."

"It would be a great waste of time to just sit around and wait for them to leave."

"Time's not really that precious to me, sir." George Sherman sat in a spacious club chair upholstered in white muslin with strips of black lacquer running down the middle of the arms. He carefully watched Barry Alum move around the table. He was mostly interested in keeping an eye on the back end of the pool cue whenever Barry came to George's side of the table. "I don't see the value of time compared with the safety of the ladies."

"A classic mistake, buddy," Barry chalked his cue and laughed. "Don't ever let them use the women against you. Women are liberated today. That's what they want. So I say, forget 'em. Let the cards fall where they may. This is an exercise in survivalist thinking."

"This is about surviving, I'll agree with you there. Do you agree, Captain?"

The two men turned when there was no response from their companion. Captain Sloe was unaware of the question, as he had fallen soundly asleep. Barry continued to set shots on the table. George, as if persuaded by the Captain, leaned his head back and closed his eyes. In a short time, he too had drifted off.

Striking the cue ball sharply, Barry watched the white ball ricochet from bumper to bumper; gradually slowing until it gently smacked the green number six. The six ball rolled at an angle away from the cue ball and stopped well short of a corner pocket. He tossed the pool cue onto the table and fished in his shirt pocket for a cigarette. The pack was empty. He crumpled it and tossed it into a potted plant and paced the day room with great agitation.

Chapter Nine

Plans Are Laid Out

Barry Alum had never had anything given to him. His life had consisted of finding out what he wanted and then going after it. When he needed the cash in order to date girls, he had researched what was selling big in New York and Los Angeles. He would then contact the distributors and be out selling the latest item in his home town of Omaha. It was a lucrative affair, and he made more money than he could spend on the girls. Once the money began to grow, he taught himself the real estate market. Where sales had been a gifted and money-making hobby, real estate became a talented and empire-making career.

He knew now what he wanted. He wanted to beat these stage acting pirates. He did not want them laughing at him. He was sure *The Jenny's* passengers were all reacting like most of the passengers on prior cruises. He wanted to be creative. He wanted to shock and impress these imposters; turn the tables on them. It really wouldn't take much to do, he calculated. There were very few pirates; a cost cutting move by the penny-pinching managers of the cruise that would prove to be their downfall.

But how was he to go about it? The only ones willing to help were that bunch of irritating women. There was Tom, the porter. He could be useful. Could two of them do it? He had never before had to subdue a man. But if they could get just one of the pirates alone, and get his gun, then that might be all the actors needed to give up. They couldn't start shooting. So they would have to cry uncle and applaud their bravery.

It was a singular characteristic of Barry Alum that he never considered the possibility that the pirates were genuine. He had read the pirates' invasion as entertainment the whole way, had relaxed and enjoyed the show, and was now ready to join the fun on stage.

As he paced about the sleeping forms of the Captain and Mr. Sherman, Barry heard someone passing in the hall. He listened and heard a door open. There was a shuffling noise, as if a struggle were involved. Barry hurried to the door of the day room and flung it open, believing a fellow passenger was in trouble and needed assistance.

To be more precise, a fellow shipmate was having trouble and could certainly have used some assistance. It was Tom. He was trying to store the skeet machine in a storage closet near the aft stairs. The closet was already full leaving very little room for the oddly shaped contraption.

"Tom, watch out there." Barry rushed forward and grabbed at some fishing rods that were about to fall upon the poor young man.

"Thanks, sir. It's always an adventure putting this darned thing away."

"Look, let me pull this out first. Now, push it in." After a few more well orchestrated maneuvers, they had the closet door closed and were standing in the empty hall.

"Who let you out to roam around?" Barry asked suspiciously. He suspected the crew was being allowed to go about their daily activities during the show. It wouldn't do to let them loaf about while on the clock, he shrewdly guessed.

"No one. I just left my room. There's no one watching us down here at the moment."

"You haven't seen any pirates?"

"Yeah, I saw a few amidships, on deck. They were talking to someone on that sub. It's back alongside us. I just wanted to get this thing back inside. The salt tears it up."

"Follow me," Barry stepped along the passage, until he came to a door. He knocked softly, and no one answered. Trying the handle, he found it was locked. "What room is this?"

"Alice's closet. Keeps the cleaning stuff in there."

"You got a key?"

"Nope. They accused me of stealing chocolate mints from the jar she keeps them in on the bottom shelf."

"Mints? Like for the pillows? How do you know they're in the jar on the bottom shelf?"

"Because that's where I was stealing them from."

"Right," Barry moved to the next door and looked at Tom.

"That's a stateroom. It's empty. Some old guy canceled out last week."

"Canceled out? Why?"

"He canceled out. Died."

"Okay. Key?"

"Yeah, but why not just use your room? This one's right next to it."

"You've got a lot to learn. A good man never plots anything in his own house."

"What's Never got to do with this? I left him in our cabin." The porter pulled a keychain from his pants pocket and inserted the key. They moved into the room and Barry snapped shut the door.

"Never's not plotting, we are."

"What are we plotting?" Tom whispered.

"You were willing to fight back against the pirates in the dining room, right?"

"Well, don't exaggerate my offer." Tom felt a clarification was important. "I agreed we should all do something. I was not exactly saying I should be the one to do it."

"Well, it may just come down to that. You and I are the only ones willing to do it. And I think we could." Barry could be a persuasive man regardless of the sales pitch. He gave Tom a full scale assault, appealing to his duty, his manhood, and other virtues the young man never knew existed. By the end of the speech, Tom was reluctantly on board.

As far as he could tell, Montane was certain the electrical failure was due to corroded wiring in a panel on the port side of the electric motor room. There was no sign of sabotage.

His chief electrician verified the wiring was old, and should never have lasted as long as it had.

"So this is no simple rewiring job?" Montane leaned back against the battery cabinets in the close quarters and knew the answer to his own question.

"I wish it were that simple. The ground caused a phase that burned out the starter on the electric battery charger." Castle, the electrician, pointed out the chain of events and ended with his hand on the charger's start button. He pushed it several times. "And we don't keep a starter like that in stock, you know."

"So no charger?"

"No charger. We're at full charge right now. But as soon as we dive, we're on a countdown. Once the batteries are empty, we'll have to surface, and we'll be unable to dive again. And at that point, anyone can find us. I have what I need to rebuild the thing. But it takes maybe a day, maybe more. Can't tell till I really get into it."

"Well then get into it." Montane pressed himself against the cabinet and allowed Castle to pass by, then turned and made his way through the diesel motor room and into the control room. Hamlet was standing at a small chart table.

"We're close enough to rendezvous with Shastov if we come about and make for here." Hamlet pointed to a grid on the map that was about one hundred nautical miles out from Martha's Vineyard. "We could be there tomorrow morning. If he can find what we need, then we pick it up from him, and be back early the next day."

"Castle thinks he can rebuild the starter."

"I doubt it."

"But you're talking about traveling the whole distance while surfaced. You're bound to be spotted. And we need to be making more in this direction. We haven't slipped the shipping lanes enough to my satisfaction."

"So, you keep on your heading, we'll meet with Shastov. We'll be traveling mostly at night. Once we make the repair, we submerge and meet up with you again wherever you like."

Montane looked around at the crew that was moving

about and shook his head. He motioned for Hamlet to climb the ladder into the conning tower. Once Hamlet ascended Montane followed. The tower had very little room for more than three people. Besides the main periscope, a smaller navigation periscope ran through the tower as well. The ladder leading to the exterior platform of the tower added to the crowded conditions. Montane kicked the heavy hatch closed between the control room and the conning tower cutting them off from the rest of the crew.

"I don't think we can split up. About the only way I would do it was if I split up the twins. But then I would have to send either you or Matvie with the sub. Either way, I don't like it."

"You need to throw those two in the sea." Hamlet was serious, and hoped Montane would take his advice.

"I can do this without bloodshed. But those two are giving me ulcers."

"So?" Hamlet waited. Montane had never been this indecisive. It concerned him to see his friend this way. Maybe it really was time for him to get out of the Captain's chair, he thought. He was not being disloyal with such musings. He was aware of Montane's desire to get out. He wanted to see it done on the Captain's terms, however, not on Lear's and Macbeth's. Theirs would consist of little pity or mercy. And as far as Hamlet was concerned, Robert Montane had been a Captain worthy of a little mercy.

"I'll stay aboard until he breaks the starter down and can give me a better estimate of his rebuild time." Montane climbed up the ladder and pushed open the hatch leading out to the top of the conning tower. With one arm supporting the hatch, he climbed up and out of Hamlet's view. Gone only a few seconds, he dropped back down and secured the hatch.

"Making sure Lear didn't drive off with your experiment?" Hamlet laughed.

"You laugh, but just remember, if this experiment doesn't work, you're likely to miss out at assuming command." Montane dropped down into the control room.

Hamlet blinked in surprise. He knew Montane would not joke about something like that unless he meant it. He grabbed the rungs of the ladder and climbed down with a great deal to think about.

Chapter Ten

During the Delay

Like a brooding, silverback gorilla, Matvie stood hunched over, watching the sub. His broad shoulders and thick arms matched his tree-trunk thick legs. He was as silent as he was solid. His face, covered in the same black curly hair that covered his head, led one to believe he held no sentient thoughts. He was more related to some statue discovered buried in the vines of a jungle than to his fellow man. Heavy-lidded eyes suggested Oriental descent. His hands were enormous. He wore a pair of white coveralls that had seen so much oil and grease and other blackening agents that they were now more black than white. A Greek fisherman's hat was smashed down on his large, round head.

He had been the loyal companion of the Captain for over twenty years. In truth, his loyalty was to the office of the captain. Montane had only been one of many whom he had served. No one could remember from where he had come. Matvie never spoke enough to give anyone even a hint as to his background. He was a workhorse; always there, ever faithful, and a mystery to them all.

Matvie had a simple and tenacious grasp on what the Captain wanted. His greater ability lay in understanding why the Captain wanted anything. Though he often acted like a simpleton, he was in fact a complex thinker; an ingredient that contributed to his melancholy manner. He never asked clarifying questions when given an order. He obeyed; but most importantly, he understood.

His gaze rested on the sub, yet all the while he was thinking. He knew what the Captain had told him. *Watch Lear and his brother. No one is to harm the prisoners.* That would have been simple enough for any one of the crew, but Matvie knew there was more at stake than the prisoners' safety. He had heard enough in the last few months to have a basic outline of the Captain's plans. Even Montane made the mistake of underestimating Matvie's capacity for logical thought. On more than one occasion he had spoken openly with David while Matvie was present.

The office of the captain was where Matvie's loyalty lay. He did not care who was captain. He would serve any man who could take and keep the office. Matvie did not have an opinion on Montane's desire to leave. His one abnormal thought was a hint of reservation in seeing Montane leave. He had treated Matvie with greater respect than any captain before him. Yet, Matvie knew that to be the Captain of a Pirate crew one needed a hard heart and a cold, swift hand. Montane, once possessing both qualities, had softened over time. It was a good thing he wanted to leave. He would not be able to maintain his captaincy if he continued to soften.

And so Matvie, knowing that the Captain was devising a way to abdicate, was ready and willing to aid him in any way he was asked. Until the last moment that Montane was captain, he would give himself to that end. But there would be no remorse once he was gone. There would be a new captain and he was ready to give service to whoever that might be. He held no ambitions of his own. He would give aid to Lear, Hamlet, or any other who might dare to lead the crew.

Just as the Captain had requested, Matvie brought two crew members with him on board *The Jenny*. Kit and the Old Man were chosen for their loyalty. Kit was in his early twenties, and Matvie knew him to be eager and willing to please. The Old Man was the eldest of the crew. Speaking with a heavy French accent, he was wise, skilled and despite his French heritage was more cheerful than anyone else on the crew. The Old Man had been around longer than Matvie and was the only one of the crew to know any details of Matvie's life. Yet there was an unspoken pact between the two men. The Old Man never told anyone anything about Matvie.

"This is all kind of odd," Kit stood on deck and dug the point of his small buck knife into a wooden railing he chanced to be standing near. "What is it we're doing?"

"That's none of your business." The Old Man watched the knife point dig into the wood and spat contemptuously. "Now why do you want to go and mar that woodwork? Have a sense of decency. When you see beautiful wood like that say 'ho ho, how wonderful'. Do not just dig into it like a termite. "

"What's a matter? I don't mean nothin' by it."

"That's the problem with a toy knife like that. It's just something you play with." With speed he did not appear to have, the Old Man pulled a large bone-handled knife and touched the tip of it to Kit's knife. "A real knife like this doesn't need to be played with. It's a serious tool that asks only to be used in earnest."

"You Old Nut," Kit jerked his hand back; the Old Man made him nervous. "What do ya need a sword for?"

"You think that's big? You should see Othello's. He-he! The man could reap wheat with that blade."

"Speak of the black devil." Kit watched Othello approach them. He was easily unnerved by the big, black man. Many stories were told of Othello by the crew that made Kit want to keep his distance.

"Is there something we're supposed to be doing here?" The Old Man spoke casually to Othello. He held no rank yet his years of service gave him certain liberties that crew members like Kit dare not take.

"Watch the stair. No one comes up."

"I'll make sure of that," Kit promised with fire in his eyes.

"Harm no one. Only, do not allow them to pass." Othello left towards the back of the boat. His movements were as economical as his words.

"Guard duty," Kit spit the words. "When do I get to do something interesting? What a waste of time."

"Interesting is overrated. I don't mind the guard duty. When you get to my age," the Old Man spoke as if he were Kit's tutor, "a chance to sit back and rest your feet is a good thing. My only objection is being paired with a whining kid."

Kit shot a pouting glance towards the elder crewman and sat down at the entrance to the stair leading down into the boat. The Old Man reminded him too much of the teachers he had run away from in school. What luck, he thought; I run away to become a pirate and get saddled with another teacher. He leaned against the entrance framing and stuck his knife into the deck between his legs. It would be a long and dull afternoon.

David sat in the dining room, his thoughts on the coming trial. Judging by the way the debate had gone about fighting to retake the yacht, he knew the passengers would have been surprised to hear he actually wanted the trial to take place. More shockingly, he really did want to see Montane forgiven. His heart yearned to see his plan work.

It would be difficult work, he knew. All defense attorneys knew what it meant to fight for a man's innocence; but what of their forgiveness? Little attention was ever given to the sentencing phase of a trial. There was definite interest in the sentence, though scant attention given to the arguments presented. *Fry him! Lock him up and throw away the key! Give the guy a break.* Most people, David thought, dealt out sentences with pure gut reaction. There was no thought put into the why and the how. Although justifications were a dime a dozen, there wasn't the least bit of mercy to be found in the public square. Put all together, the judgment laid down by society was more often swift and random as opposed to the ideal set down by Solomon.

And here, now, David saw a chance to change that. He had no idea why that change should come. This squabbling, petty rabble was every bit the prime example of the public square. Yet, he saw the merest hint of a chance. Just the fact that the opportunity was real gave him hope. There would be no court of law binding the proceedings. Surely, outside the structure of a State run affair, couldn't forgiveness be given a chance? It would vindicate everything he had told Montane during those first, unadorned dialogues they had engaged in over the phone.

"I want to give up my evil ways," Montane had simply said that first night he called the counseling center.

"What's stopping you?"

"There doesn't seem to be a point in stopping. Not if my life is ruined for good; if I must live on the run, or turn myself in for punishment. If that's all that awaits me, then stopping my life of crime has no personal benefit. The crimes will continue without me. This gang of cutthroats and rogues will carry on just as well without me. In fact they'll carry on far more than I ever let them." Montane's tone had been such that David heard no hypocrisy or selfishness in his words. "If I'm damned to hell, that's well and good. But why then should I cease my current life?"

"But you aren't damned to hell!" David still felt the passion that had driven his response. "That's the glory of God's grace. The prodigal son is always welcomed back."

"In the hereafter, you may be right; but not in this world. Men expect justice. They want to punish. They don't believe a man can change, and they wouldn't have him even if he could. There's an elitism at work that protects society from the likes of me. The whole system of law is based on apprehension and retribution."

David had been forced to admit Montane was right.

"So what good did this sacrifice do?" Montane had asked in regards to the Christian teachings of Jesus. "If a price was paid for me, it fell rather short. Or would you say that was God's plan; to save a man in the afterlife, but to leave him in his misery in the here and now?"

"You're confusing men with God. His forgiveness does not begin once life here ends. His forgiveness begins when you turn to him. In fact, it began at the cross. It's only men who fail to forgive. Don't attribute men's weakness to God. That's like suggesting the crimes you committed proved that God was a pirate."

"Now you've stepped out on a branch that won't hold your weight, Father." Montane had used the erroneous title for the first time during that conversation. "What you suggest is that my crimes are equal to those in society who fail to forgive. That may not have been your intention, but it is the logical progression."

"But it was intentional!" David's voice had risen earnestly. "Unforgiveness is the forgotten sin. But it's every bit as reprehensible to God."

Those words still echoed strongly through David's mind. Could he succeed in making these people on this boat believe that? He knew the key lay in their view of themselves. He was afraid that although he may be able to hold up a mirror to the jury, too many would fail to see their own reflection like the well-trained vampires they had become.

The time for theory had come to an end. He would find out what chance he had very soon. He began to be anxious for the outcome. As it appeared Montane was delayed for a time, David decided to seek out some of the would-be jurors. Maybe he could learn more about them before it all began.

When George Sherman awoke, he stared around the day room with mild curiosity. He was aware that Captain Sloe still slept on the couch behind him, though he could not see him. He was also distinctly aware that Barry Alum was gone. He did not need to sit up and stare down every corner of the room to know that. The annoying Mid-Westerner was not in the room.

If Barry Alum had been from the South, George would have labeled him *white trash* without a second thought. It mattered little that the man had money. His social status was ingrained in his bones. No amount of success or material trappings would ever cleanse such a stain. George had met many like him. They were easy to spot, and easier to disdain. But Barry Alum did not originate in the South, and so George withheld the actual label; he did, however, consider him a close Northern cousin to the South's white "niggers."

George himself came from important Atlanta stock. His father had been a prominent minister, his mother an imported Creole Belle from New Orleans. With the backing of his father's friends, he had been schooled privately. When the time came, his mother's substantial inheritance became the foundation of his entry into the city's upper stratum. Before long, he had married into an even greater family, formed a deeper network of influential friends, and become a fashionable widower at the age of thirty-five. Three decades later he could look back on a life of the most proper and acceptable kind he could imagine.

Standing in order to regain some much needed circulation, George stepped around the billiards table with an easy gait. He looked upon the balls laid out on the table with apathy. He had little interest in billiards. His game was gin rummy. He saw the pool cue Barry had thrown on the table and smiled. Yes, pool was more properly associated with the likes of Barry Alum, right down to the use of a wooden club.

The door to the day room opened, and for a moment George expected Barry to appear. Stepping into the room instead was the pirates' priest.

"Are we being summoned?" George asked.

"Nothing like that." David crossed to the table and surveyed the positioning of the balls. "I don't know much more than you. Just that there's some delay. Are you playing?"

"No, no." George laughed a little with his reply. "I was hoping to scare up a card game but my companions—well there's one, quite unaware of his surroundings, and I seem to have lost the other one."

"I'm aware," Captain Sloe's voice rumbled up from the couch.

"Who did you lose?" David asked with some concern.

"The profoundly average Barry Alum," George pronounced with some amusement. "He was here, at any rate, for some stimulating conversation. But that was something like an hour ago."

"Probably went to his stateroom." The captain raised himself to a sitting position and scratched at his beard. "What's this about a summons?"

"No summons," David answered. "Montane is delayed

for some reason."

"That doesn't seem right for that character. As a captain, I can tell you, that fella runs an efficient operation. No sloppiness on his watch. It's a shame his efforts are applied to the criminal trades."

"Since I was *encouraged* to join him and his crew, I have noticed the same thing. He's no ruffian. He is not what you would associate with a man of the pirate profession." David sat beside Captain Sloe on the couch as he spoke. "I have always understood piracy to be an act of rebellion and even anarchy. That doesn't seem to be the case with him."

"But to be a pirate captain," George Sherman interjected, "suggests the desire for power—unfettered power."

"I might argue against that," Captain Sloe smiled.

"Oh, I think there's truth in what Mr. Sherman says." David caught a nod of thanks from the Georgian and acknowledged him with one of his own. "Montane certainly is in control; not by accident either."

"Young man," George stood eyeing the bashful geisha on the pedestal with his back to David, "is he serious about this trial business? I'm not sure I understand it all."

"He's deadly serious. He is putting his own life on the line."

"As well he should. He seems to be doing the same with our lives."

"Not as you suppose. He has no intention whatsoever of bringing harm to any of you. I have heard him repeatedly tell his crew that no one is to be harmed. I do not condone his decision to take the boat by force. I'm sure he feels some justification in the fact that it was only by *implied* force. But I wish he hadn't done it, all the same. What matters most now is that everyone comes out of this safely. There's no stopping him, so I really hope everyone cooperates."

"But what can he hope to gain?" George was completely baffled by Montane's actions. "We will all sit silently through the whole of the trial, and quickly give him what he wants."

"Back to the gun pointed at your heads, is that it?"

"It dominates the discussion."

"That does seem to be an obstacle," David conceded reluctantly. "I wish there were some way to change that. He really is interested in a genuine outcome."

"It does make one think," Captain Sloe seemed more intrigued by Montane with every passing hour. "He may not be very different from any of us. What he's looking for seems quite natural to me."

The three men said nothing after that. Their private thoughts left no place for audible comment. David knew what the captain was driving at; it was what he had been saying all along. But George's thoughts ran very differently. He puzzled over Montane's goals seeing no sense to the matter. The Pirate Captain was certainly of better blood than someone like Barry Alum. He may not be quite to his own level of value—George knew this instinctively—but Montane did have a measure of class about him. George recognized that Montane had enough class that he should never have to subject himself to petitioning this group of social misfits for absolution. It was not a course of which he would have ever conceived nor would he have ever submitted to it.

"What will happen to us, sister?" Mrs. Kaufman, never sure of herself on normal days, was growing more anxious as this day wore on. The two elder ladies were in their stateroom. Mrs. Kaufman sat in a wooden rocker in a corner; she had the look of a trapped animal. Her dull, brown eyes kept a steady watch on her sister Ida who stood in front of a full length mirror and fussed over her rather substantial hairstyle.

"I don't know, dear." It pained Ida to have to admit this to her sister. "This is all so irritating. It's hard to believe men are allowed to go about kidnapping boatloads of good people. But I can assure you, my sweet sister, I won't take this lying down. I certainly won't cooperate with these animals. Did you see that big black one they dared to call Othello? The audacity! As if a black man could be an Othello. Shakespeare would roll in his grave."

"Wasn't Othello supposed to be black?"

"What? Don't be sassy, Erma. You understand me well

enough."

Mrs. Erma Kaufman never understood her sister, yet she always deferred to her. It was the mark of her poor self image. She had grown up in the shadow of her overbearing sister, and had only found the courage to leave her when she'd met Herman Kaufman. It was Herman who convinced her she could dare to move out from under Ida's influence. She had only traded one dominating driver for another. Herman had succeeded in getting her out from under Ida by his own overpowering personality.

Erma never realized her total dependence on other people. She would never have thought of it on her own, and neither Ida nor Herman would have ever dared to mention it to her. A woman like Erma was likely to begin seeking her own way if she was ever given the seeds of self determination. Even after she gave Herman thirty-five years of faithful marriage, Herman never considered arming her with the knowledge that she was perfectly capable of making her own choices. His last words to her had been only more of the same. "You'll still have Ida. She'll take care of you."

"What do they want from us?" Erma looked at her sister. She was no bigot in her heart, but Ida's tone convinced her Othello's skin color made him all the more sinister. "Are we in terrible danger?"

"Now Erma, don't go on like that." Having heightened her sister's fears, Ida was now able to take on her role as protector and comforter. "You don't need to worry like that. I won't let anything happen to you. They wouldn't dare oppose me. You just let me take care of things. There's a dear." Ida reached out a hand and stroked Erma's soft grey hair.

Ida took her role as Erma's older sister quite seriously. She too had come to believe the demeaning and controlling words she had spoken to her sister for a lifetime. Crushed when Erma had been taken from her, and fully aware the banker had taken her by force, Ida had seen no choice but to marry Colonel Claire. She was too capable a woman to simply run her own life. She readily turned her attentions to her new husband.

Clashing constantly with her husband's military superiors, Ida pushed her phlegmatic Colonel from one post to another. Dissatisfied with his lack of ambition, she sought out opportunities where he could shine and bullied him into seeking them. Before long, she had convinced him to ask for combat experience in the Mekong Delta where he was mercifully liberated from his brow-beaten life by a North Vietnamese rocket-propelled grenade. Ida had stood proudly at the memorial service. It had been whispered amongst the officer's wives that Ida expected to be decorated for her own sacrificial valor.

Two more husbands followed, both men bearing the weight of her immeasurable capabilities to their graves. Her two children, fathered by the ill-fated Colonel Claire, found the courage none of her husbands had ever been able to summon. By the time Isabelle and Isadora were old enough to be shipped off to boarding school, they had fought their mother to a draw. Ida's only option to avoid confessing defeat had been to send them away. The children knew they had won; Ida had known it too. She rarely spoke to either of them again.

"Whatever happens, my gentle sister Erma, we shall come through in the end. We weren't born and raised as Applewhites for nothing. We'll make Papa proud." Ida turned from the mirror and planted both hands on her hips, pulling back her shoulders in a defiant pose. "No pirate ever got the better of an Applewhite, and this little Montane won't be the first!"

A woman's shrill voice cut through the paneled walls. Ida swung her head in the direction of the startling noise.

"What is it?" Mrs. Kaufman cowered in fear.

Ida stepped quickly to the wall and placed her ear against it with both hands spread out to balance her carefully and noiselessly.

"I think *it* is that crazy Fanny Odston. What a perfectly disagreeable woman. Have you ever seen a peacock with such aggravating manners?"

Ida jumped back suddenly as something struck the opposite side of the wall with great force.

Chapter Eleven

Fanny Loses her Baubles

"Gone! They're gone!" Fanny screamed.

"Now, don't throw anything else, dear." Wavel crossed the stateroom and picked up a cast iron statuette that Fanny had just tried to throw through a wall. "Try to make sense, my love. What are you going on about?"

"My jewelry, you dolt!" Fanny stalked up to him and snatched the statuette from his hand. It was the figure of an old sea captain; the captain's pipe now bent at a most curious angle. "The pearl earrings, my mother's diamond bracelet—all of it. It's all gone!" She raised the cast iron captain and tried to hurl him through another wall. Wavel's hand caught it a moment before it left hers

"That's counterproductive." He set the captain down on a small table behind him and stood between it and his frantic wife. "Where were your jewels? I'm certain you only misplaced them.

"They were right in the top drawer of my dresser."

"The top drawer?"

"Yes, what's wrong with that?"

"Well, you certainly made it easy for them."

"For who? What are you babbling about?"

"For whoever stole them." Wavel looked into the opened drawer and rummaged through what remained. "At least they didn't steal your stockings."

"You're taking this rather well, aren't you?" Fanny pushed him away from the drawer and slammed it shut.

"I'm not very surprised, if that's what you mean. We have been boarded by pirates. What did you think would happen?"

"Don't start making excuses, Wavel Odston. Those pirates have nothing to do with it. I've been robbed." Her voice shook as the injustice of it all began to overwhelm her. When the indignity of it all washed over her as well, she could take no more. "If you won't do anything, then I will."

Fanny nearly ripped the door off its hinges as she yanked it open and stormed into the passage. With her hands balled into fists, she stared down both directions of the passage. Anger was rising in her. Wavel's decision to book the cruise, the pirate attack, getting locked up in a closet by that brute Othello, and now the theft of her precious jewelry were creating a rage within her that she finally had to vent. Wavel, watched from inside the stateroom as the vent broke free.

"YOU COWARDLY THIEVES!" Her scream flooded the boat from stem to stern. "I won't take this anymore! Show yourself! Somebody will answer for this!"

As Fanny continued to scream, doors opened along the passage. The three men in the day room hurried into the narrow hallway fearing violence had been committed. Ida Claire stuck her nose out her door and watched as Never Gamble rushed to Fanny's side. Tom showed up only a step behind him. Martin Vale was asking questions before he even made it to Fanny's end of the passage. There was general discombobulation throughout the passageway.

"You cretins! You pigs!" Fanny swung her arms as if conducting an orchestra, striking several people in the close quarters with her wild gyrations.

Captain Sloe and Never Gamble tried to pin down her arms in order to keep her from injuring anyone. As Never reached for her left arm, she swung it over his head and Never missed his aim. His own arm came down on her bosom as he lost his balance and fell into her.

"You little pervert!" Fanny fell back into the captain and smacked Never over the head with her fist. "Help me, Wavel! I'm being raped!"

The blow to Never's head knocked him momentarily senseless, and as he clutched Fanny around her waist with both arms he slid unconscious to the floor. His watch caught the zipper of the woman's skirt, both of which were compelled to follow him down in his descent. Fanny kicked in self defense, fearing for her honor. Young Tom, blushing at the sight of her slip and stockings, rushed in to disengage Never from the skirt. A push from Martin Vale, who was trying to get close enough to discover the cause of the commotion, toppled Tom head first into Fanny.

"Wavel!" Her scream of primal fear pierced the hull of *The Jenny*. Mrs. Kaufman nearly fainted at the sound. Wavel stared with knowing dread as the clump of passengers fell back into the stateroom. Fanny was under the pile, fighting and scratching, desperately searching for freedom. With some detachment, Wavel watched as each person scrambled to break free of the scrum.

"Don't just stand there, Wavel! Help me!" At any other time, those present would have understood Wavel's hesitancy to help his wife. But at that moment, caught in a small space listening to her shrieks, everyone grew angry with him for leaving her.

"Pull her out, for heaven's sake," Martin Vale insisted. Tom wished anyone would follow that command. His hand was trapped embarrassingly beneath Fanny, her nails scratching his back.

Wavel reluctantly reached into the pile and grabbed Fanny's wrist. As he began to pull, she cried out.

"What are you doing? Who's trying to rip off my arm?"

"I am, Fanny darling. Don't worry about a thing, I'll get you out."

A whimper of pain escaped her lips. "Thank you, Wavel. You're going about it all wrong, but don't stop now."

Never Gamble regained consciousness. His watch was still caught in Fanny's zipper, and as she tried to stand, the skirt around her feet tripped up her high-heeled shoes. Fanny fell to one knee; it landed squarely in the middle of Never's chest. A great *oof!* bled from his lungs. Unaware of what had happened since being knocked in the head by the hysterical lady, Never looked up and saw Mrs. Odston, half-dressed, and straddling him.

"Mrs. Odston!" Never croaked in shock, unable to breathe enough to speak with a full voice. """Have you gone nuts?"

"Oh, shut him up, Wavel." Fanny stuck out her hand and pushed herself up using Never's stomach for support. As her knee freed up his lungs and her hand compressed his stomach, Never let out a howl of pain.

"You crazy hag!" Never lay on his back and his eyes met Wavel's as he spoke. "No offense meant, Mr. Odston."

Wavel winked at him but said nothing.

Fanny, back on her feet, reached down and yanked her skirt away from the steward. Ida stood in the doorway, grinning at Mr. Sherman with satisfaction over Fanny's humiliation. She herself had not gotten caught in the melee.

"Entertained, Ida?" George asked under his breath.

"Highly entertained," Ida said, loud enough to be heard by everyone, including Fanny.

"One of you people," Fanny spat contemptuously as she struggled back into her skirt, "has stolen my jewelry. I want it returned immediately."

Never was the last to get to his feet. He was still bent over when Fanny announced the theft. Like everyone else, he froze in place and stared at her. No one spoke. For a moment, Fanny had everyone's attention. She glared at them one by one, her eyes finally coming to rest on the steward.

"I'd bet you did it." She leveled the charge as if it were a loaded pistol.

"You can't be serious!" Never straightened himself and looked around with an appeal to the others. "She can't be serious! She's actually accusing me of stealing on a ship that's been overrun by pirates! In what kind of world can I be accused of stealing when there's pirates running around?"

"He makes a very good point, Mrs. Odston," Captain Sloe said cautiously. He had no desire to attract Fanny's ire. "It's really most likely that the pirates have taken them."

"Unlikely," a voice said from behind.

"Who said that?" Ida turned and peered into the darkened passage. She did not like to hear anyone who might support

Fanny's side of the story.

"It's only me," David stepped into the room.

"Are you defending the pirates?"

"No, Mrs. Claire. That is not my intention. I only want to point out that Montane specifically told his men not to take anything. He was quite clear about that on several occasions. His men do not disobey orders."

"I hardly think the word of a pirate is worthy enough for us to begin suspecting each other of nefarious activities." Wavel tried to calm everyone down. "There are pirates on board, and they have had the run of the boat. No one has had opportunity since that sub appeared to steal the jewelry besides them."

There seemed to be general agreement on that point. Even Fanny had to cease her accusations in the face of her husband's reasoning. Only David disagreed with Wavel, though he chose to say nothing further on the subject.

"Speaking of pirates," Martin Vale looked suspiciously around him, "where have they all gone? Why have we been allowed to run free below decks?"

"Have they all gone?" Mrs. Kaufman asked with some reticent eagerness.

"Surely they heard all this ridiculous screaming," Ida glared at Fanny.

"One could feel quite insulted that they don't care to find out what is troubling us." Mr. Sherman's light remark was taken seriously by several of those listening.

"I believe two of us should go take a look," Captain Sloe suggested. "Perhaps they took all the valuables they could find and left us after shutting us in our staterooms."

"Don't get your hopes up," David cautioned them.

"Never," Captain Sloe addressed his Steward, "please come with me. We'll poke our heads out and see what there is to see."

Never's eyes widened at the frightful prospect of poking his head out above decks without the expressed permission of the pirates. He had no trouble imagining what might happen to his head.

"I'll go with you, Captain." David could see Never was in no condition to go trolling for pirates.

"Very well, Mr. David Wayne. Let's take a look-see top side, huh?" Captain Sloe made his way past the others crowding the Odston's stateroom door and approached the forward steps which led above decks.

Captain Sloe reached the stairs and ascended them rapidly, David close on his heels. At the top of the steps the captain stopped and raised a hand behind to keep David from running into him. Sitting at the top of the steps, backs turned, were the pirates Kit and the Old Man.

"There's two of them, young man. Are they dead?"

They did indeed look dead, David thought, both sitting slumped against posts, their heads cocked at what appeared to be uncomfortable angles. David pushed ahead of the Captain and moved quietly next to one of the pirates. He kneeled and watched carefully for some sign of life.

"Well? Dead?"

David shook his head in response. They were only sleeping. He put a finger to his lips to make the captain understand. At that moment, Othello appeared in front of him. He had made no noise and David had no idea from where he had come.

The captain looked up in time to see Othello raise a finger at David. The signal was unmistakable—get back below deck. Immediately, the two men backed down the stairs. As they turned back to the passageway, they heard Othello's heavy voice wake the sleeping pirates. From the sounds coming down the stairs, Othello was evidently meting out punishment for their dereliction of duty.

The others had hardly moved from their spots when Captain Sloe and David returned. There was great disappointment all around when they gave their report. It was decided they should all go back to their rooms. As a few began to leave, Fanny tried to stop them.

"But what about my diamonds? Captain, you can't let everyone go on as if nothing's happened. I've been robbed!"

Captain Sloe left the stateroom without reply.

Chapter Twelve

Plans Go Awry and Matvie Intervenes

As soon as he heard Fanny Odston's screams, Barry Alum knew just what he had to do. Much to his disappointment, the young porter Tom ran off to investigate. Barry himself could not have cared less why the bilious lady was upset. He knew it was time to act, and was not going to miss the opportunity.

As quietly as possible, yet with the speed needed to take advantage of his window of opportunity, Barry returned to the closet where he had found Tom. In the brief time he had helped Tom with stowing the skeet machine he had caught a glimpse of one, small, particular item.

Opening the closet door, he reached out and grabbed the item, a very used and very old starter pistol. Barry did not bother wondering why there had been a starter pistol on board. It looked old enough to suggest it would not even work. But he cared nothing about that. It had only to look real enough for him to convince one of the pirates, one of the *stage-acting* pirates, to give up his weapon and surrender.

The starter pistol did, in fact, work. It had been used for organized activities such as swim races, but that was for cruises with much younger passengers. It had not been used for over a year.

At the aft stairway, Barry climbed until his eyes were level with the deck. He scanned for movement. The back end of the boat (Barry did not know enough to think of it as the stern) was empty of pirates. He stepped out on deck and knew exactly where he would go. Gliding along the starboard side of *The Jenny*, he edged closer to the wheelhouse.

He heard the two brothers in the wheelhouse before he

could see them. They were arguing, then laughing. Barry was not sure how to approach them. He did not think it really mattered, but wanted to pull off his coup with style. He stood back in the shadow of the wheelhouse and thought out his next move. He was concentrating on the door to the wheelhouse and never saw the figure move in behind him.

With his hand clasped around the starter pistol grip he took a step towards the door. He'd given up on the idea of style. He could hear muffled shouts and movement from below decks and did not want to lose this chance. If the pirates heard the commotion they might investigate, or simply become more on guard. He had to surprise them without delay.

Taking another step, he raised the starter pistol to hip level. Barry felt the thrill of the game and congratulated himself on outsmarting the cruise directors. He would be the toast of the cruise.

Othello had seen Barry Alum as soon as his head was visible above the opening to the stairs. Sitting so as to be able to see the whole of the stern and most of the midships, the big African watched the little noisy American as he began to walk down the starboard side. Unobserved by his quarry, Othello watched until Barry had crept past. He noiselessly slid up to Barry and stopped, unsure what Barry would do next.

Othello listened to Lear and Macbeth in the wheelhouse while he considered Barry, who seemed to be holding something in his right hand. Pulling his fourteen inch knife from its sheath, Othello intended to stop this passenger from going any further. The brothers could not be trusted around the passengers. Othello knew he must not let this one get any nearer to those lunatics.

A sudden gust of loud music rushed out of the wheelhouse. The brothers had found a radio. A Beetles song rang out with high energy—*Twist and Shout.* Covered by the loud music, Othello stepped quietly up to Barry and reached around him with the knife, allowing Barry to see the knife as he held it three inches from his neck.

Barry instinctively spun. Othello saw what appeared to be a gun angling into a shooting position and put out his free hand to stop it. Barry squeezed the trigger with very little effort or thought, shaken at the sight of the knife at his throat and the big man's attempt to wrest the gun from his hand. The starter pistol fired harmlessly but Othello reacted, driving the knife down into Barry's back with one motion.

Barry's mouth opened wide but no sound escaped his pierced lungs. He stared briefly at Othello, as if he meant to ask a question, then dropped lifelessly to the deck.

Othello looked up to see if the brothers had heard the struggle. They did not open the wheelhouse door. The music had covered even the pistol shot. But his deadly actions had not gone unseen. Off to his left, Matvie stood watching, his eyes resting on the body of Barry Alum where it lay on the teakwood deck. Othello knew he had made a grave error. Not only had he disobeyed Montane, but he had allowed Matvie to observe him. His fate was in the silent man's hands.

Matvie was motionless for no more than a minute, then came to life. The great bull of a man approached Othello and looked at him with saddened eyes. Reaching down, he pulled Othello's knife out of Barry Alum's corpse and held it in his hand.

Othello was sure that Montane's loyal bulldog would swing the knife. There was no excuse Othello could give—and it would not matter, even if he could. Othello had heard enough to know this would be the end of Montane's plans. If Matvie swung the knife at him, Othello knew there was not one man strong enough to stop him. He stood waiting; resigned to his fate.

"Clean your knife and your hands." Matvie flipped the blade and offered Othello the massive knife's handle.

Othello took it reverently. He knew there was nothing to say. Matvie had made a decision, for reasons that did not include mercy. Whatever they were, Othello determined to make no more mistakes. Matvie was giving him a second chance; no matter the reason, he would earn that chance. He would make sure Matvie never regretted his decision.

"What should I do?" Othello was indebted to Matvie; his subservient role to Matvie was forever cemented.

"Stop that."

That was a sound of squawks and yammers coming from below. Othello understood Matvie and asked for no clarification. He did not wonder what Matvie would do with the body. It no longer concerned him. He trusted Matvie to take care of it. He would see to the passengers. Matvie had not needed to remind him there was to be no further violence. Othello understood this all too well and focused his attention on being more careful.

The sun was beginning to sink into the western expanse of the sea as Matvie stood alone over the body of Barry Alum. Although Othello's fatal mistake threatened to undo his captain's plans, Matvie did not panic. He kept calm, patiently looking at the foolish, dead man. Othello had made a colossal error, but Matvie would nullify it.

With rock music from the wheelhouse providing a surreal upbeat soundtrack, Matvie stepped over to the starboard side of *The Jenny* and noted a small wooden boat sitting on the low roof of the staterooms. It was not a lifeboat; it was too small for that. Most likely, it was used primarily by the crew to make inspections around the hull and for other small excursions that required only one or two crewmen. This small dinghy was covered with a blue tarp and lashed to the roof with bungee cords. Matvie pulled the tarp back and loosed the dinghy from its cords. Effortlessly, he lifted the boat by hand and set it on deck.

As if all had been arranged beforehand, a rope lay coiled on the plank seat. Matvie tied one end of it to one of the dinghy's oarlocks and secured the other end to a post of the bulward rail. Raising the bow of the little boat so that it sat on its squared transom, Matvie rammed his fist hard against the pine wood, cracking it just below the seat. He pried the wood back until he could strip out a large portion of it. He repeated the process a foot closer to the bow. When he was finished, there were two large gashes in the bottom of the dinghy. Again, Matvie lifted the boat, but this time he tossed it into the sea.

A soft splash was all it made. With complete trust in the knots he'd tied, Matvie turned and walked away, never looking to ensure the dinghy remained alongside. Matvie saw a closet at the rear of the wheelhouse and opened its door. As before, all seemed set up for his personal needs. He spied several large and heavy shackles and carried them to the body in one hand. He bent and lifted Barry Alum with the other, carrying him to the rail as easily as a child would carry a stuffed cotton doll.

Untying the rope, which now kept the half-sunk dinghy afloat, he threaded the rope through the shackles and wrapped the rest of it around the corpse. One final knot secured the shackles tightly to the lifeless torso. Without ceremony, without remorse, Matvie extended his arm and dropped the body into the sea. The body and the dinghy did not sink right away. They both rolled in the swells, just visible below the surface. In time, they would sink; Matvie gave them no more thought.

He returned to the scene of the killing and looked down at the pool of blood. There was a good deal of blood on the teakwood deck. Matvie went back to the closet and grabbed a mop and bucket and a nylon rope. Tying the line to the handle of the bucket, he dropped it over the side and filled it with seawater. Hauling it out of the water, he wet the mop and began to scrub the bloodied deck. Like a schoolhouse janitor, he moved slowly, letting the blood soak into the mop's cotton head. Never once did he glance about in fear. If he were seen by any of the passengers, or even any of Montane's crew, the whole game would be lost. Either he would finish his task without detection, or he wouldn't. Fate would determine the outcome. All Matvie could do was attempt to remove all traces of the killing.

With deliberate swipes of the mop, Matvie erased the stain of blood. After two or three passes, he would rinse it in the bucket. The water in the bucket became increasingly darker.

When the last of the blood had been sopped up, Matvie dumped the bucket over the side and retrieved another bucketful of saltwater. This bucketful he splashed on the deck, allowing the water to spread and run off through the scuppers. He repeated this several times until he was sure there was no longer any sign of Barry Alum's death.

He threw the mop and bucket over the side. All that remained was the starter pistol, lying to one side where Matvie had nudged it while mopping. Picking the little gun up with his thick fingers, Matvie dropped it into the sea as well. Turning his back on the discarded evidence, he gazed at the now sanitized starboard deck, sweeping it from left to right with a practiced eye. He had missed nothing. Barry Alum had disappeared.

Chapter Thirteen

A Conspiracy of Twins

"What do you think, brother? What is the captain up to?"

Macbeth stood at the large window of the wheelhouse, staring east into the darkening horizon. His triangular face came to a sharp point at his chin. A high hairline accentuated the width of his forehead; his hair was swept straight back with a gentle wave. He was the spitting image of his brother Lear, yet it was his eyes that set him apart. They were dead eyes; there was no light in them, no spark of humanity. They were dark brown; so dark one could hardly tell where the pupils began. But more unnerving was the lack of reflection in them. They absorbed light, refusing to give it up; black holes that consumed all they surveyed and gave nothing in return. His question was not one of concern. Macbeth was never concerned. He was simply looking for an angle. Strategy was uppermost in his mind. He looked to his brother for the answer.

Many believed that Lear had stolen the light that was missing from his brother's eyes. If Macbeth's eyes absorbed light, Lear's created their own. They shone with a white fire. They could be mesmerizing. Most of the crew avoided them as if they were living specters that sought to steal men's souls. Only Montane had the courage to look into them without fear. That had been one of the reasons Lear had felt compelled to follow Montane. It was the same reason Lear had come to despise him. Once in awe of Montane's rock solid gaze, he had grown to hate this one man who dared to look into his very soul. The two men had been locked in a Mexican Standoff ever since. Montane would not give in to Lear's blinding presence, and Lear could not change the nature of his growing madness.

But in that locked stare, Lear believed he was slowly gaining the upper hand. He felt the truth behind Montane's schemes and sleight of hand. Lear was beginning to see what the others could not.

"Smoke and mirrors;
the webs he weaves.
The Picture is cleared
by the trail he leaves."

Macbeth was used to his brother's way of talking. He knew the poorly constructed rhyme said nothing useful but he gave no indication to that effect. He knew better than to push his brother. His brother had become more unstable over time, and Macbeth tried to keep from adding to his brother's mental swings. He kept his eyes on the expanse of the Atlantic.

"What makes you say he's up to something?" Lear smiled as if he were serious and really wanted an answer.

"He doesn't want this boat. Not anything aboard her. We should have taken what we could and left already. He's restricted the crew from leaving the sub. Keeps us up here. You know exactly what I mean."

"I do. I would say he's losing his nerve, but that's not it. He's too cagey; he keeps Matvie and Hamlet too close. There is purpose to his dead calm. He reveals nothing; but Hamlet is not so hard to read. I have seen him watching us. He does this with the look of a predator. Sometimes I think he is trying to compose a eulogy for us. He treats us like we're dangerous."

"We are." Macbeth reminded him.

"Sure. We're more than that. And so what if Hamlet or even Montane know it? So long as we give them no reason to move against us. Not yet. Not yet. When we're ready, then let them move."

"We should strike first." Macbeth yearned to be given the freedom to act.

"Unless you really think you can kill that freak Matvie, you'll listen to me and wait. Matvie will not stand for treachery. Self-defense he'll understand. He'll have no choice. I will kill Montane when he moves against us. Until then, I'm telling you to wait."

"I could kill that beast. Matvie is not immortal."

"I like your spirit." Lear cocked his head and it was obvious the idea did excite him.

"Then I'll do it." Macbeth said this with total faith in his ability to carry out the threat.

"I wouldn't be surprised—if you really did try it, anyway. I suppose I should be ready to deal with that big darkie in case you actually succeed. I'll have to think about that."

"And what if I don't succeed? You'd better think of how you'll deal with Matvie then." Macbeth was teasing him.

"If you don't succeed, my deadly little brother, then I won't have to deal with anything ever again."

"Name one man that I set out to kill who isn't dead?"

Lear did not even attempt to come up with a name. He knew there was no one who could stop Macbeth from his business. But he knew Matvie was not simply a man. The thought of their inevitable clash took his breath away. It would be something to see. Macbeth was nowhere near Matvie's size, but he had killer instinct. It would not be a matter of shooting him. They had seen Matvie hit by bullets before. His mass merely swallowed them, and they had very little effect on him in the short run. No, Lear calculated with growing excitement, Macbeth would have to take him by force. But would he die trying?

Lear cared deeply for his brother. They were twins, after all, and they had rarely been apart. The thought of Macbeth losing his life shook Lear, but he could not deny his eagerness to see if Macbeth could actually kill Matvie, like a pit bull owner who wants to see his most beloved prizewinner take on a grizzly in the ring for sheer pride. Though the odds were against them, it made him giddy to think of that one chance in a thousand that his prizewinner would triumph. If he did-- if Macbeth could actually rid them all of Matvie—then the *Prowler* would be Lear's, and Montane would be at his mercy.

Lear began to laugh as he thought more about Macbeth's plan.

"I never took you for a dreamer. My brother—the Giant killer. And people think I'm crazy."

Despite Lear's pronouncement, Macbeth was no dreamer. He was, however, fiercely protective of his twin. He knew Montane was driving Lear to a disastrous edge from which he would never be able to return. There were times he already feared that line had been crossed. Macbeth could remember a time when his brother had not always been so near to lunacy. Lear had once been an open-hearted boy, eager to please those he admired. Lear had rejoiced to see Montane take command. He believed Montane was nothing like their former leader; Captain Black. Black was cruel, he was indifferent to those under him. And most painful to Lear, when he found tenderness, he beat it until it became as hard as rock. He hounded hope into the grave, and shredded gentle souls. Much to the crew's relief, Montane had put an end to Black's reign of terror.

But the damage, though not so easily recognized at the time, had already been done. Lear eagerly gave his loyalty—one might have even called it love—over to Montane. But no one suspected that beneath his sensitive spirit there were cracks slowly widening into a chasm that would consume both mind and spirit. Captain Black had left a poison that was now threatening his successor—Montane.

Macbeth placed no blame on Montane. He knew Black was the sole murderer of his brother's spirit. But he could see that Montane was, through no real fault of his own, the catalyst that kept pushing Lear towards greater darkness. And so he chose to help his brother if at all possible. And he knew they could not wait for Montane to make the first move. Lear's warped mind could conceive of Montane making such an unjustified and rash action; Macbeth knew the captain would never do it. And the longer they waited, the less time Lear had before his mind crossed the point of no return.

Yes, it was impatience that drove him. Macbeth knew

that. But it was his only choice. He set himself to the task of killing Matvie. He was not concerned with losing his own life; he focused on saving Lear.

Chapter Fourteen

Getting On With It

Paul Castle was a careful man. He took his role as the *Prowler's* electrician seriously. He knew his duties were nearly as important as the chief mechanic's; without battery power, the sub could not submerge. And a submarine that could not submerge would eventually be found. That was unacceptable for pirates. And so Castle was extremely careful in responding to the Captain's question about the starter.

"Having torn the starter apart and examined it, I will be able to fix it. But I must add that there is no guarantee that it will last very long. By some time tomorrow, I will certainly have it working. It will start. But as to how many times it will start—I cannot say."

"That's all I needed to hear." Montane gratefully slapped Castle on his shoulder. He knew the refused guarantee was nothing to be concerned over. If Castle said it would work, he could be sure it would work for quite some time. Montane knew that his men made a habit of exaggerating the possibility of failure. Pirates, as a general rule, were men who had left the overachieving world of society in order to live a life devoid of responsibility. Taking pride in one's work and insisting on its quality were never the virtues of a pirate crew. Getting the job done but disowning association with it in light of the slightest chance of a mistake was more in line with the pirate nature. Montane knew all of this and accepted it without passing judgment.

It was high time he headed back over to the captured yacht. Montane could feel that this affair had slowed down too much. The crew would soon become restless. The passengers were already quarrelsome; there was no knowing what they may devolve into. Then there were Lear and Othello; Montane could not keep them at bay forever. If even one thing went wrong now, he would have gained nothing.

"If you don't mind," Montane informed Hamlet, "I think I'll leave you in charge of the *Prowler*. I'll keep the others with me. And don't worry—Matvie will watch my back."

"I'll take care of your sub."

Montane had no idea just how much things had changed on board *The Jenny* when he stepped back onto her deck. Hamlet had no way of knowing what had occurred either, but he was uneasy as he pulled the gangway and gave the order for the sub to drop back to her position behind the yacht. He chided himself for not waiting until he saw Matvie come on deck and meet with the Captain. *The Jenny's* empty decks gave him pause. He had decided to follow Montane's command and drop back because it was the practical move. If somehow Lear had taken control of the boat, there was no reason to keep the sub within his reach.

As the sun began to disappear behind the horizon, Montane stepped across the deck and stood at the head of the main stairs leading down into the cabin passage. There was no sign of Kit or the Old Man. Before going down the steps, Montane made his way to the starboard side and looked towards the bow then back to the stern. He saw no one. He heard nothing. Going forward, he reached the wheelhouse and stepped boldly inside. It was empty. The wheel was lashed, and Montane looked at the boat's heading. They were on the course he had ordered. He walked back out of the wheelhouse and all the way to the stern.

Aside from noticing the skeet machine had been removed from where Captain Sloe had disassembled it, nothing else was out of place. His only choice was to go down into the cabin and see what was going on, unless he signaled Hamlet to join him. Montane was no coward, and he easily decided that no matter what he found, he would go down the steps. He was no fool, though, either. He used the aft stairs and stepped lightly. The last light of day left the sky as Montane descended the steps.

The passageway was silent. Every stateroom he passed was empty. He opened several doors and looked into the darkened rooms. The flip of a wall switch revealed signs of looting; some ladies' garments were strewn about the floor and the drawers of a bureau hung open. Montane turned off the light and kept moving forward. The day room was dark and empty. There was a faint light coming from under the dining room door but he heard nothing. Firmly grasping the brass knob, he swung the door open.

To his astonishment, the room was full. Every one of *The Jenny's* passengers and crew sat at the tables. Even more astonishing was the fact that not one of them spoke; they weren't even moving. Montane saw all of this at once, and at the same time saw that Matvie, Othello, Kit and the Old Man were all standing around those seated. He noted immediately that Lear and Macbeth were not present.

"What the devil are you all doing?" Montane would never have admitted to being worried, but he was greatly relieved to find Matvie still firmly in command.

He expected a chaotic response from the gaggle of men and women who could not shut up the last time he had seen them. To his surprise, no one answered, until David Wayne—who had been seated next to Captain Sloe—rose from his chair and crossed the floor.

"I'm glad you came back," David said solemnly. "It's not going so well here."

"What happened?"

David led Montane away and spoke softly.

"Someone's escaped."

"What?" Montane looked over his shoulder at the group. "Hold on. Before you go any further, where are Lear and Macbeth?"

"The last I heard, they were going into the galley to get something to eat. That's why we're all in here. They insisted on going into the galley together. Seems they won't split up. I think they're as paranoid as you are. Matvie moved everyone in here in order to comply with your orders to keep everyone away from the brothers. That's when we discovered

Barry Alum missing."

"Who's that?"

"One of the passengers; he was nowhere to be found. Matvie sent Othello and the Old Man to search every corner of the boat. He's simply vanished."

"Do you think those two lunatics had anything to do with this?"

"No, and I think I can prove that. You see, no one can remember seeing him since the fight."

"The fight? I'm going to regret asking this. What fight?"

"Well, that's partially my fault. I really should have called for Matvie's help when it was discovered Mrs. Odston's jewels were stolen."

"Her jewels were what?" Montane was trying to keep his temper in check.

"Well, she insists that someone has stolen her jewelry. The funny thing is, I believe her. I just don't believe one of your crew did it. And then after Othello broke up the fight—"

"What infernal fight do you keep talking about?"

"Mrs. Odston—" David sighed heavily and rubbed his temples as if recalling the incident were as painful as a migraine headache, "Mrs. Odston attacked Mrs. Claire when the latter made a suggestion that the former's missing jewelry was fake. Once these two ladies started to go at it, some of the men tried to intervene. Before I knew what was going on, the whole bunch of them were kicking and hitting. I think someone even got bit. That's when Othello showed up and pulled everyone apart. He made them all sit down here and won't let them say a word."

"Now that's impressive. I'd like to know how he managed that." Montane stole another glance at those seated around the tables. "So now there's a jewel thief among them? You're right. This isn't going so well."

"No, let me finish. The missing boat tells us that none of them is the thief."

"Missing boat?" Montane did all he could not to shout. "Is there anything else I should know about?"

"Well, not really. It just seems a safe bet that the missing passenger took the jewels and left in the boat."

"Missing passenger? I'd nearly forgotten about him amidst the rest of this chaotic story. Well, it could have been worse. At least they haven't taken to killing each other yet." Montane wearily ran a hand through his hair. "Father, I should never have boarded this cursed boat. Matvie!"

Summoned, Matvie approached his captain.

"This Barry character; are you sure he's no longer aboard?"

"Yes." Matvie looked straight into Montane's eyes.

"And tell me now, not later. Did one of us take the jewels?"

"I have spoken with Othello and the others. No one has taken them."

"What about Lear and his brother? Have the passengers been kept away from them?"

"Yes," Matvie's reply was short and very much the truth.

"Thank you, Matvie." Montane stopped his taciturn soldier with one more question. "Is there anything else I should know?"

Matvie turned and looked at him in silence. It was his manner, and so Montane could read nothing in the man's hesitance. Finally, Matvie gave his answer. "No, Captain. This is nothing further for you to know."

"Thank you, Matvie."

Matvie said nothing more. He felt no guilt. As far as he was concerned, he had told no lies to his captain. He was sure the dead man was no longer aboard. None of Montane's crew had stolen the jewelry; they really did not have an opportunity, they had all been occupied with different jobs. The passengers had been kept away from Lear and his brother; this included Barry Alum whom Othello had fatally stopped from getting near the wheelhouse. And Matvie told no lie when he said there was nothing further the captain should know. Having done his duty, Matvie returned to the other side of the dining room and stood watch over the prisoners.

Othello gave Matvie a quick look; he wished to know

what Matvie and the captain had spoken about. Judging by the captain's demeanor, Othello realized that the real story of Barry Alum's death had not been revealed.

"I see everyone's eaten." Montane referred to the remains of a light meal scattered over the tables.

"Yes, they have. I suppose it is too late in the day to get started," David remarked.

"I don't see why. I say let's get this thing going."

"I'm not sure I would recommend them in the mood they're in."

"At this point, Father, I don't really care. Can you believe it; one of them making a grab for some jewels and fleeing in a small boat in the middle of the Atlantic Ocean? Somehow, that actually makes sense with this crowd. So why shouldn't they be the ones to decide my fate? And why not just cut to the chase and get it over with?"

David could see no point left to argue. He went off to inform Captain Sloe that he should start the proceedings.

Montane sent Matvie and the other crew members out of the room. He gave orders that they were not to be disturbed. The pirates left the room. Montane was alone with his fate.

Chapter Fifteen

The Jury Gets a Bailiff

Much to Captain Sloe's relief, the passengers were in a subdued mood. Othello and Matvie's dreadful presence were not easily forgotten. And although they had left the room, their influence remained palpable. The captain asked that one end of the room be set up as a court. A table was placed for Captain Sloe. To his left, a chair was set for witnesses. Defense and prosecution tables were put in place and two rows of chairs were put on the Captain's right for the jury.

Unfortunately, the work stirred their blood and the controlling presence of the feared pirates receded in their minds.

"We're back to eleven again!" Never Gamble said with a sudden exclamation. He had just set the twelfth chair down to complete the jury box.

"Oh, don't start," spat Ida Claire.

"What does he mean?" asked Mrs. Kaufman?

"That jewel thief's gone," Tom said with building excitement. "We really are back to eleven."

"We agreed this would be done right," complained Fanny Odston. "Captain Sloe, we can't go on like this."

"Are we sure of that?" Wavel wasn't so sure.

"Don't question me like that," Fanny was getting back to her old self. She smacked Wavel on his shoulders as verification of the fact. "This should not surprise you. We all agreed. There must be twelve jurors. It just can't go on since that thieving poltroon stole my lovely diamonds and jumped boat."

"Jumped ship, my dear," corrected Wavel.

"Don't correct me—I've been told again and again this is a boat, not a ship. Don't you listen?"

"I know it's a boat. I was only pointing out the proper phrase. You said *jumped boat* but the idiom is *jumped ship*."

"I think," Cora Vale waded into the debate, "you could say he *jumped Jenny*."

"Don't be crass, Cora." Martin Vale growled at her drunken lewdness.

"Oh, I don't know," Mr. Sherman came to her defense, "That's just the kind of joke Barry Alum would have loved."

Cora looked George Sherman over with a sensual leer. "Where did you get such a deep and lovely tan?"

"From centuries of living in Africa," George replied quickly before anyone could scold her for her queer remark. He could not be offended; not at the moment. He was still enjoying the fact that Barry Alum had turned out to be what he had known all along—a no good thief. It was a bonus to find the man had fled.

"From centuries of living in Africa? My, you look great for your age." Cora ran her long fingers over the lapel of his dinner jacket and let out a throaty laugh.

"Hussy!" huffed Ida. "Shameful—and in front of her husband."

"I doubt very much her husband cares," Wavel said quite seriously, pushing his glasses back up the bridge of his nose.

"Captain, we can't go on with a short jury." Fanny announced with defiance.

"What are they talking about?" Montane had not been paying attention to their banter and looked to David for an explanation.

"They thought they had to have twelve on the jury. Otherwise, it wouldn't be a jury. Details like that seem to drive them to distraction."

Montane walked over to the center of the dining room and called out sharply—"People! I don't know what you think this it but it is not optional. Twelve jurors, ten jurors—I don't care. Everybody just sit down." With a crowd composed of such stubborn children, tone can be everything. Montane's was sufficient. Everyone found a seat.

"Alright now," Captain Sloe sat at his table and tried to quiet the jury. David Wayne and Captain Montane sat opposite to Sloe at the table off to his left. Martin Vale sat alone at the table just to Sloe's right. The jury sat in the two rows of chairs. The six men sat in the back row: Wavel Odston, George Sherman, Never Gamble, Tom the Porter, Melvin the Pilot, and Bob the Cook. The five women sat in the front row: Fanny Odston, Cora Vale, Ida Claire, Mrs. Kaufman, and Alice the maid.

"Please, people." The talking continued.

Montane barely suppressed his anger as he looked at Captain Sloe.

Captain Sloe leaned to one side, removed one black wingtip from his left foot, and slammed the shoe on the table three times.

"Order in the court!" He felt rather foolish but it was the only way to get their attention.

"Is that a gavel?" Mrs. Kaufman asked; her eyes not being what they used to be.

"It's not a gavel. What are you, blind?" Never Gamble groused.

"Don't you call my sister blind," Ida turned and threatened to smack Never, who was sitting behind her.

Montane glared at the jury.

"What's going on?" he asked David. "When I came into this room, they were all *behaving*. Now they're back like this."

"Bring Matvie back in here," David offered in suggestion. "They seem to be afraid of him."

"I can't—not with Lear on board. I need Matvie to keep an eye on what's happening topside. But I could get Othello back in here. Were they afraid of him?"

"Unsettled, I would say."

"That's good enough. And I'll tell them I'll call Matvie if they won't shut up. Tell me, are you ready for this to really get started?" Montane looked at David with a hint of vulnerability.

"I'm ready. But what about you? And what about them?" He nodded towards the bickering jury.

"I was ready for this the moment you first came up with the idea. You know, something in me clicked when you said it. I knew right away I really wanted to try this."

"Well, you may have had me kidnapped at gunpoint, but in a way I'm glad. I really would like to see you find what you've been seeking."

"You're the best priest a guy ever had."

The sniping and whining came to an abrupt halt when Othello walked back into the room. He stepped directly up to the rows of jurors and stared down at them. With arms crossed, he moved just enough to where he did not block their view of Captain Sloe.

Those in the jury could not seem to keep their eyes off of him. Othello mesmerized them, though none of them knew why. Ever since he had driven the knife into Barry Alum, Othello had drawn himself into a shell. He had always appeared distant to those around him. Now, it was as though he were light-years away. All that remained was his living, breathing body, with eyes as empty and lifeless as those of the dead Barry Alum's. But aside from Matvie, no one knew the reason. His coldness left them with a kind of nagging fear. The evidence that something was wrong was all over him; but as to what *it* was, no one suspected the truth.

Othello's effect on the jurors was more than Montane had hoped. He was so pleased they had finally ceased to speak he did not notice the change in Othello. He allowed himself to focus on what was to come.

"I'm not sure how I am to proceed." Captain Sloe said with some apprehension. He looked from the jury to Martin Vale and finally rested his gaze on David Wayne. "How official do you want this? I'm not very schooled in court procedures, you know?"

"Whatever you decide is fine," David said reassuringly. "But you should try to stick to a manageable order; something that can be followed with uniformity."

"Should we start with a prayer?" Captain Sloe asked.

"Absolutely not!" Martin Vale spoke up as the prosecutor

for the first time. "This is no prayer service. There's no need to try and legitimize this illegal trial by praying over it like it was some religious rite. I refuse to allow it."

The jury watched Othello nervously as Martin Vale made this bold stand. They were expecting a painful response. Captain Sloe waited for a response from Montane or Othello. He tried to think of something to say when it was evident that the pirates were going to allow Vale to speak his mind.

"O—Okay, that seems only fair. No prayer then." The Captain raised the shoe to hammer the table when he remembered it was not a gavel and it was in fact his shoe. Dropping it softly to the floor and slipping it back on, he settled on smacking the table with his open palm. "Any further items?"

"I have something." Martin Vale rose from his chair and stepped out in front of his table. He looked back at Montane as he addressed the Captain. "I think we need this trial explained in greater detail. I doubt any of us really knows what this pirate has in mind. I just want some solid ground rules laid out."

At some point in the trial, Captain Sloe ceased looking at Montane for an answer and he began to act as if he really were in charge. But for the moment, he still glanced in Montane's direction before making a decision.

"I will make that the number one item once we get underway. Is that okay?"

"Well, let's not waste time," Vale said impatiently.

"So then, let this court come to order."

Chapter Sixteen

The Case For and Against

Captain Sloe sat at the judge's table and looked over the jury with trepidation. The faces of the eleven men and women were a mixture of anger, fear, confusion, and even some bemusement. All told, he was unsure of how everything would proceed. Yet, as a captain, he had faced storms of unknown power with phlegmatic courage. He would do the same in this trial. He addressed the jurors in a soft yet authoritative voice.

"I'm aware that it is in the proper order of things for the prosecution to begin with their opening statements. But as there are certain guidelines that need to be laid out by the defense, and the defense is the party that will be dictating the order of these proceedings, I'm going to ask Mr. Wayne—the counsel for the defense—to give us his opening remarks first."

There were no objections. Both the jury and the prosecution wanted to hear a clear statement from the defense. David Wayne stood up at the defense table and nodded to the judge.

"Thank you, Captain Sloe. I think I can keep this short, and I hope I can satisfy everyone at the same time. The goal of these proceedings is not to find Robert Montane guilty of piracy. The defendant pleads guilty already. What we are asking of this court is a recognition of forgiveness. While we recognize society's right to demand retribution or mete out punishment, we respectfully suggest that society can also waive both rights incumbent upon a mutual decision to forgive.

"It is my objective to lay out the case that forgiveness is

justifiable and a common resolution in society today. I only ask the jury to give the matter serious consideration as they hear me out.

"At the conclusion of this hearing, Robert Montane agrees to abide by the findings of this jury. If he is refused forgiveness, he will allow himself to be handed over to the authorities to be imprisoned for piracy. If, however, the jury finds they are able to release Robert Montane from his guilt through forgiveness, he will retire from his pirate ways and leave the sea thereafter."

David finished speaking and stood in front of the jurors with his hands at his side. He made eye contact with a few of them, but most of them were staring at Montane.

Montane sat silently at the defense table. Sitting back in his chair, the usually stiff jaw dropped down upon his chest. His eyes were closed and his hands were folded in his lap. For the first time since seizing *The Jenny* he did not appear to be in command of the world around him. Those in the jury could sense this and it made them realize this might actually be for real. The thought emboldened them. It emboldened Martin Vale as well.

"Captain, before this young man starts to beg forgiveness on behalf of his pirate client, I insist I be given the chance to lay out the particulars of his crimes. It's all well and good for Montane to confess to his crimes but the jury deserves to know the full extent of his guilt."

"That seems appropriate, Mr. Vale. However, in the future, let's not refer to Mr. Montane as a *pirate*. No matter that he admits to it, the label carries with it a spurious and damaging connotation."

Vale gave Captain Sloe a look that clearly said *you must be joking*, but he refrained from speaking the actual words. Instead, he addressed the jury.

"Ladies and gentlemen, I want you to be sure that I will not stand idly by while this man appeals to your sympathies. I intend to hold true to society's insistence that punishment must follow crime. Without this tenant, order is lost. No matter how you *feel* about this man, you must hold him to account for his actions. I'm confident you will see through his selfish demands for forgiveness."

There was a subtle shift amongst the participants of this mock trial. As each one of them took their positions in the room and as each one of them played their part, a degree of believability began to overtake their dislike and distrust of the proceedings. Martin Vale was evidence of this as he took his opening statement seriously and began to adopt a stentorian tone. As the trial progressed, he became more and more a real prosecutor with all of the zeal and passion for justice that any district attorney would immediately recognize.

"In short, I remind you the defendant has taken all of us as his prisoners. He looted our staterooms and now he's laughing at us as we consider forgiving him. I proudly stand here and say *NO!* We cannot forgive this reprobate until he has paid his rightful debt to society."

A little out of breath, Martin Vale cast a quick glance back towards Montane to make sure the pirate was not going to interfere with his incendiary speech. To his masked satisfaction, Montane said nothing.

"Is that it then?" Captain Sloe asked the defense and the prosecution simultaneously. "Well then I believe that in consideration of the special circumstances that we find ourselves in, it would be proper to allow Mr. Montane to step up to the stand and tell us in his own words what he is confessing to." Captain Sloe held up a hand to cut off Martin Vale's objection before he could begin. "Just be patient, Mr. Vale. I'll let you say your piece after Mr. Montane is finished. If you feel you have information that needs to be added to what Mr. Montane gives us, you will have full freedom to do so."

The jury came to life at this point. They had forgotten Othello's presence as they focused more on what was being said. Othello himself was listening intently; his Captain's intentions were a surprise to him and he wondered just what the other pirates knew about it all.

"How can you allow this pirate to speak before Mr. Vale can elaborate on the crimes he is guilty of?" Ida Claire's question burst from her with great indignity.

"I wouldn't mind hearing Montane first," Wavel offered in opinion.

"Hold it!" Captain Sloe raised his voice and cut them off before the whole jury could really begin to squabble. "The jury will remain silent. This is not a debate. Mr. Montane will take the stand and deliver his confession *without* interruption."

A hand slowly lifted into the air. Captain Sloe saw it and lowered his gaze in agitation. "Never, put your hand down. This is not a grade school class in which you can raise your hand at anytime to ask a question."

"I'm sorry, Captain. Only—there's no Bible."

"No what?"

"I don't believe we have a Bible for swearing in witnesses."

Everyone in the room turned to look at Never Gamble. He shrugged his shoulders and shook a little nervously, smiling apologetically with those who made eye contact.

"I'm sure we have a Bible on board," Captain Sloe said with gentle correction. He looked at Montane. "Would it bother you if we fetched a Bible? I think everyone would feel better if we had one for swearing you in."

Montane lifted both hands a few inches as a sign of reluctant surrender to the request for a Bible.

"I'd give odds they can't find a Bible between the lot of them," Montane said in a hushed voice to David.

"Would one of you ladies have a Bible in your luggage?" Captain Sloe smiled easily at the first row of jurors.

None of the women answered him. They all fidgeted in their seats and kept their eyes shifting about in order to avoid eye contact with anyone.

"Well," Ida Claire straightened her spine and finally spoke up, "I don't see what that has to do with us. Why we should be expected to have a Bible I'm sure I just don't know. There's nothing says we have to bring a Bible on a cruise. And why shouldn't the *men* have one? That seems sexist of you, Captain. As if only the women would be silly enough to carry a Bible. We're as liberated and progressive as any man!"

Captain Sloe and most of the other men thought it odd

that anyone would suggest that Ida Claire was anything but liberated.

"Now Ida," George Sherman offered her a kind word in her time of distress, "don't you worry. I haven't a Bible on board and I don't feel the least bit embarrassed at the fact."

"I must say, as Captain of this boat, I'd be embarrassed to discover we haven't a Bible on board. I seem to recall there is one in my office—"

"Not anymore, Captain." Never shook his head. "Mr. Vale demanded it be removed on the grounds that it might offend one of the crew or passengers."

"A reasonable request," Vale defended himself. "You have to be careful about these things nowadays."

"Way to go, Marty." Cora saw an opportunity to abuse her husband publicly and as a rule she never passed those up. "Of all the lousy things to do—casting Bibles overboard. I married a communist."

"If I might make a suggestion," David Wayne stood and waited until he had everyone's attention. "If we absolutely must have a Bible, there are several onboard the submarine, but I think we could just as well go on without one. The Bible itself forbids swearing by anything, so I don't think we really need one."

"Now I am embarrassed, Mr. Wayne." Captain Sloe chuckled at the irony. "To find that a pirate ship has a Bible or two while *The Jenny* has not one Bible is truly telling, don't you think?"

"What's a pirate ship doing with a Bible? What an ungodly oddity!" Fanny Odston saw nothing odd in her profane remark.

"What would a pirate do with a Bible?" asked Mrs. Kaufman.

"Read it, I presume." Wavel Odston could not refrain from offering the obvious answer.

"Captain Sloe?" A small voice broke through the murmuring crowd.

"Yes, Alice?" The Captain looked at the maid with the kindness of a grandfather. Alice rarely spoke, and it was evident she was hesitant to do so even then.

"I know we weren't supposed to—I mean the rules said so and all. But I did bring a small Bible on board. It is in my room. I'm very sorry."

"Not at all, Alice. Don't be sorry. It restores my faith that we're not all atheists on board. Could you run out and bring it back quickly?"

Alice nodded in reply. With Montane's reluctant and irritated permission, Alice hurried from the dining room and came back in just three minutes. In her hand, she clutched a small baby blue leather Bible. She laid it down on the captain's table and held her hand over it for a moment before taking her seat.

Chapter Seventeen

Montane Takes the Stand

Despite having been kidnapped by pirates, despite having been robbed and held at gunpoint, despite having been forced to participate in an illegal court proceeding, everyone watched Montane take the stand with great anticipation. Even Martin Vale could not help but watch in fascination as Captain Sloe swore in Montane. This man was, after all, the reason that everything had happened since being boarded. This man, who ruled a band of cutthroats, had taken over their lives. Yet now, if he was to be believed, he was giving over his life into *their* hands. And for all of that, they knew very little about him. It was not so much that he was a mystery to them; he was more like a blank slate. There was eager expectation to see those blanks filled in.

As Montane sat down, those in the jury really got their first good look at this pirate captain. Their interactions with him up until that time had been veiled by fear and anger. No one had really felt like scrutinizing their captor, they were far too worried about their own personal futures to bother with such details. But now, as the trial settled into a somewhat familiar routine, they all began to relax in one way or another. And one of those ways was to inspect Montane's physical characteristics.

Robert Montane was a man of medium height and looked to be nearly forty years old. He was thin; his gaunt frame suggested that he smoked more than he exercised. His face was long, and a cigarette hanging from his lips would have accentuated the deep lines in his cheeks but he had kicked the habit long enough by then that he did not reek of nicotine any longer. A thick mat of wavy black hair lay easily on his head. Just a slight bit of it threatened to cover his right eye. His large, brown eyes contrasted with his small nose that turned up ever so slightly at its end.

He wore a black-ribbed, turtleneck sweater that fit him like a glove. There were black elbow patches that were hardly perceptible. A pair of black jeans with white and black canvas tennis shoes completed his wardrobe.

As he put his hand on the Bible, those sitting close enough to him could see that his hands, though thin, looked as hard as if they were made of a steel armature wrapped with thick sailcloth. The nails were well cared for, however, and there was no evidence of nervousness in his movements. Sitting in the improvised witness chair, Montane was relaxed without being careless. He was no coiled spring, yet he was no lounging slacker. He seemed naturally able to combine grace with purpose. He tilted his head and waited for Captain Sloe to allow him to speak.

"I ask everyone here to please allow Mr. Montane to speak without interruption. As your captain, I would remind all of you that the fewer interruptions there are, the quicker this will be over."

Captain Sloe had no illusions that his admonishment would do much good. He only hoped to be able to stem the tide in some way. Shaking his head as he contemplated just how long this could drag along, he turned and nodded at Montane.

There was silence in the room. Montane did not speak right away. He gave David Wayne a long glance as if he were drawing resolve from his counselor. David gave him an encouraging nod. Montane's head snapped up with sudden conviction and he addressed the jury.

"I won't bore you all with a sad story of childhood. I won't bother wringing my hands in great despair. You will not have to sit through a recantation of some religious conversion story. I don't think that's what you want to hear. And more to the point, it's not something I can do.

"What I can do, however, is get straight to the point. You know I'm a pirate. It's not something I have ever denied.

I've never flown false colors. I've always dealt honestly on this point. So that's what I'll do here. You can be assured that I won't back down from my confession. I won't water it down. I will not deceive you in anything I say. I won't have the audacity to suggest you should trust the word of a pirate. But all I can do is be open and honest, and then what you do with it will be your own choice.

"Captain Sloe, I readily admit to illegally seizing many dozens of ships and boats over the past fifteen years. Never once having to sink one of my targets, I have always left the passengers unmolested. I am guilty of looting my victims, taking all things of value from their possession. I have beaten or have had beaten six men in order to make them reveal the whereabouts of hidden valuables. None of these men were permanently harmed. And on one occasion I set fire to a vessel and marooned the crew on an oil platform. The ship was later recovered as were the crewmembers by my own call to the authorities. The firing of the ship was a direct result of my having lost control of my temper.

"While it is true that as a crewmember under Captain Virgil Black I witnessed several murders and assaults upon female passengers, I never participated in the acts. These few incidents were the reasons I finally took control of this pirate crew. My one violent crime was committed the night I put a revolver to Captain Black's temple as he slept and forced him overboard where I am certain sharks ended his life very quickly. I felt no remorse at ending his life after watching him beat my fellow crewmembers. He was vicious, cruel, and without humanity.

"I'm not suggesting I'm a saint. I have had members of my crew beaten. I have caused much grief and stolen great amounts of plunder. But as I said before, I don't deny that. I don't weep over it either. What I have done is in the past. I very much want it to remain there. I will not pirate anymore. My reasons are personal; some might rightly say they're selfish. But that is beside the point. I am resolved to quitting the pirate life."

Montane's abrupt conclusion left everyone momentarily

unsure of the next step. Captain Sloe had been caught off guard as well and it took him a moment to speak.

"Is that all, Mr. Montane?"

"Yes. But I know that there will be plenty of questions, and I will try to answer every one."

"This is exactly what I warned you about!" Martin Vale came swiftly to his feet and charged around his table and up to Captain Sloe. "You see what he's done? This…criminal has nearly made himself out to be Mother Theresa. What kind of a confession was that? I never did this and that. No one was *permanently* harmed? I've never heard such —"

"Mr. Vale." Captain Sloe cut him off in the middle of a particularly unsavory euphemism. "That's enough. You have every opportunity to bring all of this to light. You don't need to raise your voice and lower your vocabulary. I must admit I was expecting a little more from Captain Montane, but that really doesn't matter. You are free to ask him anything you like. Is that possibly something that could satisfy your anger?"

"Nothing would satisfy my anger short of seeing Montane hang from the nearest yardarm!"

A few soft murmurs slipped out from among the jurors.

"Mr. Vale," Captain Sloe spoke with a heavy tone, "please sit down. You are out of order. I have no option left to me but to suspend this hearing until tomorrow morning. Hopefully by then, you will be in better control of yourself."

The captain's timing could not have been better. Ida Claire and her sister Mrs. Kaufman were both beginning to nod as weariness threatened to overcome them. Cora Vale, unable to get a drink, diverted her thoughts to George Sherman and kept turning in her chair to catch sight of him. Twice she managed to force eye contact with a smile. Both times he gave her a curious look.

As a group, the jurors were simply losing focus as the night wore on. The captain's announcement to break for the night was greatly welcomed.

Disappointed with the early end to the evening, Montane stood up and immediately took charge of the room. No longer the subdued defendant, he resumed his place as commander of the pirates.

"Othello, go get Matvie. I want everyone taken to their rooms. Captain Sloe, are there any empty staterooms?"

"Two."

"Lend me your steward, then."

"Never, show Mr. Montane the empty staterooms. He will decide which one he wants to use."

"You read my mind, Captain." Montane followed Never Gamble from the room. In the passageway he met with Matvie. "Take them all to their rooms. No one is allowed to be out and about. I want Othello and Kit to take the first watch. When you and the Old Man have had enough sleep, you take the rest of the night. After the steward shows me the room I want, I'll send him to you, and he can show you the remaining room. Oh, and if the brothers should ask—tell them one of them should get some sleep as best they can in the wheelhouse."

Matvie listened carefully to his instructions and nodded just once after Montane finished speaking.

Unlocking a door, Never pushed it open and showed Montane the first room.

"Is the other room closer to the aft stairs?" asked Montane.

"N-no sir."

"Then this will be fine." Montane watched Never try to leave in a hurry. "Hold on there, Never. That is your name? Never? I like that. It's definite."

"Yes, sir." Never stood in the doorway wishing he could run from the pirate. His back was to Montane and he closed his eyes as if it would make Montane disappear.

"You don't like me, do you?"

"Well, you're a pirate." Never winced at his own clumsy reply as he turned to face Montane. "What I mean… that is… it's just like sides on a football game. We're on different teams."

"Are you always this nervous?"

"Practically." Never wiped his brow on his sleeve, then

quickly reversed his answer. "No! It's very stressful being murdered by pirates."

"Murdered? No one's murdering you, kid. What's got you so worried about murder?"

"Oh, nothing very much, thank you. It's all well and good for you, *a pirate*, but your life's not being threatened. You aren't waiting for the hammer to fall. You do the threatening; you've got the hammer." With every word he uttered, Never expected Montane to lash out at him, but for some inexplicable reason, Never could not shut up. "I know all about pirates. I know they're bloodthirsty, cruel, murdering, raping, pillaging—" Never nearly choked on the words as they tumbled out of his mouth with greater and greater speed.

"Never! Get a grip. Just what do you really know about pirates? What you see in the movies?"

"My uncle was in the merchant marines. He'd been attacked by pirates. They were murderers; did unspeakable things!"

Montane could see the real disgust in Never's face and knew this was a prime example of what he was up against. No matter what his particular crimes were, he was labeled a pirate, and all the connotations of that title followed with it.

"So you think I'm like the pirates in your uncle's story, eh?"

"You *are* one of the pirates in his story. He said the pirate captain's name was Black."

Montane took a breath and let the words of the steward sink in. *Black.*

"Do you know the name of your uncle's ship?"

"No. But you did kill one of my uncle's friends; Willie Bee, they called him."

Montane's mind flashed to the sound of a gun being fired and a sailor calling out – *Willie! For God's sake, no!* There was no image with the memory; just the flash of a gun and a man crying out for a dying friend. Montane had not pulled the trigger; but what did that matter?

"Black was ruthless. He *was* bloodthirsty. It's why I killed him. But you're wrong about something. My life's threatened every day. And there's a hammer waiting to fall on me as well; both from my crew and from society. And society wields the biggest hammer of them all. Now go on and get out of here."

Never left.

Chapter Eighteen

What Goes On When the Lights Go Off

Othello stood watch in the main passageway. The last of the prisoners had been shut in their rooms. With Matvie and the Old Man down for some sleep, and Kit most likely sleeping while on guard at the head of the forward stairs, Othello was alone with his thoughts.

The day had not ended as he had thought it would. The incident with Barry Alum had shaken him, and so he was unprepared as he stood listening to the opening of the strange court proceedings. It had taken no effort to conceal his surprise at what was being said. That was his nature. He had always concealed his emotions and reactions. And so no matter how much the news of Montane's decision to abdicate disturbed him, no one had noticed it. But it had disturbed him. And he had to decide what he would do about it.

There was no reason to consider the right and wrong of protecting Captain Montane any longer. Othello felt immediately that Montane had stepped out from under that protection. His intention to leave the pirates nullified any loyalty that Othello should have felt for his captain. Othello could see that any consideration for the future had to be made with his own future in mind, not Montane's.

He was sure that Montane had thought far enough ahead to who he would name as his replacement. And he was equally sure it would be Hamlet. It was a good choice. Hamlet was fair, he had a keen wit, and the men respected him. The big African would have gladly given his loyalty over to Hamlet. He would have, if not for the brothers.

The one thing Hamlet did not have was the will to rule. And without it, the brothers would defeat him. Hamlet would never cement his role as captain of the *Prowler* before Lear and Macbeth overpowered him. Othello did not see it as *if* they would take command, but *when* they would take command. He had no illusions that the *when* would be later than sooner. And when it did happen, it would not be bloodless.

Othello knew where this line of logic was leading. He did not shy away from the final conclusion. As much as he wanted to see Hamlet succeed Montane, it would have only been short-lived and could have meant his own death as an ally of Hamlet's. The answer, though repulsive, was simple. He would have to help Lear become the captain. If he worked towards that end, he might get everyone through the change of captains without anyone losing his head.

He would have to be careful. Matvie would see his actions as treacherous until Lear was firmly in place as Captain. But Matvie was asleep right then. It may be this was the only chance he had to approach Lear. Othello waited a few minutes to ensure there were no longer any sounds coming from the staterooms, then silently left the passageway in search of Lear.

Martin Vale lay in his bed staring into a ceiling he could not see. The room was pitch black. He had been sleeping, but a troubled stomach woke him. Indigestion ate him from within, and he knew why. Montane. The man infuriated him. He had cost him a great deal of money. Even more so, he had singled out Vale's vessels as targets, making him the boob of Montane's pirate war.

Vale felt sweat bead on his forehead. The sickness in his gut was more than indignation. It was fear. But he wasn't afraid of Montane. He was afraid of himself. Afraid that what he had set out to do just might happen. He had privately been filled with satisfaction when Montane had seized the boat. It had been just as he had hoped; things were going according to plan. And as expected, no one had suspected that he had a gun hidden on board. No one would have believed it. Vale smiled at the thought. And the gun wasn't the only trick he had up his sleeve. There was still the professional he had hired.

But now he had to wait. Montane's move to hold a mock trial had been as unexpected as his attack on *The Jenny* had been expected. Vale could not understand Montane's move, but he saw in it an opportunity. All he had to do was ensure that the jury refused Montane's request for absolution and then make sure Montane really did turn himself in. Only if he refused to hand himself over to the police would Vale have to return to his desperate plan. If it came to that, Vale wondered, could he really do it? He thought of the gun tucked neatly away behind his desk. Yes, he decided, he could do it. He only hoped the professional knew to wait until the outcome of the trial as well. Vale had been unable to get alone with him long enough to make his wishes clear.

A nagging fear began to march across his thoughts. What if the gun had already been found? It would be just like Montane to smugly remove it and say nothing. Vale reached out in the darkness and switched on his bedside lamp.

Beside him, in a separate bed, he expected to see Cora deep in an alcoholic sleep. To his great shock she was not there.

"Cora." He said her name out loud as if she were still there. Sweeping the room with his eyes he saw no sign of her.

"Where is my wife?" he asked no one. Understandably, there was no reply. He sat upright in bed and swung his legs over the side where his feet slid into soft leather slippers. In one motion he stood up and threw a robe on, cinching the belt at his waist. He scratched his head and stared at Cora's empty bed with narrowed eyes. He raised one eyebrow as he ciphered out the mystery. "Probably trolloping with that buccaneer Montane."

Marching boldly through the passageway, Vale stopped and pounded on the door of a stateroom. After some fumbling around, Never Gamble pulled the door open a crack and stared wide-eyed at his employer.

"What is it, Mr. Vale?"

"What room did you put Montane in? Tell me quickly."

"Room 12, the one that we prepared for that guy who died."

"There's going to be a death alright." Vale hurried towards number 12 with no real plan in his head. He began to wish he had retrieved the gun from the desk. He could have ended things right then and there. Nearing the door to number 12, Vale began to shout Montane's name. "Where are you, you cuckolding sea-rat! Get your hands off her!"

Before he could pound on the door, Montane yanked the door open and stood in the doorframe. He raised his head and stared down Vale.

"What are you yelling about?"

"You've got Cora in there. I've come to take her back where she belongs." Vale was out of breath, the stress was wearing on him.

"You both flatter and insult your wife at the same time. What a fine husband. I should have you thrown overboard for this. But like I said, I'm trying to get away from that kind of thing. And in the interest of getting a good night's rest, I'll gladly let you look in this room for your wife. You will not, however, find any sign of her."

Vale pushed past the pirate and stomped around the room for a few moments. Montane had been right. There was no sign of Cora. By this time, a few others had come out into the hall and watched with curiosity. George Sherman was standing at the door to his room in a paisley, silk robe. David Wayne stood in the doorway of the day room where he had been sleeping on the couch. Tom the porter stood beside Never and suddenly pointed out the missing lady.

"Mr. Vale. There's Mrs. Vale in your own room."

Cora stood just a step inside her doorway in a full length satin night gown with a matching shawl thrown over her bare shoulders.

"Marty, what is going on? Come back to bed. You're making a fool of yourself."

Vale stared at her suspiciously. He stalked down the passageway and came near enough to touch her, which he did, as if he needed verification she was not some high society specter.

"Where in the world were you?" he demanded.

"I was right here in bed, you idiot."

"You weren't. I saw you gone… I mean I saw the bed empty."

"You're dreaming, Marty. Go back to sleep."

Vale gently shut his door without saying a word of apology to anyone for the night's interruption. Enduring a stream of insults from his wife, Vale dropped his robe to the floor and pulled his feet from the slippers. Laying back in the darkness, he ran over the scene in his mind. For all he could remember, Cora had not been there. Yet, there she was. It was only when he was half asleep that he remembered he had forgotten to make sure the gun was still in its hiding place.

After Vale shut himself in his room, David Wayne stood in the corridor and looked at George Sherman, whose door was next to the day room. George stood watching the drama with an air of complete peace. He hardly seemed to mind being awakened at such an hour. After a short while, George noticed he was being watched and he turned to David and spoke.

"Quite the scene, don't you think? Get's one's blood moving enough to make it hard to get back to sleep."

"Want to join me in the day room?" David asked.

"As long as that big African doesn't object. I don't feel like being beaten this early in the morning."

"I think I can guarantee your safety. Besides, I don't see Othello anywhere."

"Then let's have a drink," George headed into the day room.

"I don't drink, but I'm open to conversation."

George headed straight for the wet bar and dug a glass out of the lower cabinet. He grabbed an elaborately cut glass decanter and poured two inches of bourbon.

"You need something to get you to sleep?" David eyed the glass with a hint of a smile, "or is it to steady your nerves?"

"I'm sorry?" George turned around and studied the younger man.

"It's just that I suppose there are two things going through your mind right now."

"And those two things would be what?"

"Well, first, that it was extremely lucky that Vale pounded on Montane's door and not yours. And secondly, it was more good luck your room was located in such a way that Vale's back was turned to you so that she could make it safely back to Vale's room without being seen."

George stared silently at David. Almost as an afterthought he raised the glass to his lips and poured the bourbon down his throat.

"For a crisis hotline telephone counselor, you don't miss a trick, do you?"

"Simple circumstance. She had to pass the day room to get back to her room. I heard her footsteps as I was about to open the door. I saw enough after I looked out. You two were taking a great risk."

"That's what I told her," George relaxed a little as the bourbon worked its way into his system. He poured another shot as he spoke, then sat down in the white muslin club chair. "I didn't encourage Cora. She knocked on the door and I tried to send her away. But she was standing there looking so…"

"Needy? Afraid?"

"No, no. Nothing as noble as that. I was going to say attractive. She may not appear so to a man of your youth, but at my age, Cora is an absolute delight. Oh I realize she drinks too much, but that only seems to be an indication of a soft and broken heart. Inviting her in was the only decent thing I could do."

"Ever the gentleman." David said with no trace of sarcasm.

George was surprised that David was not scolding him, though he did not feel in the least as if he had to defend his and Cora's actions. This perspective allowed him to lower his guard far more than he had intended.

"I know you're a religious man, Mr. Wayne, so I don't suppose you'd understand. Taking another man's wife into your… room is a very deliberate action. Moral people always leap to the side of the husband; the injured party. But it only takes a little logic to turn it all around. Why should Cora have wanted to knock on my door? You might as well ask why she drinks. She's been tossed aside. A beautiful and vibrant woman like her has been left along the road. Not for another woman. For something far more humiliating: money. Martin Vale is so wrapped up in his little empire that somewhere along the way he left Cora behind. I don't feel one bit of guilt at having the decency to pick up what another man has so ignorantly let fall."

"She does seem very lovely," David conceded. He could not condone George's philosophy, but neither could he condemn him.

"You're being very discreet, young man. I notice you aren't asking if anything went on between us. Forgive me if I remain discreet and don't offer any details."

"I wouldn't think you'll need *my* forgiveness," David said with the hint of a smile.

"Very clever thinking." George held his glass up to gesture a toast. "What you mean is, if I felt Vale should forgive me—or even could forgive me, then why not forgive Montane? Isn't that it?"

"You're reading more into that than necessary."

"Oh, of course. My mistake. But I suppose you like the idea all the same. My indiscretions and Montane's crimes; there's nothing like a little metaphor to help wash down the bourbon." He threw the liquor back and swallowed it in one quick motion. "But before you congratulate yourself, David Wayne, on scoring a point for the defense, understand something. My indiscretions, as you called them—"

"That was your term," David inserted the correction.

"—as I called them, are nothing in comparison to Montane's crimes. That's a different animal altogether. It's not even apples and oranges. More like apples and lions. Cora was a consenting adult, as was I.

"So what now? Rushing off to tell Vale? No, that doesn't seem your style. I wonder why, then, you bothered to mention it at all."

"It helps people to talk about their stresses. I guess that's the crisis counselor in me showing. It's my way of helping."

"And I need help? You're a nice enough young man. But lord, you are self-righteous, aren't you? I mean, look at this Montane affair. I'll bet you really think we all ought to let bygones be bygones. You really think we should stamp forgiven across his forehead. What was it you said earlier? The idealist in you thinks you're both an idealist and a pragmatist? That might be the real problem. You really think you're both. But I know that's not the case. How old are you, Mr. Wayne? Twenty-five?"

"Twenty-seven."

"Never married?"

"Not even for a weekend." David smiled; he knew what the older man was going to say next. He was used to it.

"That's exactly what I thought it would be. You're obviously a man of great moral conviction. But the trouble is, you've never really seen anything of life. You've never known real suffering, never had to deny yourself very much. I'll even go so far as to wager you've never had to *forgive* anyone for anything substantial."

"You might lose that wager," David said softly.

"Oh, maybe. But you've surely never had any experience forgiving a man like Montane."

"How do you suppose a pirate in the Atlantic Ocean came to call the Cleveland Youth Crisis Hotline?"

"I assumed Montane was from Cleveland," George said in ignorance.

"No, he'd never been to Cleveland. Montane found a card with the Hotline's name and number printed on it in a purse that had been stolen on a raid of one of Vale's cruise ships; *The Jenny's* sister ship *The Missy*."

"Well that makes sense. What is the significance of this?"

"Montane dialed that number and when someone answered at the hotline, he asked for the name that was penciled in on the card; he asked for David. He asked for me."

"I think I see. Your mother's purse, perhaps?" George guessed.

"Nothing so dramatic. It belonged to a girl I had helped through a very difficult divorce. She was very young, and I had convinced her that there was still good in this world. That there were still men out there with compassion and love. And more importantly, I convinced her that God loved her. She seemed to have gotten her life in order. As a kind of therapy, she took a cruise. Montane raided *The Missy* while she was a passenger. During the raid, she was sexually assaulted. Somewhere out here, as *The Missy* made its way back to Boston, this young girl jumped into the sea."

George cursed aloud. "What was her name?"

"Elise."

"I notice Montane left that little item out of his confessions."

"He doesn't know about it. He's heard a few rumors, but nothing concrete. I've come to believe one of the twins raped her when Montane was attending to other business. And I think he suspects that as well. But regardless of what Montane knows, he was certainly culpable to some degree; to a very large degree."

"And still you argue for his forgiveness? Did this girl's death mean nothing to you?"

"Just the opposite," David's tone became softer, his naturally positive aspect faded. "Elise was very important to me. I had hoped one day she might marry me."

"Damn Montane to hell," George offered as sympathy.

"No," David replied, looking around as if he were breaking out of a trance. "You're right, I am an idealist. And for me, the ideal is still forgiveness. I convinced her to take that trip. She didn't want to. But I manipulated her into going; for her own good, I thought. I found a way to forgive myself for that. And when Montane called me, I knew right away who he was, and I knew I would have to find a way to forgive him as well. But at the moment, either I'm getting very tired, or this story is beginning to sound too sappy for even me to believe."

"Does Montane know your connection to this Elise?"

"I don't think he has any idea. I certainly have no desire to tell him."

"Well, I'm no doctor," George stood up and looked down at David, "but I would prescribe a double shot of this bourbon before you went to sleep."

"Thanks all the same, George. I'll be fine. And I'll be discreet."

"Good night, David Wayne of Cleveland. Here's to discretion." He finished off one last shot of the liquor and left for his room.

Chapter Nineteen

Three Pre-Dawn Encounters

Hamlet sat at a small table in the small compartment generously labeled as the dining room. It was in fact simply the officer's quarters where a table had been erected between the bunks on both sides of the submarine. The table stood on a pedestal that could be removed when the table was not in use. Four men could sit around the table and eat on it. Only two men could sit with a measure of comfort.

Hamlet sat at this table with a pencil in his hand, scribbling listlessly on a sheet of paper. His mind was focused on other matters.

"You wanted to see me?" Castle, the Electrician, stepped through the bulkhead doorway and leaned over the table. Castle was too tall for submarines. He was nearly six feet six inches tall. With long thin red hair that fell backwards over his scalp and neck, and a well receded widow's peak, he looked like a character out of an old MGM Viking movie. A sparse red beard completed the costume.

"Have you eaten breakfast yet? I know it's a little early, but I bet you haven't been eating much." Hamlet slid a plate of eggs and biscuits towards Castle and motioned for him to sit.

"Haven't been sleeping much either." Castle dropped onto the bunk opposite Hamlet and pulled a cigarette pack from the left breast pocket of his faded blue coveralls. "Living off these cursed things right now."

"Have you been at the repairs all night?"

"Nearly," smoke fell between them as he exhaled while speaking. "That starter's worse than my mother-in-law. Gives me a headache."

"Paul, you're not married, remember?"

"Wife left me—the mother-in-law never got the memo. She nags me to death every time we get into port." The smoke hung over the table like a cloud. "You didn't just want to feed me. What did you want?"

"Let's go up and get some air."

Castle waved his hand through the pall of smoke, stirring up the cloud. "I thought that's what this stuff was called."

Once out on the conning tower, Hamlet allowed himself to speak with a little more freedom. They were alone. He kicked the floor hatch closed the same way Montane had done the day before.

There was a good breeze blowing dead against the bow. Castle's cigarette smoke evaporated back along the length of the submarine. Both of the men watched *The Jenny* in the early morning darkness. Her stern lights were partially obscured by a light mist, but her silhouette was easily discernible, though it was only a dark shadow to them.

"What's the timetable on the starter, now?"

"Working all night has its benefits." Castle said with a good portion of pride. "Another couple of hours and we'll be done."

"And will it work?"

"Three years or thirty-six thousand miles."

"The Captain's leaving." Hamlet intentionally said the words without preamble. He was watching Castle's response. The big electrician sucked on his cigarette and blew out the smoke, watching it dissolve in the wind.

"Was it something I said?" Castle smiled and shook his red mane. He abruptly dropped his smile and sighed. "Just like that, huh? Early retirement?"

"That's about the sum of it. I'm going to need your help."

Castle's thoughts went right to the heart of the matter: Lear. "You're not kidding. We're all going to need help. Do Lear and Macbeth know about this?"

"No. And that's something we can use to our advantage. But as for the rest of the crew, this isn't common knowledge yet. It's gotta stay like that for now. But there are some things we can do."

Castle threw his cigarette into the sea and put his hands on the lip of the conning tower railing. He turned his head and stared at Hamlet. After muttering a curse, he shook his head and dug into his pocket for another smoke.

At that early hour, there was another soul up and wondering what he could do. It was Tom, the porter. With a face as fresh as an underclassman in high school, Tom looked into a small mirror mounted on the wall beside his top bunk. He was still very young, and he knew it. He looked young. And he knew he still acted young. He was not bothered by how he looked to everyone on board. There was only one person whose perspective mattered: Alice.

Yet here he sat, doing nothing while pirates overran *The Jenny*. What must Alice think of him? He knew he was playing the part of a child, doing all he was told and keeping out of the way when he wasn't wanted. But that could not be all that he was capable of. He had offered his help to Barry Alum, but what a disaster that had turned into. He had inadvertently joined up with a thief. At least no one knew of his association with the man. Tom shook his head at his reflection and wondered just what he could do to help Alice. Because after all, if he couldn't help Alice, there wasn't any point in doing anything.

Alice was a few years older than Tom. And though she didn't look it, she certainly acted as if she were. She was quiet, demure around others, and had an unshakable gaze during the few times she ever looked at anyone. Most people mistook her for window dressing. Tom knew there was more to her than that. But his own inhibitions around girls forced him to keep his distance. Of course he talked to her, but it was always about their duties on the boat. He was always asking if she needed help cleaning a room, or offering to fix the wheel on her cleaning cart. She was always polite, and often accepted his help. But at all times she held back from any personal communication.

None of that mattered to Tom. In his young mind, she

did not actually belong to him, but he had earned the right to watch over her by his own diligent efforts.

He was simply biding time with his thoughts. He knew what he was waiting for. Even though the boat had been turned upside down by the pirates, he was certain that Bob and Alice would be up at the usual hour to prepare breakfast. It made sense to Tom that their schedule would not have changed. He was rewarded for his forward thinking when he heard Alice's soft steps coming down the passage. It did not matter that in reality the footsteps could have been anyone's. Tom knew when it was Alice. And knowing it was her, he slipped out of his room just as she came abreast of his door.

"Oh, good morning, Alice. Is it time for breakfast already?" Tom was not the best actor. Alice recognized his efforts at sounding natural, however, and allowed him to think he had fooled her.

"Yes, nearly 5:30. Bob will be expecting me to get things ready." Her voice was gentle, and those who knew nothing about her could immediately recognize her kindness after hearing her speak only a few words.

"Does Bob get up at this time, too?"

"No," she gave a guarded laugh, "he will expect all to be ready when he arrives at ten till six."

"I was having trouble staying asleep. I suppose my mind is too busy to sleep. This whole trial is very hard to understand. Would you like my help?"

"Yes, that would be nice."

He had done it again. He was acting as her servant. He did not know how to approach her in any other way. Shrugging off the suspicion that he was nothing more than a hired hand around her, he brightened at the prospect of spending a few minutes alone with her. Once they were in the galley, he pestered her relentlessly about what she needed done. He did his best to keep her from having to do any work at all.

He could think of nothing more to say to her. She was apparently of the same mind. She never said a word until the cook walked into the galley.

Dressed in a green, floral, polyester house coat, Ida Claire walked resolutely down the passage and climbed the main stairs that led to the deck. She carried a large beach bag that was covered with hundreds of glued-on beads. Slightly favoring her left leg, she stepped heavily up the stairs. Before she reached the last step, a voice spoke to her out of the darkness.

"And where are you going?" The voice, a heavy French accent, was more curious than ominous.

Ida lifted her head and saw an old man—one of the pirates—and hesitated. After thinking it through, she decided she cared very little about what this pirate could do to her. She was tired of giving in to them.

"I'm going to the front of the boat, now get out of my way, you dumb Frenchie."

"And you think I am dumb enough to jus' let you wander all over the boat?" The Old Man leaned towards her and reached out a hand to finger the beads on the bag. "What are you hiding in here, eh?"

Ida smacked his hand and jerked the bag away from him. "Get your filthy hand off me!"

"Now," the Old Man rubbed his hand and smiled with a light in his eyes, "that's a saucy spirit in this one. A beautiful woman who knows how to hit a man— that's something, *oui*? What's in the bag?"

"Oh for heaven's sake, it's just a camera. I just dare you to try and steal it from me. You won't though. Your captain has promised that nothing will be taken. Now, out of my way! I'm going to get a picture of the sunrise, and time is running out."

"No, no, *mademoiselle*. I am duty bound to keep you away from there. Now run off—shoo, shoo—back downstairs you go. No click-click with the pictures."

"Don't you push me!" Ida's voice rose in pitch as well as volume. "I will not go—shoo, shoo! You listen to me. I paid for this vacation, and I intend to treat it like one. I want a picture of the sunrise, and I swear you aren't going to stop me!"

Ida charged up the last few steps. The Old Man backed

up and allowed her to get one step past him before he put a hand out and blocked her. He was grinning, obviously enjoying her gumption.

"You know, I like you, *chérie*. Do you know what? I do not see why I cannot let you take some pictures. I tell you this: I will personally take you to the bow. I can see, yes, the sun it is about to rise. What a beautiful and romantic picture it will make. Come, come. You follow me."

The Old Man motioned for her to fall in behind him and he began to make his way along the port side. They made an intriguing couple. The Old Man moved with a quiet carefulness, stepping lightly. Ida followed him with heavy steps, proudly jutting her chin out and keeping her spine rigid, unwilling to skulk about the boat. She had trouble seeing her guide in the pre-dawn light.

"What are you doing, sneaking around like that? Get back here. Stop acting like a—well a pirate." Ida's voice caught in the stiff breeze and carried back over *The Jenny*.

The Old Man shushed her gently. "But I am a pirate. And you are talking so loud, you must not. You must think and be discreet, huh? Think as if we were sneaking into each other's bedrooms, ha-ha!"

"I will not! And don't you think of it, either." Her voice was not growing any softer.

"Alright, alright. Just please, not so loud."

They approached the port side door of the wheelhouse and the Old Man allowed Ida to pass him. She marched on towards the pointed bow and began digging in her bag for her camera. The Old Man cocked his head towards the window of the wheelhouse and nodded at a figure inside. The door opened and Macbeth's image appeared in the doorway. He was backlit from a small light in the wheelhouse, but the Old Man could still see his dark empty eyes. The Old Man was one of the few members of the crew who could stand to look at him for any length of time; he was not afraid to talk to him, either.

"I have a little company, you see? Don't mind us. Just having a little fun, huh?"

Macbeth said nothing. He shifted his eyes and stared at the elderly woman fussing with her bag and then looked back at the Old Man.

"Don't you say a word, then. What else could I do? A beautiful creature like her seeks me out in the night? Ha-ha! I've still got it, you know! But, that is hardly a surprise."

Macbeth watched him join the woman at the bow. Closing the door, he stood watching them. He was sure that if his brother were awake, Lear would make a joke or two about the crazy Frenchman. But in the absence of Lear, Macbeth just stared at them with indifference.

"Only a little wait, now." The Old Man drew in a deep breath and let it out as he looked for the coming sun. "You have a poet's soul, to seek out the rising sun. I like that."

"Huh! I don't know what you mean." Ida glared suspiciously at her unwelcome companion. He was certainly older than she was, though how much older she was unable to guess. His short, white hair was scattered across his spotted scalp as if sprinkled there by a salt shaker. The wrinkles around his brown eyes lay in sagging circles. He was thin, but he still had strength in him. Whenever he spoke, his entire face danced with the words.

"Oh, you are not fooling me. What is your name, or shall I just call you my little Rose?"

"Now who's fooling who? Rose, indeed. Though I object to fraternizing with a pirate, I don't suppose it would hurt to tell you. My name is Ida. *Mrs.* Ida Claire."

"Ah, a delicate name. Ida." He repeated the name with delight. "I like that very much. But I do not like that Mrs. in the name, I think."

"Well, I can't just call you pirate. What is your name?"

"Oh, they call me the Old Man."

"Ridiculous. You're not old enough for a name like that. Now you tell me, what is your name?"

The Old Man smiled at her, embarrassment showing in his eyes. "You would be surprised at how old I am. It is a fitting name. Just call me Old Man. I will not be offended."

"Oh, don't be proud. You tell me your name right now."

"*Mademoiselle*, I have not told anyone my name in many, many years."

"Well, I haven't been alone with a man before the sunrise in many years. Now if you want to keep standing here with me you'll tell me your name."

"I cannot stand up to you, that is clear as the bell." The Old Man scratched behind his ear and looked at his feet. "My name is Maurice. Maurice Baptiste. But you mustn't tell, huh?"

"I don't see why not." Ida looked at him with a raised eyebrow. "It's a perfectly good name. More so than letting everyone call you Old Man."

The Old Man thought about what she had said. Maybe she was right. There was pride in her words, but then, maybe he needed to be reminded that even though he was old, he could still have some pride. He kept silent as they waited for the sun to rise and wondered at such thoughts. In time, the colors of the sky transformed their shrouded vigil into a bright and magnificent morning.

Chapter Twenty

A Shave with a Chance of Showers

David Wayne felt along the crest of his thick hair and gauged just how much of it was standing up. With a few attempts at forcing it all into some kind of order, he stepped from *The Jenny's* day room and looked down the passageway. He was not surprised to see Matvie standing near the end of the dark hallway at the base of the stairs leading to the stern of the boat. There was not much light by which to see, but David could tell that the large shadow was Matvie. It had to be, David thought with some amusement. There was very little else it could be.

"Morning," David said softly, touching two fingers to his forehead in a lax—and what he hoped would be received as a friendly—salute. The slightest hint of movement was all David could see as a response. He was always trying to make headway in cracking the great and somber Matvie's stolid façade. To date, he had neither cracked it, nor had he even scuffed its paint.

At Montane's door, David rapped on the doorpost twice and walked right in. He had no doubt that the Captain was already awake and ready for the day. Montane never lingered in bed.

"I expected to see you a little earlier than this." Montane was standing in front of a mirror, his hands engaged in shaving with a straight razor. Only a thin strip of his neck was still covered in white foam. David knew of precious few men who still used a straight razor. He knew of none who used them on a moving boat save Montane.

"I was up a little later than I had planned. I had an interesting talk with one of your jurors. Sorry to have kept you waiting."

"I didn't mean anything by that. You're not late." Montane did not bother to ask who the juror was. He cared very little about them. He cared very little about most people. "It's just that you're always early to rise like me. Do you want to shave? You look dreadful." Montane finished with the razor and washed it out in a porcelain bowl on the dresser in front of him.

David ran a hand over his chin and down his neck. It had been several days since he had scraped his face clean. But the thought of the razor held him in check. He declined the offer.

"You know," Montane looked into the mirror at David's reflection and spoke with the resigned tone of a father speaking to a disappointing son, "it wouldn't hurt you to learn to use a straight razor."

"That's exactly what I'm afraid it will do: hurt me," David countered.

"What happens is you get dependent on the manufacturers of safety razors and electric shavers. Now sit down." David did as he was told, sitting in the chair that Montane placed in front of the mirror. With the practiced movements of an old barbershop cutter, Montane draped a towel over David's shoulders and began applying shaving cream to David's face with a soft bristle brush. "A man becomes more independent when he learns to keep a good razor of his own that he can sharpen and use for a long time. And the more independent a man can become, the greater his life becomes."

David watched with some fascination as Montane began to carefully run the sharp edge of the blade down from his left ear to his jaw line. He felt the blade scrape his skin just enough to make him aware of what could go wrong. He resisted the temptation to wince knowing it would increase the chance of a wayward cut. Montane worked with a slow and patient stroke.

"So what do you think of last night?" Montane asked.

"I think Vale pounded on the wrong door."

"No, I don't care about that. I was talking about the trial."

"Well, I don't really know what to think, yet. Vale is going to be hard to handle once he gets up a head of steam. But I'm not so sure there are many on the jury who would not see through his histrionics. He sure did not like your statement, Robbie. But do the others think you're as disingenuous as he does? I don't know yet."

"And what about you? Am I disingenuous?"

David waited to reply while the blade finished passing on his upper lip.

"I know you too well, now, to doubt your sincerity. But I have been thinking about it a little; from their point of view. I think that if I were them, I would be looking for something else. A piece of the puzzle is already missing for them, I think." David's eyes met Montane's, and they locked for a moment in the mirror. The blade stopped moving.

"They already have my confession. I've already surrendered to their judgment. Your missing piece of the puzzle can only be one thing."

"Which is?"

"You think they want to see remorse." The blade began to move again as Montane pulled it against the grain of David's neck. Montane's face darkened as he said the word.

"Is that word so distasteful to you?"

"It's not distasteful. But it is rather alien to me. Why do they need remorse? What purpose does it serve?"

"That's what I've been thinking over. The only thing I can figure is that it's human. It's necessary as a sign of humanity—a sign that there is a heart somewhere inside of you."

"But David, you know better than I do—did Jesus ask for remorse or repentance?"

"Repentance." David spoke the word quietly as if he were hearing it instead of speaking it. "I know your heart, Robbie. You've shown it to me enough that I know you feel remorse; regret even. All I meant was that you should show them what I've seen. Let them see your troubled heart."

"Remorse that is conjured up for an audience only comes

off as selfish regret. I know how I feel. But that's all it is—how I feel. What they see of that should not matter. Is forgiveness only based on the measure of a man's remorse? I've known men with murderous hearts who could cry a river after they had killed. But that river always dried up until the next kill. Such tears never helped any victims."

"I was only thinking of how the jurists will view it all."

"I won't appeal to them with high emotion. Call it pride. Call it whatever you like. I will stay the way I am."

"And remain independent?"

"Do you really think that's my goal?" Montane scraped the last bit of the shaving cream from David's face and held the razor just below the young man's jaw line. "I know how to use a straight razor and you don't. I hold the razor, and you have the razor at your throat. Which of us is the more independent?"

As David watched, Montane pulled the blade away from his throat and held it up, inspecting the sharpened blade with a scrutinizing gaze.

"I've given this group of idiots the razor and they now hold it to my neck. I would never have done that if I'd wanted to remain independent. And even if they find in my favor and release me—forgiven—my life will always be dependent on that verdict. That, in itself, will be a heavy burden to bear."

Montane washed the razor in the water and pulled the towel off of David's shoulder. He turned his customer's head from one side to the other and inspected his work.

"All done, Mr. Wayne. And not one cut. I hope you're a big tipper. I don't get a lot of business on this boat."

"Is it any wonder? Not too many people here crazy enough to let a pirate put a razor to their throats."

"Arrh," Montane growled from the side of his mouth.

Macbeth stood in the open door of the wheelhouse and looked over the bow. The Old Man and the Old Woman were gone now; back below deck. The sun had been up for a little while. The last shades of night were only hanging on far to the west. The morning breeze began to pick up.

A stream of curses cut through the sounds of *The Jenny* as she cut through the wind and waves. Macbeth turned to see his brother Lear sit up on the deck of the wheelhouse and rub at his neck. More curses followed.

"Would you shut that stupid door? I dreamt it started to snow in here!" Lear rubbed his hands over his knit sweater.

Macbeth realized the temperature really had dropped even as the sun came up. More importantly, he noticed that what little humidity had hung in the air over night was now gone. He shut the door and looked at a barometer on the panel under the pilot's window. It had begun to drop.

Lear stood up and leaned on the sill of the window scanning the horizon.

"You know what? This place looks familiar." Lear looked back at his brother and let out a wicked laugh. "I know this place, I just can't put my finger on it." He reached out a shaky hand and stuck his finger against a pane of glass. "There, now I got it. I've put my finger on it. It's the ocean."

As if the thought had just occurred to him, Lear reached down and throttled *The Jenny's* engines back to one-third power. Turning his head from left to right, and repeating the motion with a loose and celebratory manner, he sang out "We're here!" A last jerk on the throttle killed the engines.

"Watch this—" Lear pushed open the portside door and motioned for Macbeth to follow. At the portside rail, Lear leaned out and looked back at the *Prowler* as it followed in *The Jenny's* wake. Macbeth did the same and saw the *Prowler* begin to overtake the smaller boat as she drifted to a stop. The *Prowler* came on at full speed.

"I'll bet fifty dollars Franklin is at the sonar dead asleep." Lear watched with eager anticipation as the sub appeared to be heading on a collision course with *The Jenny*.

Macbeth did not accept the bet. He watched and waited, curious to see if they would be rammed by the old submarine. Both brothers stared as the collision seemed imminent and unavoidable.

Just as Macbeth was sure the *Prowler* had passed the point of no return, the great beast heeled ever so slightly to port, her screws churning a frothy wake as they were thrown in reverse. Lear laughed and bounced on the deck as he watched the *Prowler's* bow just miss *The Jenny's* stern as it angled away.

"A foot! A foot, Macbeth! One more foot and they would have rammed us. That was great!" Lear danced a few steps in celebration.

Macbeth ignored his brother's antics and watched the sub. Its forward momentum allowed it to come abreast of *The Jenny* as a figure appeared on the conning tower. He had expected what would happen next. Lear was hoping for a tantrum from Hamlet. In fact, Lear had been looking forward to hearing Montane's pet officer curse a little. Macbeth knew Hamlet would never give them the satisfaction.

"Good morning, boys." Hamlet shouted down to the brothers with a pleasant smile on his face. "Engine trouble?"

"Not at all," Lear's reply was polite and ingratiating. He accepted the fact that Hamlet had been able to stay in control of his emotions with ease. "We didn't startle you, did we?"

"Not in the least."

"This seemed as good a place as any to stop." Lear waved a hand around the great vista that was the sea. "I would certainly say we are well out of the shipping lanes."

"We certainly are." Hamlet turned away from Lear and raised a hand in salute. "Good morning, Captain."

Montane came on deck. He looked at the brothers as he waved in acknowledgment to Hamlet. "I expect everything's in order. Is it?"

"We are right where you said you wanted to go, Captain. I took the liberty of halting our progress. This little valley has it all—plenty of grass, a nice little wooded hill, and all the water we can want. I hope my actions meet with your approval."

"Thank you, Lear. I couldn't have asked for anything more."

Hamlet crawled down the conning tower's ladder in order

to speak with Montane without having to shout as loud. He pointed north, over his shoulder.

"Do you see that?"

Montane looked into the strengthening wind. It had shifted by then and was coming from the north. A low bank of clouds could be seen on the horizon.

"What do you think? Is it serious?"

"We'll have to keep an eye on it," Hamlet warned.

Montane nodded at Hamlet and turned his attention to Lear. He walked across the deck and came to within a few feet of both brothers.

"What was our heading all night?" Montane asked.

"Due east, Cap'n." Lear tried to sound like a movie pirate.

"Bring her around to a south by southwest heading. Take her easy at about six or seven knots." Montane examined the cloud bank to the north. "We'll try to keep out of that. If it looks like it's going to catch us, let me know."

"I'm here twenty-four hours a day, Captain, seven days a week. Me or my associate would be glad to assist you in any way we can."

I'll bet you would, thought Montane. He smiled politely and left the open deck.

Lear and Macbeth watched Montane descend the stairs. When he was out of sight, Lear spoke in a completely different, deadly serious tone.

"You don't suppose that big African is lying to us, do you? He may be setting a trap."

"I believe Othello." Macbeth had never known Othello to be anything but a straight shooter.

"I suppose he's telling the truth. He never was one to be crafty. It was a shock just to hear him say as much as he did. Montane giving himself up? I thought I was the crazy one. I don't like this. Maybe you'd better hold off killing Matvie, huh?"

Macbeth made no reply. His empty eyes stared back at his brother. Lear felt a chill, though whether it was from the wind or his brother's look he did not really know.

"Well, maybe not. You do what you want. I've gotta think about what I'm gonna do."

Chapter Twenty-One

Fireworks for Breakfast

Tom carried tableware for the place settings as the early-birds arrived. Ida Claire and Mrs. Kaufman came into the dining room in that order. Mrs. Kaufman was always a few steps behind her sister. Ida walked briskly ahead talking to her sister the whole while and never once looking back to see if she was heard.

Ida pushed her way into a chair at the table closest to the galley door and loudly called to Tom for some coffee. Tom hurried towards the galley and soon discovered Ida's chair was partially blocking his way. He hesitated, wondering if he dared ask her to move off to one side. In the end, he turned himself sideways and slid past her without saying a word.

"Aren't you in that boy's way?" asked Mrs. Kaufman.

"Just dreadful, Erma. I don't know what to say." Having declared she did not know what to say, Ida disproved this statement by continuing to ramble on. "Yelling in the hallways, pounding on doors—that's no way for a man of Mr. Vale's stature and position to act. He was acting like a lunatic. What did you ask, dear?"

"Isn't it hard for the porter to get by your chair? Shouldn't you move?"

"Don't be silly, Erma. Imagine me being in the way of a porter. No, that just can't be. He's perfectly able to find another way around me. That's his job. He must in no way inconvenience me. If he does I can assure you Captain Sloe will hear of it."

As she spoke those very words, Tom pushed the galley door open and it bumped into Ida's chair. She bristled at the contact. Tom managed to keep the coffee from spilling and set it down in front of Ida with enough charm and humility to stifle her protest.

Martin Vale entered the room as if he did not wish to be seen. He was pleased to see the sisters were the only ones already seated for breakfast. He headed straight for a corner table, placing himself in shadow. He put an elbow on the table and cradled his head in one hand as if nursing a great headache. When he looked up, Captain Sloe had arrived and approached his table with an outstretched hand.

"Good morning, Mr. Vale." He shook his employer's hand with the affability of a man who has slept through the night and awakened refreshed.

"Oh, yes. Yes. Morning." Vale stumbled through his reply.

"Ladies," the captain moved on to the sisters' table and hovered over them with a warm smile, "I hope you slept well. I trust everything is shipshape?"

"Hardly shipshape, Captain Sloe." Ida raised a brow in disapproval of his optimism. "There are pirates aboard this ship. I hope you haven't forgotten the fact."

"Well, yes. There is that. But I hope to have that cleared up very soon. Are you very hungry, Mrs. Kaufman? Our cook makes wonderful crepes."

"Should I be hungry?" Mrs. Kaufman was unsure of her own appetite.

"We can hardly be expected to eat at a time like this." Ida answered for her sister. "This is all too upsetting. Porter! Give us some of these crepes the Captain was just talking about, and give us each two eggs, poached. An English muffin for my sister and a waffle for myself. Now go along and just add two slices of ham and a large fruit cup for each of us."

Others began pouring into the dining room as Tom squeezed his way past Ida and ducked into the galley. He heard Fanny Odston's voice even after the door swung closed.

"Alice, more of them are coming in," Tom said, alarmed. He was willing to take a cup of coffee or two out, but he was too nervous to start carrying orders out to the passengers. He relayed Ida's order to Bob the cook—as much as he could remember—then looked at Alice with wide eyes.

"Thank you, Tom," Alice said simply, grabbing an urn of coffee. She stepped past him and gave him a smile. It was not a big smile, but to Tom it was the most exciting sign he'd gotten from her since the start of the voyage.

Alice pushed open the swinging door and deftly avoided hitting Ida or her chair as she eased out into the dining room. Smiling demurely at Captain Sloe, she made her way from one table to another taking orders and pouring coffee.

"There's just nothing else to be done, Fanny." Wavel Odston stared at the coffee as it filled his cup. He waved off Alice's offer of creamer and sipped the black coffee. "This fellow Barry Alum obviously has your jewels. What did you want me to do? Jump overboard and follow him?"

"I'll bet he didn't even take them." Fanny poured enough creamer into her own coffee to turn it white. She scooped sugar with a vengeance. "The thief is probably right here in this room. You ought to do something about it, Wavel. Don't just sit there slurping your coffee. How many times have I said to quit slurping your coffee?"

"I've lost count, my love. What would you propose I do about this thief? Should I begin to strip search the sisters over there?"

Fanny ignored his vulgar suggestion and kept at him. "You can do more than eat breakfast; that's something."

"Not really. You want me to do more than eat, but you don't say what I should do more of. Unless you mean you want me to do more eating. But I doubt it. So until you specify what it is you want more of, it's not *something*; it could be *anything*, but it's not *something*." Wavel's explanation was patient and delivered without sarcasm, as if he were a professor going over a student's poorly written essay.

"Wavel, I really don't have time for your idiotic ideas." Fanny continued to demand he do something about her jewels. Wavel continued to do nothing.

Tom showed up again with more coffee. He was able to

pour some for Montane and David Wayne as they sat down at a table slightly removed from the others. Melvin the pilot appeared suddenly and stood in the center of the room as if he were lost. Alice came to his rescue, guiding him to an empty table and making sure he was comfortable. *The Jenny's* old pilot smiled at her and nodded in appreciation. Alice was the only one on board at whom he would not growl.

Cora Vale stepped slowly through the door. Her eyes were half closed, she was hardly awake, but she gave the entire room a thorough glare before coming completely into the dining room. After staring down her husband, she crossed directly to his table and sat opposite him.

"I hope you can be civil, Marty." She picked up a coffee cup and shook it in the air as if it were a bell. Tom caught the gesture out of the corner of his eye and rushed to the galley to get a fresh urn of coffee. His foot snagged one of Ida Claire's chair legs. Ida grunted with grave disapproval.

"I did apologize, you know." Martin would not plead with his wife but he did wish, at least, to procure a ceasefire. "I've said I won't say another word about it. I'm under a great deal of stress. I don't know why I couldn't see you in the bed."

"I will not let you make a fool out of me again. If you ever publicly accuse me of something like that again, you'd better be able to back it up, buster."

"I said I was—"

"I know you're sorry." Her emphasis on *sorry* struck like a sword thrust.

Alice was bringing out plates of food by then. She glided past Ida Claire with arms full and never once bumped into the older woman. Tom, however, nudged her several times and once dropped a fruit cup when his elbow jammed against her high-backed chair.

"No bacon, Wavel." Fanny snatched the offensive meat from Wavel's plate and set it out of reach.

"Thank you, darling." Wavel stared at his empty plate. "I nearly ate that."

"If that boy hits me one more time," Ida threatened, "I'll

see that Captain Sloe runs him off."

"Where would Captain Sloe run him off to?" Mrs. Kaufman asked. For once, her question was most appropriate.

Captain Sloe, unaware he was so close to running anyone anywhere, finally settled down at the Odston's table. He had managed to speak with everyone in the room and was now ready to eat. Alice knew beforehand what her captain would want to eat and placed his food in front of him even as he tucked a napkin into his collar. Brushing his whiskers back, he dug into his meal with enthusiasm.

"Captain Sloe," Fanny chewed on her eggs as she attacked him, "what have you done about my jewels?"

"I'll wager he hasn't given a thought to your jewels, little heart." Wavel laid the terms of endearment on a little too thick. Fanny glared at him.

"Just the opposite, Mr. Odston." Captain Sloe cut his ham into equal-sized pieces as he spoke. "This whole business of the jewels is bothering me. You know, I admit I'm not too surprised Barry Alum stole them. He did seem to me rather questionable in character. But you know, one thing about him: he did not seem stupid. Yet there he goes, off into the sea in only our small dinghy. Preposterous, you see. Where did he expect to go? That dinghy's only good for puttering around in a marina. But you can't really navigate across the sea in it. What the man was thinking I'll never know."

"Well, that's thieves for you, Captain." Wavel eyed the distant bacon and made plans for its recovery. "Alum was no brain surgeon, that's plain as day."

"There's no proof. We should begin searching everyone." Fanny held her ground.

"My wife has suggested I strip search everyone beginning with the delightful Ida Claire."

"Really!" Captain Sloe let out a sharp laugh at the idea. His face curled into a full smile as he leaned over towards Fanny. "You do know how to make a man laugh. Really, Mrs. Odston, you shouldn't make such jokes. It's highly inappropriate for me to be laughing at such an idea. You're wicked, Mrs. Odston."

"Call her Fanny, I insist." Wavel winked at the Captain.

Before Fanny could object to the two men's banter, she spied Never Gamble coming in through the door. She lowered her chin and stared fiercely at the steward. She had not forgotten the incident with her skirt.

"There's that brain-dead delinquent Gamble. He's more than likely to be the thief. Captain, I implore you to place that man under arrest and have him watched."

"Fanny, love of my life, if the man were arrested, what would be the use in watching him?"

"Don't start, Wavel."

"Oh," Captain Sloe tried to mollify Mrs. Odston, "Never's an alright young man. He tends to get a bit nervous at times, but he's perfectly okay as stewards go. Doubt very much he'd ever steal anything. The strain would kill him. The first person to say *boo* to him would give him a heart attack. Good morning, Never."

Never tried to smile as he nodded towards the Captain and his companions. Once he saw Fanny Odston's icy stare, the smile faded to a look more suitable for a hunted rabbit. He tried to mumble out a 'good morning' but nothing really came of it. He abruptly cut to his left and tried to make for the galley. Concentrating on getting out of Fanny Odston's line of vision, he never saw Ida Claire until it was too late.

"Little Devil!" Ida shouted as Never's feet tangled with her chair's feet and he fell sideways into her lap. Ida, holding a fork in her right hand, instinctively defended herself, jabbing the fork into Never's hip. Never howled as if he'd been shot. It wasn't the fork that set him to howling. But once he'd been stabbed, he jerked his arm back to bat the fork away and knocked over Ida's cup of coffee, splashing his hand with the scalding liquid.

Tom tried to dash into the dining room to investigate the commotion and only succeeded in ramming the galley door into Never's skull. In the meantime, Ida had gathered enough strength to shove the steward off her lap and he slumped into a heap under the sisters' table.

Wavel and Captain Sloe arrived at the table simultaneously

and bent down to extract the unfortunate young man. Ida Claire smacked him on the head as he emerged.

"You clod-headed little creep!"

"If you please, Mrs. Claire," Captain Sloe admonished her, "don't abuse the boy any further. It was an accident, I assure you."

"I'm abusing *him*?" Ida's voice shrilled in protest. "The fool launched himself on top of me!"

"Check your necklace, Ida!" Fanny Odston would have enjoyed seeing Ida so humiliated if she hadn't suspected Never of being the thief. As it was, she believed the steward was up to his old tricks. "I'll bet he ripped it right off your body."

"I wasn't wearing a necklace," Ida crossed swords with Fanny, whom she was beginning to hate. "And just you mind your tongue. There's no call for suggesting he ripped something off my body loud enough for everyone present to hear. It's simply disgusting."

"Never, are you all right, my boy?" The captain had managed to sit Never upright and was snapping his fingers in front of Never's face.

"All things considered," Wavel assessed the situation, "having just lived through intimate contact with that woman, he'll be lucky to come out of this with only a few bruises. Of course, he'll be emotionally scarred for life."

Montane sat at his remote table and watched the action with disinterest. None of what he saw surprised him. He held a plain biscuit in one hand and chewed it, washing it down with black coffee. His only reaction to the scene had been to shift his glance over to David Wayne, as if to ask, *do you see what I've been trying to say?*

"I've never seen a group like this." David shook his head. He was both dismayed and amused at what he saw. "They're like nitroglycerin. The slightest rattle sets them off."

"It gives me comfort to think you talked me into letting them be my jury."

"Doesn't say much for you that you listened to me."

"Beginning to doubt yourself?" taunted Montane.

"It does strain my faith. But didn't I suggest they might

not be the ideal bunch to work with? As I recall, yesterday you said something about no group being worthy of this role so we might as well use them."

"You have a bad memory. That was what you said about me. I called them puddin' heads and the label stands."

They watched in silence as Captain Sloe and Wavel Odston helped Never Gamble to his feet. The wounded man limped out of the dining room as both Ida Claire and Fanny Odston hurled insults into his line of retreat.

Chapter Twenty-Two

Never Spies a Thief

Like a prize fighter who has taken a great beating and lost his title, Never Gamble sat alone in his stateroom nursing his wounds. One hand, blistered by the spilt coffee, held a towel to his swollen head with ice wrapped inside, thereby doubling the effects of the ice. He used his free hand to probe the soft flesh of his hip where the fork had pierced his skin.

His wounds were situated so as not to allow him to lie back and rest his head. He was forced to sit on the lower berth twisted at the hip to keep pressure off the throbbing wound. He sat painfully in this cockeyed way for five or ten minutes. His end of *The Jenny* was quiet. Everyone else was in the dining room. Never had almost drifted into a fitful sleep when he heard a door close outside his room.

What struck him as odd was the lack of footsteps he should have heard. He had heard no steps before the door closed and he had heard no steps after the door closed. Someone, Never decided, was being awfully quiet.

Rolling gently off his berth, Never eased open his door and peeked around the doorframe in both directions. The passage was empty.

Holding his breath, he could hear nothing save the muted sounds coming from the dining room at the front of the boat. The engines of *The Jenny* purred quietly, it was obvious to one of Never's experience that they were not being driven very hard.

A low, dull *thud* sounded from across the passage, but Never could not say from which stateroom it had come. He carefully shifted the ice pack on his head; the moving ice rumbled like thunder. Never froze.

The passage remained empty and devoid of sound.

He had finally decided to step out of his room, and very nearly did so, when a door near the dining room opened. To his shock, Never watched George Sherman slip out of Martin and Cora Vale's private room. The distinguished gentleman patted the inside pocket of his suit jacket and cast a lazy glance up and down the passage. Never just managed to duck back into his room without being seen.

When he dared to peer out of his room again, George Sherman had disappeared.

Never took two steps into the passage and stared incredulously at where he had just seen George Sherman. His mouth hung open, his eyes wide with disbelief.

"If I hadn't seen it with my own eyes," Never mumbled aloud. "Imagine: the old bat was right. That wonky woman knew what she was talking about. There really is a jewel thief on board this ship!" Never was upset enough to forget it was only a boat.

"Who will believe me when I tell them all Mr. Sherman is the thief?"

The towel full of ice slipped from his hands and fell to the floor spitting ice cubes in every direction.

"Good morning, Mr. Sherman," Captain Sloe stood up and reached out a hand. "Getting a late start, eh?"

"I never make it a habit to rise early when there's a perfectly good bed underneath me." George pulled out a chair from the Odston's table and sat down with a broad grin.

"That's a lazy attitude," Fanny pronounced.

"I admire it," Wavel offered in an effort to annoy his wife. "I would love to stay in bed more often, but for some reason I always feel compelled to flee it as soon as I awake." He gazed evenly at Fanny.

"I don't mind being lazy, Mrs. Odston," George addressed her with his best society air. "You see, I believe my ancestors rose so early and so often in their pursuit of cotton that I feel I need to make up for their industriousness by pulling back a little."

"Well," Fanny huffed, "it's good to know someone in your family knew how to work. Maybe you could learn a little something from them."

"Now Fanny, my love," Wavel smiled benignly at his wife, "we have no idea how hard Mr. Sherman works. Why, who knows? There are all kinds of labors a man may be called upon to perform in the dead of night; though I can't remember the last time I was called upon in the middle of the night."

"Really, Wavel! You say the queerest things. I don't know what you're talking about."

By the measure of Captain Sloe's smile, he had a good idea what Wavel meant. George merely busied himself with his coffee and made no reply.

Making his second entrance of the morning, Never Gamble limped into the dining room and stood gaping at Captain Sloe's table. He stared hard at the captain trying in vain to get his attention, making several quick hand gestures but failing to catch the captain's eye.

"Look at your steward, Marty." Cora Vale watched the pale steward as a woman might watch another woman's idiot child. She seemed to be enjoying herself. "Only you could hire a dope like that. First he picks a fight with that old hag, and now he stands in the middle of the room like a deranged mime."

Martin Vale raised his head enough to look at his steward. "I don't hire them, Cora. I just pay them. I've said before the boy's a fool."

"Well, you ought to go help the poor thing. Professional courtesy, you know; one fool to another."

"Don't get snippy. You're only upset he's standing there playing charades instead of bringing you a drink. Should I run over and tell him you'd like to start the day off with scotch or gin this morning?"

"Why don't you go pick a duel with the pirate captain and lose?"

"Whatever I do, Cora," Martin stole a look towards Montane, "don't be too sure I'm going to lose."

They watched Never cease his hand signals and reluctantly approach Captain Sloe.

"Captain, sir." Never tried his best not to look at George Sherman. "A moment of your time?"

"Feeling better, now, Never?" The question seemed to confuse everyone at the table for a moment. "What can I do for you?"

"I'd like to speak to you." Never felt his mouth going dry and his head begin to spin.

"Well, go ahead. What is it?"

"Sir, it's—something you need to see—I mean, I need to show you what I have to say."

The Captain had very little idea of what Never was trying to say. Those at the table were just as lost. "Is something wrong?" Captain Sloe stood slowly and set his napkin down on his plate.

"Outside the door, sir—I've got to show you a word." Never suddenly turned and strode from the room.

"Pardon me, everyone. I think the boy's head injury may be more extensive than I had hoped." The captain followed Never through the door and caught up with him halfway down the passage. "Never, hold up, young man. What's this all about?"

"Thief." Never pointed a finger repeatedly at the door of the Vales' room. The knot on his head began throbbing with greater intensity.

"A thief?" Never nodded. Captain Sloe's eyes narrowed. "He's in there right now?" Never shook his head. "Well, speak plainly then, son."

"Mr.—I saw the thief—jewels in his pocket. Robbing the Vales'—I saw—" Never had not taken a breath during this stilted announcement. Finally, the strain became too much, and Never's eyes rolled up into his head and he fell gracelessly to the floor.

Never heard voices.

"It's all my fault. I hit him with the door."

"Easy, Tom. A hard rap on the head couldn't damage

Gamble's head anymore than nature did when he was born."

"Thank you, Mr. Odston."

"It's likely that anything the young man says from here on out will be nonsensical. This story about a thief in the Vales' room is a prime example."

"Yes, that's bound to be the case, Mr. Sherman." Someone gently touched one of Never's eyelids and pulled it back. Never saw Captain Sloe peering closely at him. "Are you awake now, Never?"

"Yes, sir," Never was barely able to say. He opened his eyes without assistance and winced at the pain that invaded his head. He was laying on the divan in the day room. He could see Tom, Wavel Odston, Captain Sloe, and George Sherman standing over him like a bevy of anxious doctors. His unfocused gaze lingered on George Sherman.

"Now, my boy," Captain Sloe spoke soothingly, "what were you saying about a thief? You said you saw someone?"

"Yes, Mr. Gamble," George Sherman bent over him and grinned widely at him, "just what did you *think* you saw? Feel absolutely free to tell us anything. We know full well you were suffering from a head injury, and we will not fault you in the least for thinking you saw whatever it was you *think* you saw."

"Mr. Sherman's right," Wavel jumped in, a bit more enthusiastically than was his usual manner.

"The Captain says you spied a jewel thief." Tom said helpfully, trying to jog Never's memory. "Did you really spy a jewel thief?"

"No," Never whispered. The close presence of George Sherman was overwhelming. "I never spied a thief. I—I don't know what I was saying."

"We understand. This poor boy needs rest." George patted Never on the top of his head. "You try to rest, now."

"Good old Never." Tom shook his head in admiration and sympathy. "He's a little out of his mind, isn't he, Captain? When do you think he'll get back to normal?"

"I for one," Wavel observed, "don't see a difference. When did he say he saw this jewel thief?"

"I don't know, really." Captain Sloe admitted. "Everything he said made very little sense."

"I suggest we forget the whole thing." George Sherman said with finality.

"I second the motion," Wavel concluded the agreement. No one gave Never's revelation another thought.

Chapter Twenty-Three

Circumstance and Happenstance

Ida Claire picked at the last of her ham with the same fork that had stabbed young Never Gamble. She had only bothered to wipe it off with a napkin. She was not interested in the ham but did not want to give up on her breakfast. She always liked to finish what was on her plate, regardless of how much she ordered. Her sister, on the other hand, had not eaten one third of the food Ida had ordered for her.

"Now don't be stubborn, Erma. Eat the ham, at least. There's no point wasting all that food."

A figure appeared beside Ida, startling her as she stuck a piece of ham into her mouth.

"Oho! So here you are, my little Rose of the sea." The Old Man clucked his tongue as if he were playing with a pet poodle. "I have been looking for you. But what is this? Another flower? A man can have no greater luck, *n'est-ce pas*? *Enchanted, Mademoiselle.* What lovely name do they call you?"

"That's my sister," Ida said irritably. She had no desire to allow this French charmer to get to know Erma.

"Ah, just so. I should have guessed as much. Two beautiful flowers, one extraordinary family."

"Now just you go along, Maurice. None of your love making here. How do you say it? Shoo—shoo." Ida waved him off like a buzzing fly.

The Old Man snatched the last of Ida's waffle from her plate and popped it into his mouth, his satisfied grunt drowned out by Ida's sharp bark of protest.

"Get away! Get!" Ida slapped at him.

The Old Man jigged out of reach and laughed at her attempts to punish him. "Saucy, sau—cy!" he cried.

Other pirates had descended on the dining room. Othello sat down at Melvin's table, remaining silent until Alice brought him a plate. Kit, having attempted to sit beside Fanny Odston, gave up and moved to another table after she fussed and fumed at his impertinence. The Old Man joined him, laughing at his young partner's misfortune. Only Matvie did not show up for breakfast. He was nowhere to be seen.

Othello quickly ate, then ordered Alice to bring two plates for the twins. Tom, protecting her from further interaction with the pirate, took over and brought Othello the plates. An urn of coffee in one hand and two cups in the other, Tom followed as Othello left.

A signal from Montane was all that was needed to get David moving. David stood and sought out Captain Sloe. He found him coming in through the door.

"Captain, we ought to get going."

"So soon? I'm not sure that will work."

"What do you mean?" David cocked his head to one side and hoped the captain was not serious. He had a sinking feeling another silly protocol was about to delay everything.

"There's the dishes to be done." Captain Sloe said, without a hint of a smile on his face. "It really can't be avoided."

"Captain, I hardly think Montane will wait around while—"

"Young man, there is only one full set of dishes on this boat. If we were to leave this set dirtied by this morning's breakfast, there would be nothing left to eat on for lunch. Do you intend this trial to be over before noon? I really don't think you do. Now it won't take all that long. I shall endeavor to make sure the cleanup is swift, but it really must be done."

David was at a loss as to how he should respond. The people of *The Jenny* had an uncanny way of presenting their lunacies with logical arguments. He saw Montane approach and turned to explain the predicament.

"I heard," Montane said with a sigh, as if he had just overheard news that the boat was sinking. Resigned to the idiosyncrasies of his captives, Montane jammed his hands into his pockets. "Shall we take a walk up on deck?"

He led the way topside.

When Othello opened the door of the wheelhouse, Tom was right on his heels. Macbeth stood at the helm watching the surface of the ocean. Swells were beginning to form upon it. The grey blue waters were becoming more grey than blue. Lear sat in a corner on a padded bench, fiddling with a small portable radio.

"Breakfast in bed!" Lear pushed away from the bench and snatched a plate from Othello. Macbeth waited until his plate was handed to him. Lear pawed at the ham and stuffed it in his mouth. He gave Tom a quizzical glance. "Who's this?"

Othello said nothing. Lear's eyes widened in mock curiosity as the silence built. Tom stood, nervously wishing he could set down the coffee so he would not accidentally spill it on the pirates.

"Tom," the porter eventually admitted.

"Tom," Lear repeated. "Hello there, Tom. You're a young fella. Seems everyone else around here is older than my Aunt Harry. That's gotta wreak havoc with your love life, huh?"

Tom could tell right away that Lear was not to be trusted. He warily set down the coffee cups and filled them.

"Of course, ya'll got more women on board than we do on our submarine. We're kinda like a bachelor ship or something. A rowboat full of monks, if you know what I mean. Kinda makes one begin to doubt himself. Now I ain't saying those old biddies you got look good to me, but it sure does get me to thinking, among other things."

Tom did not like the tone of the pirate. It made him want to get away from the wheelhouse. He left the coffee urn by the cups and backed towards the door.

"What's your rush, Tom?" Lear moved uncomfortably close to the porter. "I get the feeling you don't like me. And that's too bad. I was gonna get your help. Tell me. Are there any young does aboard for us bucks? Montane sure is keeping us away from everyone. I can't believe that old woman I saw this morning was the youngest skirt on board. Now what's that look for? No need to get all pissed off at me."

Tom was doing his best to keep a poker face, but he was well out of his element. For Tom, guile was an alien art. Of course, as soon as Lear started asking about young does, Tom immediately thought of Alice. He was sure that just as soon as he had thought of Alice, her name had magically appeared above his head where Lear could read it with wicked delight. The thought that this pirate was making him endanger Alice was what—as Lear had just phrased it—had pissed him off.

"I think you're taking this the wrong way." Lear put an arm around Tom's shoulder. "I'm just being friendly and making small talk. You can talk, can't you?"

"Uh-huh," Tom uttered eloquently.

"Hmm. Macbeth, is it my imagination, or this guy being uncooperative? All I wanted to know was if there were any young ladies on this here boat. He don't wanna answer me. Now what is that?"

Macbeth didn't say anything. He knew full well that Lear was gearing up for his own kind of fun. He never participated in Lear's games. And he did not like the effect they had on his brother. He would never have gone so far as to oppose Lear, but he made it a rule not to encourage him.

Tom, though young and unused to such situations, had wisely decided on the same strategy. He tried to remain as calm as he could while keeping his mouth closed.

"All he had to say was *yes* or *no*." Lear's face was very close to Tom's as he added, "but then again, silence at this point must mean *yes*."

"There is a young one." Othello tried to mollify him, thinking it best if Lear did not hurt the boy. Tom ground his teeth to stifle the protest rising within him.

"That's all I was asking," Lear let go of Tom and backed up, opening his arms as if to show he had no tricks up his sleeves. "See how simple that was? I just asked a question. Go on back with the others, Tom. And try to relax, huh?"

Tom guardedly put his hand on the door handle and

twisted it. The door swung out a little, and a chill wind entered the wheelhouse. Lear said something to Othello that Tom could not hear. But he distinctly heard Othello's reply.

"I will see if I can bring her."

Tom's chivalry got the better of him and he shouted out, "You leave her alone!" He rushed from the wheelhouse. Lear pushed Othello after him.

"Go get that boy!"

"So who was your late night visitor?" Montane enjoyed David's clueless expression. They stood at the stern, watching the *Prowler* following a short distance away.

"Late night visitor?"

"You said something about a talk with a juror last night."

"Oh, *that* visitor." David had forgotten that he had mentioned his late discussion. He was not surprised that Montane had remembered. He was learning more and more that very little escaped Montane. "Let's just say I was doing some research for your defense. Maybe laying a little groundwork for my closing arguments."

"Well then, tell me all about it. It is *my* defense we're talking about here."

"Now, Robbie, you sound as if you're getting nervous. Don't you trust me?"

"David," Montane leaned on the stern rail and spit into the wake, "that's all the value I've ever put in trust. Maybe I just never had occasion to use it. But I think I can safely say you are the first person I've trusted in a very long time. Does that make any sense? I don't even really know you."

"Oh, you're being dramatic. You trust Hamlet. And Matvie."

"I trust Hamlet to a point. I would never trust Matvie. He's like a wild dog that attaches himself to you. For now, he's at my side and watching over me. But I have no control over him. Since you're my priest, I won't hesitate to confess to you; Matvie scares the dickens out of me. But, for now, he's on my side."

David laughed a little at that. He was intrigued to find

that Montane's pirate life was as full of politics as his own life among his school's faculty. He said as much out loud.

"Similar politics, I would agree. But I don't think your fellow teachers are always worrying about someone literally stabbing them in the back."

"Well, not the teachers. If you've ever taught in an inner city school in Cleveland, you'd know it's the students you have to watch out for instead of your fellow teachers. But what I want to know is: if your life is this full of tension, why do you do it? Why be a pirate?"

"There's a simpler answer to that than you might imagine." Montane sighed and shook his head. "Do you ever wonder why someone is a garbage man? Why someone cleans out septic tanks? Do you think those people set out to work amongst garbage and sewage? Do you think they like the stench? Or take something less foul, and say a factory worker; a man who stands in one place and does one monotonous job all day long. Did he say – 'that's my ideal job'? 'That's what I aspire to be'? A few of them, maybe. But more of them are there simply because it was available; or it was all they knew. Dad was at the factory; that's where I'll be. Circumstance and happenstance."

"Was your father a pirate?"

"No," Montane laughed at the question. "My father was a sanitation worker. Doesn't that sound clean? *Sanitation*? We knew it meant *Sewage*. But I wasn't going to follow him. I literally ran off to the sea."

"Like Robinson Crusoe? A classical choice."

"My first time out on a container ship we were attacked by Captain Black. The choice was simple; join up or go into the sea. Circumstance and happenstance."

"But you've had enough."

"Maybe I'm beginning to believe that I can change my circumstance. I already did that when I killed Black."

"But that was years ago. Why did you keep on? Why didn't you quit then? What drives you to give it all up now?"

"You're going back over waters we've already sailed. As a priest, you're not very subtle. This is not just about saving my own skin. The only reason I'm in danger from my own crew right now is because I haven't done the logical thing and killed Lear and Macbeth. I could do that, and no one would oppose me for a long time. But killing Black, no matter how justified it was, has never sat easy with me. It still eats at me. And I know what two more deaths on my hands would do to me. Yes, I know. That sounds suspiciously like I have a conscience."

"Of course you do." David had heard all of this before, and he knew that Montane was just shoring up his resolve to continue with his plan. "It also suspiciously sounds like you're experiencing remorse."

"Is it showing? And it's just my luck the jury's nowhere around."

Chapter Twenty-Four

Which Way the Wind Blows

"Where's Tom?" Alice stood in front of Captain Sloe. Worry shrouded her pleasant face. Her top lip pulled under her bottom lip and her large eyes were full of questions. "Shouldn't he be here?"

"I suppose he should," Captain Sloe watched Alice stacking dishes in a cabinet. Never Gamble was standing at the sink with a white apron tied around his hips and his hands elbow-deep in suds. There was no one else in the galley. "It's not like him to let you clean up by yourself."

"Well, she's not by herself," Never made sure everyone understood that. "I don't mind helping out, but Tom is the porter, after all. And I'm injured, too. He ought to be helping."

"It's not like him," Alice's concern rose as she thought more about it. "He would be helping, you know how he is. Something must be keeping him."

"I'll go have a look around, don't you worry none about him." Captain Sloe flashed her a smile and added a wink for reassurance. He had to admit he was curious as well. Tom never let Alice work if he could help it. In fact, the captain was beginning to worry about the boy the more *he* thought of it.

"Mr. Odston, could I have a moment?" Captain Sloe approached Wavel, who was still reclining at his table. Fanny had left to use the ladies' room and Wavel was enjoying the peace and quiet. "Have you seen my porter anywhere?"

"Misplaced him, have you? I thought it was customary for the porter to misplace the luggage."

"No, no. We don't do that sort of thing aboard *The Jen-*

ny."

"I was only joking," Wavel felt the need to add.

"Oh yes, well, I see. I suppose that is rather funny—misplaced the porter. I'm afraid I'm rather preoccupied. It would put my mind at ease if I could just find young Tom."

"He's likely in his room. Have you checked there?"

"His room? Yes, I'm sure that's where I'll find him. Only—"

"Only what?"

"Nothing, sir. I'm sure that is where I'll find him. Sorry to have bothered you."

A quick search of the porter's room and the day room resulted in proving that the porter had indeed been misplaced. Captain Sloe reentered the dining room and stood in the center of it perplexed. Wavel could see his consternation.

"No luck?" Wavel asked.

"I did not see him anywhere. I wonder just how he could have gone missing."

Before long, everyone was pressing around Captain Sloe with questions or advice. He had to ask several times that everyone quiet down. In the ensuing silence, an unexpected voice spoke up.

"I saw him." It was Melvin, the pilot.

"And?" Captain Sloe encouraged him.

"Went with that there black fella. Arms full of coffee." Melvin, having said what he felt had to be said, returned his attention to his pipe that he had been preparing to light.

"Mr. Sherman," Alice turned to the man from Georgia with eagerness, "do you know where Tom went?"

"Miss, I believe this man was speaking of another black fella." He emphasized 'fella' with a nod. "If we could find Othello, we should be able to find Tom."

A full scale search began in earnest. Every stateroom was examined. When they finished, every space below deck large enough to contain the porter had been poked and prodded. It was obvious Tom was topside.

"Now Alice, there's no need to worry," Captain Sloe continued to make the effort to calm her fears. "I will take Mr.

Sherman with me, and we will go up on deck. More than likely, we'll find him working at some maintenance task that he just could not pass up. You know how diligent he is. We'll be right back."

The Captain and Mr. Sherman did not, in fact, come right back. Having climbed out of the stairwell and onto the deck, they were surprised to see the sky had begun to lose its color. The only blue left in the sky was off to the south. A strengthening wind was pushing it all from the north. A great bank of storm clouds, though still some distance away, were obviously bearing down on them. Captain Sloe's thoughts switched from his porter to his boat.

"I don't like the looks of that." His mind took in the approaching storm and position and speed of *The Jenny* at the same time. "What the devil is Montane doing?"

"I'd prefer to know what the devil *that* one is doing." Mr. Sherman was watching Othello as he appeared from the starboard side. He was moving quickly along the deck and casting furtive glances as if he were afraid of being seen. Startled when he saw both Captain Sloe and Mr. Sherman, Othello froze, seemingly confirming their suspicions.

"You there," Captain Sloe called with authority to the pirate, "where's your captain? I want to see Montane right now. Does he realize what is heading this way?"

Othello had no idea what the rosy-cheeked captain was talking about. He turned his head, following Captain Sloe's gesture, and eyed the cloud bank. It was no matter to him. He could do nothing about the weather. He could, however, get rid of these men.

"You go back below." Othello pointed to the stairs with a jerk of his arm.

"I will not. I will talk with Captain Montane."

Othello was not a man to suffer arguments. He grabbed Captain Sloe by the collar of his coat and began to push him towards the steps. He did the same to Mr. Sherman.

"Take your hands—" Captain Sloe's protest was cut off as Othello jerked him to a stop. Montane stood staring at them; how long he had been there no one knew.

"Why are you up here?" Montane was more angry at Othello's mishandling of Captain Sloe than at the fact the captain had disregarded his warnings to stay below deck. He had no intention of saying so. Othello was only doing as he had been told.

"And why aren't we getting out of the way of *that*?" Captain Sloe pointed north.

"We're watching it." Montane, after seeing the cloud bank was much closer and larger than he had last seen it, had the same questions as Captain Sloe. He wondered why Lear had not sent him word. Maybe he had not been paying attention. Hadn't he and David just been standing at the stern and never noticed it either? No, Montane thought, he and David were guilty of not paying attention. But he was certain Lear had failed to tell him of the storm's changing position on purpose. He needed to move fast to spoil whatever Lear had in mind. If it was not already too late.

"Captain Sloe, follow me. I want to address your concerns immediately and hopefully to your satisfaction."

Captain Sloe and George Sherman shrugged off Othello's large hands and walked off with Montane.

"Maybe," Montane tried to soften Captain Sloe's anger, "I'm just too accustomed to traveling in a submarine. I'm not used to facing storms in a vessel that won't go below the surface."

"Believe me, Montane, *The Jenny* will very easily go below the surface. Have no delusions about that."

"I see what you mean." Montane yanked open the door of the wheelhouse and decided the best way to deal with Lear would be to overplay his role as captain. He gave Lear and Macbeth a withering glare. "You two, what are you clowns doing? I told you to keep me updated on the weather. Did you fall asleep?"

"Now hold on—" Lear watched the wheelhouse fill with the commanding presence of Montane and the others following in his wake. He backed down without a fight.

"Captain Sloe. I will allow you to take command of *The Jenny* to the extent that you may take whatever actions necessary to avoid the coming storm. Do you require the use of your Pilot? I could have him sent up."

"No, no. If you'll just allow me a few minutes." Captain Sloe stepped back out of the wheelhouse and stared into the wind. He watched the waves, the deepening swells, and gauged the wind. After allowing his five senses to take in all the data available, he ducked back inside and turned his attention to the modern technological gauging devices.

In the end, Montane did send for Melvin. Captain Sloe set a course designed to keep them out of harm's way. Montane hoped the old captain's skills were sufficient. By his own estimations, he was not so sure.

Wavel watched the captain and George Sherman leave in search of the porter. He sat back in his chair and closed his eyes. He could hear Ida Claire nagging her sister.

"Eat what's on your plate. Don't order it if you aren't going to eat it."

"Didn't you order all of this?" asked Mrs. Kaufman.

"I don't see what that has to do with anything."

Wavel tried to ignore the frivolous chatter. It would be pleasant to be able to shut everything out. He was wondering just how long he could hope Fanny would stay in the powder room when he heard steps approaching his table and despaired. What would Fanny find to go on and on about next? Whatever it was, he was certain it would be droll.

"Would you join me in the day room?"

Wavel opened his eyes and was pleasantly surprised to see Martin Vale standing over him. He realized he had an opportunity to escape from Fanny before she returned. He jumped up from his seat.

"Wonderful idea." Wavel hurried off, leaving Vale to wonder at the man's enthusiasm. They both settled into the comfortable furnishings in the day room and Wavel accepted a cigar from Vale. After the cigars were lit, the two men sat back and said nothing for a few minutes, concentrating on their tobacco leaf. The smoke filtered through the room, suffusing it with a heavy aroma. Martin Vale broke the silence.

"Silly business, this trial, eh?"

"Uncommon," Wavel tried to modify Vale's assessment. "I don't say unnatural, mind you. But it is uncommon."

"I'd always taken you for a logical man, Odston." Vale frowned and pulled on the cigar. He blew the smoke in frustration. "Sounds as if you're siding with Montane."

"Do you think so? Because I said it's not unnatural?" Wavel pointed his cigar at Vale, who was nodding his assent. "To begin with, I am a logical man. And that very same logic tells me your statement suggesting I'm siding with Montane does not fit in. I said this trial is natural. I never said anything to align myself with Montane. I only meant that the desire for absolution is natural."

"Alright, alright. I give in. You have no sympathies for this pirate, then?"

"There you go again. You should stick to asking questions, not confirmations of your assumptions." Wavel knew what Vale was fishing for. He simply enjoyed the verbal banter. Vale did not.

"Then let me be frank," Vale sat up and asked a direct question. "Are you going to fall for this nonsense? Would you ever consider forgiving a criminal like Montane? Or more specifically, can I count on you to condemn this degenerate man?"

"Now that you've asked a definite question, I will reply with a definite answer. Yes. And I'll tell you why. On a personal level, I understand him. Any of us would probably take something he shouldn't if given the opportunity. In fact, maybe more of us have than we admit. But if we are talking about justice, then we can't just forgive the man. He has to pay a price for his own absolution, but more importantly, he must uphold society's declaration of law and order. If you start throwing forgiveness around, everyone's going to expect it and take advantage of it."

"Right, exactly!" Vale laughed a little with the giddiness that comes from finding someone who confirms your own beliefs. "I don't quite agree with the first part of what you said. About all of us being thieves or what-not, but the last part; yes, ain't that the truth. I heartily agree. Absolutely."

Wavel smiled at his agreeable smoking partner. He raised his cigar in salute. Vale returned the salute.

"I like you Odston. You're from St. Louis, aren't you?"

"St. Louis." Wavel nodded at the name of his home.

"I give you—"Vale hesitated as he calculated in his head "—at least twenty years in banking. Am I right?"

"Accountant. Twenty-Five years."

"Now, that's almost the same thing." Vale waved off his mistake. "I knew you were a man who dealt with money. I can recognize that in other men. It's my life. It's what I do. I know when I meet other men who've had success with the dollar bill."

Wavel said nothing in response to that. He had said nothing about success. A shadow passed over his face. A release of smoke obscured the shadow so that when the smoke cleared, the shadow was gone as well. Wavel conjured up a smile.

"If it weren't so early in the morning, I'd offer a toast to success."

"That's refreshing," laughed Vale. He leaned over and smacked Wavel on the knee. "Refreshing, indeed. It's nice to spend time with someone who thinks there is a time that's too early to drink. I should get you to explain it to my wife. I must thank you, Odston. It's done me good to speak with you. You've cheered me considerably. I can't say too many accountants have done that, over the years."

Wavel felt certain that Vale's good mood sprang more from having heard Wavel's determination to condemn Montane than from any other part of the conversation. He had seen the gleam in Vale's eyes when he discovered Wavel was on his side. Let him gloat, thought Wavel, it doesn't bother me in the least if I've misled the man. Was Vale so foolish as to think there was more than one possible outcome from this affair? Wavel walked from the room chuckling silently. Vale was more ignorant than he appeared, he decided. And from his perspective, the owner of *The Jenny* looked plenty ignorant to begin with.

Vale was gloating. He was confident that he could defeat Montane. But he was less so when he thought of Montane's promise to submit to the jury's decision. That, Vale knew, was not something he could depend on. 'And that', Vale said to himself, 'is why I need my guarantee.' He thought once more of the gun hidden in his room. And the same thought from the night before troubled him. He had to make sure it was still safely hidden.

Crossing from the day room into his stateroom, Vale locked his door and stood with his ear against it. He could hear no footsteps. There was no one in the passage outside. He went to Cora's vanity and saw his reflection in the half-length mirror. He knew he was looking older every day. And he had put on a good deal of weight over the years. But no matter how he appeared to Cora, Montane, and all the others, Vale was satisfied to know that his mind was still sharp and his instincts still as great as ever.

Yes, Vale nodded at his image, you've outwitted the snake. You've been two steps ahead of him the whole way. With grace born from his certainty of superiority, Vale deftly slipped his hand between the vanity and the wall and felt for the revolver taped in its hiding place. It was not there. The revolver was gone.

A flush of despair burned Vale's face. "I hate Montane," he said aloud. But in the same instant, he smiled at the mirror. "No matter," the smile grew wider. "I didn't say I was one step ahead of you. Two steps. I was two steps ahead of you. You may have found the gun, but you still don't know about my backup plan. You still lose, Montane. And I still win."

A brief shadow of doubt passed over his reflection, but it did not linger.

Chapter Twenty-Five

Discretion is the Better Part of Bluster

Montane's mood deteriorated faster than the weather. After a fairly confident assurance by Captain Sloe that *The Jenny* would miss the storm, he had tried to get the trial restarted. It took only a few minutes before Tom's disappearance came to his attention. No one had seen him. A search of the boat had been fruitless. Questioning Lear, Macbeth, and Othello had been a waste of time as well. Montane had no way to prove it, but he was sure his crew had something to do with Tom's absence. He was losing his resolve to remain on the straight and narrow.

The foolish arguments had returned. If Tom could not be found, the jury would be even more short-handed. They were now short by three. They were missing Barry Alum and the porter, and now Melvin was staying in the wheelhouse to try and steer *The Jenny* away from the pursuing storm. Montane had to fight to keep his experimental trial under control.

"Ladies, please!" Captain Sloe hammered his table with a mallet that Tom had found amongst the boat's tools. That was Tom, thought the captain, solving the missing gavel problem. That *was* Tom? He tried not to think of Tom any more than he had to. He had seriously begun to doubt the boy's safety. "There is nothing more we can do. Montane insists we continue as we are, regardless of the number of jurors."

"He's fixing the jury!" Ida Claire accused Montane with a shrill voice. "He's had that porter killed off because the boy was going to vote against him. He's going to kill us all!"

"Mrs. Claire!" Captain Sloe shouted her name in order to shut her up. "That will be enough of that kind of talk. You have no proof of such a statement, and I might add you're wrong. If Tom was going to vote against Montane I'll be the captain of a plague ship. The fact is, if anybody was going to offer a kind hand to Montane it was going to be Tom."

Captain Sloe considered calling on the services of Othello to keep Ida quiet but thought better of it. Their so-called bailiff made Captain Sloe nervous and he did not want to start something that might end with someone getting hurt. He knew first hand just how strong and persuasive Othello could be.

Ida could see just what Captain Sloe had been thinking when she caught his glance at the big African. Those listening to her had to believe she had never in her life understood the expression "discretion is the better part of valor".

"Oh, just you try to get that brute to silence me! Shame on you, Captain. Why, it's this pirate who likely did away with the porter," Ida announced. Alice let out a gasp. Ida continued her speech. "This one was with him last. And now he's missing. He's a cutthroat! Murderer! And yet, instead of forcing a confession from the wretch, you'd tell him to gag me. To tie me to my chair! Oh, captain, I protest!"

"Now, Mrs. Claire," Captain Sloe was slightly shocked that she had read his mind so clearly. He had not thought of tying her to a chair and gagging her. However, as soon as he heard the suggestion, it appealed to him. He hoped she was not reading his mind any further. "Mrs. Claire, you are allowing panic to seize you. Let's try to be logical. Othello hasn't murdered anyone—anyone here, that is."

Othello's stone mask developed a hairline fracture. The woman's shrill accusations struck a nerve that he believed had long ago died. Could he in truth still have a conscience? The suggestion was surprising. The answer was stunning. Yes, he thought, something had been bothering him. His mind wandered to that fateful moment with the killing of the passenger with the little gun. He no longer listened to what was going on around him.

"Oh, why don't you just shut up?" Fanny Odston blurted out. "If you don't, we'll be here forever."

"It may be the best thing, Miss Ida." George Sherman leaned down and patted the woman on her shoulder. "We all want this to be over."

Finally, it became apparent that Ida did understand discretion was at least the better part of complete and abysmal failure. That she had failed to win her argument could no longer be denied. Brushing lint from the lapel of her lime-green wool dress, she sat up straight in her chair and stared dead ahead.

As Captain Sloe had predicted, Martin Vale had calmed down considerably since the adjournment of the trial the previous night. He stood now, coldly looking down at Montane, who was seated at the makeshift witness stand. Vale wet his lips and began to speak.

"I took the liberty of writing down a few of your more interesting admissions yesterday. I would like to get you to elaborate on a few of them." Vale snatched a notepad from his table and held it up to the jury. "These are Robert Montane's own words. I haven't embellished them one bit. I ask you to consider the truths behind these statements.

"To begin with," he turned on Montane in great imitation of a courtroom drama actor overplaying a district attorney, "did you or did you not say 'I have beaten six men to force them to reveal the locations of valuables'?"

"In so many words, yes."

"Describe for us this ambiguous word *beaten*. Don't you, in fact, mean *tortured*?" An audible gasp came from the row of women jurors.

"No." Montane answered. "I would have said tortured if I had meant it. But I said they were beaten. Each one of those men was more interested in hiding his valuables from me than in saving his own crew. I very simply allowed my men to strike them repeatedly with their fists until they complied. I don't mean to sound so cold in what I say, but you did ask for a description."

"Just answer the question without trying to justify it."

"I do not wish to justify anything I have done. I may explain why I did a thing, but there is no justification for my crimes. I readily accept that. Haven't I been clear on that?"

"Well, what of this ridiculous claim of 'no permanent damage'?"

"I meant what I said. Aside from bruises and cuts and scrapes, they were not harmed in any physical way that would not heal up on its own. I'm sorry to say, my assessment of no physical damage only covers that: physical damage. I do not know the deeper damage I have done to anyone. To their heart or their soul. But I am sure the damage has been done there as well." For a moment, Montane knew that some of David's highly sought remorse was showing through. Montane refused to draw upon it. He would not seek to exploit it.

"I am sure it has. But even discounting damage that cannot be measured, it would be accurate to state that you are admitting to the assault and battery of six men. Is that correct?"

"I have confessed to having this done, not to doing it myself. But while the distinction can be made, I take full responsibility for it."

Martin Vale was not done. He tried to draw out every possible detail regarding Montane's confession. He discussed at length the amount of property stolen during the fifteen years; he made Montane recount the incident when he had lost his temper and set fire to a captured ship. Through it all, Montane never held back an answer. He had no intentions of lying about his past. The only time there was an argument was when Vale accused Montane of purposely setting out to seize Vale's ships. Vale began to lose his composure.

"You have set out to destroy me!" Vale pounded his fist on Captain Sloe's table. The captain, startled, raised a brow at the sudden action.

"I've done nothing of the kind," Captain Sloe said facetiously.

"I didn't mean you," Vale grumbled apologetically.

"Then please don't attack my table." The captain smiled placidly.

"If you were directing that at me," Montane offered, "I

will have to say you are wrong. I like to think I've been quite fair in attacking the broadest spectrum of ships the ocean has to offer."

"I find that shocking," Vale's tone had changed from anger to mockery. "I was ready to believe you only stole from the rich to give to the poor."

"Nothing so noble, I'm afraid. Just stealing from whomever to give to us poor pirates."

Vale stood for a full minute without saying a word. The measure of contempt he held for Montane was plain for all to see. His breathing was irregular; his posture indignant.

"Mr. Vale?" Captain Sloe spoke softly into the silence. "Do you have anything more?"

"What?" Vale asked sharply. "What more could there be? I don't see any reason to keep going on. The man's an admitted pirate, guilty of piracy, assault and battery, grand larceny, and who knows what else. I can't for the life of me figure out what all the mystery is about. I'm not going to waste any more time on this. I don't care if his soul is in conflict. I want his bones in jail!"

"Captain, may I suggest a recess?" George Sherman raised his voice just enough to be heard. "I'm sure the ladies could use a break. I sure could."

"I think that's something everyone might just agree on, Mr. Sherman. And might I add, a pleasant thought that is, everyone agreeing on something for once." His assumption was correct; everyone was ready for a chance to stretch their legs.

Lunch was brought out. David Wayne found he could not help but wish they could have used paper plates. He knew another dishwashing delay would be inevitable. Fortunately it had only been sandwiches with a vegetable tray. How Bob and Alice had managed to get it all prepared as quickly as they did was a wonder to David.

"What do you think about the missing porter?" David asked Montane. They were seated at the same table they had used for breakfast, set far enough apart from the others in order to speak without being overheard.

"I'm worried. There is no conveniently missing boat to suggest he has escaped in the same way that jewel thief did. In fact, it makes me begin to question just how reliable our assumption is that the jewel thief did take the boat."

"What does that mean?" asked David.

"I'm beginning to suspect that someone on my crew is killing off passengers." Montane only suspected one of his crew, but he did not need to say as much. David knew exactly what he was thinking. "If I'm right, this whole mission of mine is a disaster."

"Should you have sent that pilot up there with them?"

"He's not with Lear. I sent Lear back to the *Prowler* on the pretense I wanted him to inform Hamlet what our new heading was in case we are separated by the storm."

"I thought you wanted to avoid leaving Lear alone on the sub."

"It was either that or leave him here. Considering I suspect him of murder…" Montane did not finish his thought.

"What will Hamlet do with him? Send him right back?"

"I hope Hamlet stuffs him in a torpedo tube."

David had no reply. Such a comment should have made him laugh. But Montane was more likely to be serious on that subject than not. David felt depression settling in; was it possible Montane really had no choice but to resort to violence? Was fate this difficult to escape? Deflecting the answer he did not want to hear, he turned his attention to the other tables.

George Sherman had joined the sisters at their table. With charm and grace he removed his jacket and laid it on the table, obviously entertaining them with an anecdote. They were in good humor, brought on by the attention he was lavishing upon them. Once he was finished cheering the two old ladies, he stood and made his way to the Vales' table. David was surprised to see George sit down next to Martin Vale. He could tell Vale looked just as surprised. Cora, he noticed, did not look at George. He would have liked to have been a fly on their tablecloth; what could George have to say to Martin Vale?

"Is there something you want?" Martin Vale looked George Sherman over with a steely eye. He was still irritated by the way the morning's portion of the trial had ended. He was also suspicious enough of George to wish that he would keep his distance.

"Actually, I may have something you want," George answered cryptically. "Come with me into the hall and I think you'll like what I have to offer."

"If it comes from you it had better be something of great value." There was an obvious dislike from both sides of the table. While Vale had a noticeable disdain for the Georgian, George had a very real and palpable contempt for the self-important owner of *The Jenny*.

"It's your choice whether you find out or not." George stood up and left.

"What are you waiting for, you dimwit?" Cora was in a foul mood. Montane had forbidden the use of alcohol until the end of the trial. She nursed a grudge now instead of a glass of bourbon. "It's not gonna hurt you to go find out what the man wants."

"I don't like that man," Vale said as if it were a legitimate excuse for bad manners. "He's smug. He thinks too much of himself. He's..." Vale tried to think of another insult he could hurl.

"Uppity?" Cora offered with her own smug look.

"Don't even," Vale said, baring his teeth. "You're going to say I'm a bigot now, is that it? Well, see if I care. I don't mind meeting him in the hall." Vale stood and straightened his tie. "It's no crime to try and keep your wife from making a mistake." He had only muttered that last remark, though it had been loud enough for Cora to hear. She watched him walk off with a brief look of melancholy that he never saw.

Cora did not wonder at George's desire to speak with her husband. She should have been worried that he might intend to reveal the details of their midnight rendezvous. That she did not care what George told Martin spoke volumes to her soul. There was no great eagerness for such revelations, but neither could she stir up any dread at the thought. Let Martin rant and rave, she decided. Whatever George tells him will be just fine. Cora felt a small measure of relief, but she wished she could wash it all down with a large, alcoholic drink just the same.

"You've got some nerve!" Fanny Odston's shout shook the dining room. All eyes turned towards the Odstons. "Just what kind of crack was that?"

"It was merely an observation," Wavel said quietly, well aware that they suddenly commanded the attention of everyone in the room. "There's nothing sacrilegious about it, my little angel. You've no cause to crucify me simply because I made a practical statement."

"Practical statement?" His wife spit the words out as if they were poisonous darts aimed at his heart. "You dare suggest that insurance money replacing my jewelry may be a better tradeoff? My mother's jewelry better off as cash in our pockets?"

"It was only a passing comment. That's just the accountant in me. My dear sweet wife, you keep harping on those stolen diamonds as if we'd lost a child. They're only baubles when all is said and done. And with our current situation—" he lowered his voice when he said that "—I'm just saying the insurance money may be more welcome right now."

"You're happy they've been stolen, aren't you? You always did hate my mother."

"I will cheerfully agree with one of those accusations, my love." Wavel's concession seemed to placate Fanny. She grunted in satisfaction. Her suspicions had been proved right.

Chapter Twenty-Six

Revelations

"Don't you ever give up?" Ida Claire protested the Old Man's arrival for lunch. He had brazenly sat down next to Ida and slid his chair close to her.

"No, no. I could never give up on you, my little rose. Where is your lovely sister, huh?"

"You just forget about her. She's resting—and no, I won't tell you what stateroom she's in." Ida gave him a hard stare.

"I would not have asked. I am pleased to find you alone. You would not object to my eating a little lunch, no?" He waved to Alice, who smiled and disappeared into the kitchen, only to return just seconds later with a plate of halved sandwiches.

"Well, you needn't eat so close to me." Ida tried to slide her chair away from him. The Old Man shot a hand out and grasped her wrist.

"You must stay close," he lowered his voice in earnest. Ida tensed at his rough touch. He let go of her and leaned in closer. He smelled of the sea and his breath of cigarettes. His face was covered with white stubble over a backdrop of heavy wrinkles. Yet Ida could see something genuine in his bright eyes. "There is something I must tell you."

"Well I don't know what that could be. I told you before I want no more of your love making."

"Oh, that is for another time. One day, eh? But now is the time for other matters. You must know. Things are not all as they appear. We are not the only pirates aboard."

"What kind of nonsense is that, Maurice? You make very little sense. Speak clearly, I can barely understand you with your accent as it is."

The Old Man made himself perfectly clear even as he whispered in her ear.

"Preposterous!" Ida shouted. The Old Man shushed her. Ida dropped her voice, though not nearly low enough to satisfy the Frenchman. "What's all this nonsense? I've never heard such slander."

"You will see—ho-ho, you will see." He tore off a bite of his sandwich and chewed with concentration, his mind no longer on intrigues and secrets. Playfully, he walked his fingers forward and gently tapped Ida on the back of her hand accompanied by a child's smile. Ida allowed no smile in return, but neither did she pull her hand away.

"Ah, the other flower arrives." He stood and assisted Mrs. Kaufman as she took her seat.

"How are you, Mr. Maurice?"

"He's telling stories, Erma. Don't listen to him. His foolishness is so trying."

"Have patience, little rose. And be very careful. Remember what I have said, eh? Maybe your Maurice is not as old and feeble-minded as he appears."

"What did he say?" asked Mrs. Kaufman after the old pirate left the table.

"Never you mind, Erma. Look what that fool of a Frenchman did now. He's left his coat on the table." Ida picked up the coat and stood to follow Maurice.

"Isn't that Mr. Sherman's coat?"

"Why, yes it is." Ida paused, her hands feeling the soft material. Ida's brow bent in contemplation. "I would surely have thought this belonged to Maurice. What should I do about this?"

"Shouldn't you just give it to Mr. Sherman?"

"Oh, I will." Ida hefted the jacket with one hand. She smiled at her sister's suggestion. "I'll take care of Mr. Sherman."

The jury returned to their seats. Captain Sloe sat at his

table as judge. Robert Montane and David Wayne sat together while Martin Vale sat alone. Othello still stood in as bailiff. Everything was in order. The trial resumed.

"Mr. Wayne," Captain Sloe began, "with the conclusion of Mr. Vale's questioning, I would like to give you the opportunity to ask Mr. Montane anything you like. Do you have any questions for him?"

"No, Captain. Mr. Montane has stated that he has revealed all he can and I won't argue with him. I think he's been very cooperative and forthright."

"I understand. Well I'm not sure where we go from here," Captain Sloe pondered his options. "Mr. Vale, although I find it unlikely, I feel compelled to ask you if you have any other witnesses you would like to call."

"I most certainly do." Vale stood and raised his chin defiantly. "I call David Wayne to the stand."

The jury turned to look at the young man from Cleveland with a mixture of curiosity and surprise. Even Captain Sloe could not keep from exclaiming under his breath. David himself seemed to be caught off guard. The only one who failed to respond with any real expression was Montane. He sat still, his eyes fixed steadily on Vale.

David immediately knew something was wrong. There was any number of reasons Vale was calling him to the stand and the majority of them were harmless. He anticipated questions regarding his kidnapping. That could be easily dealt with. But as young and idealistic as he might have been, he had learned enough to realize something was about to hit him without warning. He tried to think clearly as he sat in the witness chair.

"Shall we swear you in?" Vale asked, knowing what the answer would be.

"I can't do that," David replied. He was not trying to be contentious and even Vale knew it. In fact, Vale had counted on it.

"Why can't you?" Vale asked, again, knowing the answer beforehand.

"The very Bible that you ask me to swear by says quite

clearly that we are not to swear by anything. We are simply commanded to speak the truth and tell no lies."

"So without swearing, you must tell the truth, without exception, correct? We have that assurance from you?"

"Yes." David felt, rather than saw, the eyes of everyone upon him. He had proclaimed his Christian faith to everyone present and he knew what Vale was up to. Vale was making sure David remembered that he was under a deeper obligation to be truthful than the average witness who swears by the Bible to be honest. The fact that Vale placed such a value on this point confirmed David's suspicions that something was about to drop from the sky. He could do nothing but wait for it.

"Well I think that's good enough for me. If you assure me that your answers will be the truth and nothing but the truth, as the saying goes, then I'll take you at your word. Now in that spirit, let's get to the first of my questions. Can you tell me how you came to be a part of Montane's crew?"

That was obvious, David thought. He had expected that question, and he was quick to retell his story. He started with Montane's call to the crisis hotline and ended with his arrival on board the *Prowler*.

"So we can justly add kidnapping to the list of Montane's crimes."

"Yes, technically speaking." David resisted the urge to say there had been no kidnapping. But he added "I would say, however, that since I would have come of my own accord had Mr. Montane simply asked me, I do not view it as a kidnapping."

"Oh, how touching, Mr. Wayne: *if he had only asked you*. Yet, how much more of a violation was it when we consider your selfless attitude? But I will defer to you, Mr. Wayne. You are the injured party in this instance, and if you don't wish to call it kidnapping, I will concede the point." Vale had something of the used car salesman in him; no one really believed what he was saying.

David was sure that would not be all. He watched Vale's face for any hint of what might come next. The only thing noticeable about Vale was his refusal to look David in the eyes. David did not like the implications of that. He knew that somewhere in the back of his mind, a prayer was going up to God. The words were not articulated, but they did not have to be. It was enough to know God would understand it.

"I won't bother you much longer, Mr. Wayne. There is just one more matter I would like you to enlighten us on." Vale stepped in front of David and finally looked him in the eye. "Would you please tell us about Elise?"

The name dropped into David's lap like a grenade. It was hard for him to take a breath. He cut a sharp look at George Sherman. The man was seated casually, leaning back enough to appear disinterested in the questioning, but David could see the concentration in his eyes. It had never occurred to David that he should not have told anyone about the girl. Montane sat looking at him with a puzzled brow. He did not want Montane to learn about Elise; not like this. He had no idea how he could begin to speak of her.

"Come now, Mr. Wayne," Vale was thoroughly enjoying himself. He knew that George Sherman's information was genuine as soon as he saw the paleness in David Wayne's face. It emboldened Vale to a dramatic effect. "I thought we had an agreement. Didn't you just sit there and tell us all your good, Christian dedication to the truth? Why would you now fail in that dedication? Why won't you speak? You have heard of a young woman by the name of Elise, haven't you?"

"Yes," David's voice was barely audible. He cleared his throat. "Elise was…"

"Young man," Vale said in mock tenderness, "I'm having trouble hearing you and I'm only a few feet away. I'm sure these good people in the jury can't hear you. A little louder, if you please?"

"Elise was a young woman who called me one night at the Crisis Hotline. She was depressed; suicidal. She had been going through a very tough divorce. There had been abuse. I had been able to talk her out of harming herself. I don't think she really wanted to seriously end her life. But she was the type of person who had trouble facing her problems. She was very quick to want to run from them."

"And then?" Vale pressed him for more.

"Then she got back on her feet. She would call from time to time. Things were better for her. She had found a way to believe that life could be good. That she could expect more out of life than being run over by it as if it were a train and she was tied to the tracks. That was the image she once used." David's thoughts began to bring back memories he had suppressed. "I remember her saying those very words. It made quite an impression on me. I couldn't stand to think she'd come to think of life like that. It seemed like every time she would start to make progress, something would happen that would pull her back. She needed time away. She needed to get clear of her old surroundings."

"So what did she do?" Vale asked, knowing full well the answer.

"She listened to me. I don't know why. I guess in a way, I used everything I knew about her to get her to leave. I suggested a cruise. That was an easy choice. She'd always said how she wanted to see the ocean one day; how she had been trapped there in Cleveland for so long. I knew that just mentioning a cruise would cut her resistance to the idea in half. She didn't like people much. Hated crowds. It's why I recommended she take a small cruise. Like this one. I pulled her strings until there was no way she was not going to take that cruise. I'd felt proud of that. I was very proud of myself."

"Why not?" Vale asked knowingly. "What's wrong with a cruise?"

David chanced a look in Montane's direction. The pirate's eyes betrayed his suspicions. His expression said he knew where this was leading.

"Her cruise was overtaken by the *Prowler*. Montane and his crew seized her boat; *The Jenny's* sister ship, *The Missy*."

"Well, that's good news, isn't it?" Vale's mockery was a bitter pill for David.

"No." That was hard enough for him to say. His next words were even harder. "Montane's crew—to be more accurate, someone on Montane's crew raped her."

A troubled cry arose from the front row of jurors. Every woman there stared at David with disgust.

"Well, at least she lived to tell the tale, didn't she?" David wanted to jump up and grab Vale by the throat. His sick and very deliberate attempts to anger him were working.

"She didn't live. She lived through the attack, but she never made it back to the harbor." Vale's emotional attack was successful. David felt his staggered breathing and tears gathering in his eyes. He forced himself to continue before he broke down. "She killed herself after that. She just threw herself into the ocean. She'd been hit by that train one too many times."

"So now, maybe we see that Montane is responsible for a little more than some stolen goods. Isn't that right, Mr. Wayne?" Vale's question was a triumph.

"Montane knew nothing about the rape." David shook his head and tried to focus his thoughts. "He had no idea it had taken place."

"And you believe that? Are you willing to believe that this pirate captain did not know what his crew was doing? Have you asked him about it?" David shook his head. "And why not? Are you afraid of what he might answer?"

"I did not want to bring it up with him to spare him the pain of knowing."

"What pain? According to you he's not responsible, right?"

"I never said that. He's as responsible as I was. I sent her on that cruise. She did not want to go, but I pushed all the right buttons in order to change her mind. I'm as guilty as Montane."

"Why did you do that? What was she to you?"

"I had hoped to marry her one day," David admitted with a trembling voice.

"And now," Vale circled in on his prey with a meticulous choice of words, "are you really going to ask these good people of the jury to forgive Robert Montane? Do you seriously forgive the man? Do you forgive the man who caused your fiancé to be raped and then dropped in the sea?"

"Yes," David said in a near whisper.

"What? Oh come on. Do you even believe what you just said? I can tell you, no one here believes you. I'll bet Montane doesn't even believe you."

"I have to. If I don't, I can't forgive myself."

"There are many things we have to do that we are never able to do. You may think you have to forgive him; you may want to forgive yourself. But can you really do either one?"

"I don't know." The admission was impossible, but somehow David had managed to say it.

David had avoided looking at Montane since Vale had mentioned Elise. Now he looked up and stared at the pirate. He had never seen Montane so stunned. It was obvious that no matter what he may have known about Elise, he had never known that she was related in any way to David. He looked as if he had been shot in the gut. He had just discovered that the one friend he thought he had found in the world had become his chief accuser. There was no bitterness in his eyes; only hopelessness.

Captain Sloe, as stunned as everyone else, nodded at David. He watched the young man stand up from the witness seat with a new found respect. He would never have imagined the scale of what David was trying to accomplish. His initial response was to believe this was some kind of parlor game for Montane and the young counselor. That is was some kind of poker bluff gone absurd. He now knew it was not. He now understood that David had a much larger stake in Montane's scheme. There were two souls on the cusp.

"Thank you, young man." The cruel edge was still evident in Vale's voice. He was savoring the blow he had dealt to Montane. His satisfaction was evident to everyone there. For some it was understandable; a few of them would have gladly joined in the celebration. But a few others were uncomfortable watching him gloat. It seemed out of place; as if something sacred had been vandalized.

"I hope my efforts as a prosecutor are appreciated. You all wanted me to take on this role. Well, I have done the best

I could." Vale nodded at Captain Sloe and sat down with his mind at ease.

"Mr. Wayne," Captain Sloe hesitated to disturb David, "if you would like a recess—"

"No, that won't be necessary. I would like to do what I came here to do." David stood and looked at Martin Vale. "You have done your job, Mr. Vale. You have represented society in its effort to condemn this man to jail. You did an even better job than I could have hoped. But if you don't mind, it's my turn to speak."

He turned and faced the jury.

Chapter Twenty-Seven

The Priest Responds

"I won't try to tell you that Robert Montane is a good man. He's not." David stood in front of the jurors and tried to collect his thoughts. Vale's attack had certainly had a debilitating effect on him. He did not try to ignore that. He tried, in fact, to harness it. He wanted to answer Vale. He wanted the entirety of his defense of Montane to be an answer to Vale and everyone who thought along the same ruthless lines. He knew he could do it. But he had to shake off the emotional jitters that Vale had given him. He stood silently, ordering his thoughts. He felt a great desire to pray. But there was no time. The jury sat waiting for him to speak.

"I want everyone here to remember something. I want you all to consider that Robert Montane was not caught and brought to justice. He is not begging for your mercy as a prisoner in the clutches of the law. Quite the opposite is true. Mr. Montane has delivered himself into your hands. He has freely given his destiny over to you. There had been no massive manhunt for him or his crew. He was not being hounded day and night. He had, in fact, developed a system by which he could quite easily keep out of the law's reach. With his submarine, he could simply vanish when he needed to. His own freedom was as secure as any criminal could ever hope it would be.

"Yet, here he is today, giving himself up and asking you, representatives of the state, to pardon him. Why? He might have just slipped away into retirement, financially free to do whatever he liked. A quiet retreat somewhere, living a life of luxury. Surely that was a more sensible choice than the road he has chosen. It would have made it all easier on each of you. No one would have had to deal with him. None of you would have this decision before you. And yet he has turned himself in to you. And you are now faced with a question.

"That question is this: what should we do with this pirate? What should we do with this confessed criminal? What's the big deal? I'm sure you've already figured out there is no deep dilemma. There is every advantage to making sure this man is locked up for a long, long time. And there seems to be no advantage in bestowing forgiveness on him and allowing him to go free. You might be wondering, is this a trick question?" David stopped and looked several of the jurors in the eye. "The fact is, this is a trick question. And if you're not careful, you'll miss it. And the decision you make now may fill you with regret for a very long time to come."

Martin Vale shifted in his chair and sighed loud enough to be heard. He screwed up his face and acted as though he might begin to snarl like a caged dog. His antics were enough to distract a couple of the women in the front row. He gave a *can you believe this guy* look that both Ida Claire and Fanny Odston could clearly read. David, aware of Vale's theatrics, tried to focus more on his thoughts and how he could express them to the jury.

"Captain," Vale's voice was heavy with exasperation, "is this closing arguments or does this young man have anyone to call to the stand?"

"Now, Mr. Vale. I don't see anything irregular in allowing Mr. Wayne to speak his mind."

"That's alright, Captain Sloe." David saw an opportunity that he did not want to pass up. "I think Mr. Vale is right. I really ought to be calling someone to the stand. I would like to call Ida Claire, if you would allow it."

"Oh, for Pete's sake," Ida sighed without delicacy, rolling her eyes. "What could I possibly be needed for?"

"I just want to ask a few questions," David explained with gentle patience.

"That seems appropriate to me," Captain Sloe said.

"Really!" Ida extricated herself from her chair and pushed herself into the witness chair. She was shaking her head in irritation and David tried not to crack a smile as she fussed. Stretching and smoothing her dress too many times, she sat ramrod straight and finally fixed her eyes on David as if he were a misbehaving child. "Why ever did you want to talk to me?"

"Well, Mrs. Claire, I must admit I have noticed you are willing to give an opinion when asked for one. And I wanted to get your opinion on a few things. Is that all right with you?"

"Oh," Ida said at his comment about her willingness to give opinions. "Yes," she'd added in answer to David's question.

"Mrs. Claire, have you ever heard of something like this request of Mr. Montane's? This petition for forgiveness?"

"Absolutely not. It's unheard of," came her rapid-fire reply.

"Do you really think so?"

"Of course."

"Do you consider yourself a Christian woman?"

Ida's eyes widened in offense, then narrowed with anger. "Just what are you suggesting? Of course I'm a Christian woman. What sort of insult are you trying to make?"

"You are a follower of the Christian faith, then? You attend a church, partake of communion, and pray the Lord 's Prayer?"

"I do my part." What that part was no one was very sure of. "You can't try to slander me, young man. I've been a believer in God for double the years that you've been born. Well, almost double, anyway."

"I knew I had guessed right with you." David smiled and stepped up to her. He was rewarded with something close to a smile from Ida, though it was not a real smile. But for Ida, it was close enough.

"And what did you guess about me?" The apparent compliment had won her over.

"What I really wanted was for one of you in the jury to recite the Lord's Prayer for us. And I wasn't very sure who of you could do that. But after thinking it over, it was quite obvious that you would be the one to ask."

Ida stole a triumphant look at Fanny Odston.

"Would you be so kind, Mrs. Claire, as to repeat it for us?"

Ida raised an eyebrow and began:

"Our Father which art in heaven,
Hallowed be Thy name.
Thy Kingdom come,
Thy will be done
On earth as it is in Heaven.
Give us this day our daily bread
And forgive us our trespasses,
As we forgive those who trespass against us."

David watched the jurors' faces as Ida recited the prayer. Despite the majority of the listeners' seeming indifference to what was being said, he noticed Alice silently mouthing the words.

"And lead us not into temptation,
but deliver us from evil,
for thine is the kingdom and the power
and the glory forever."

David could hear Alice conclude the prayer with a whispered "amen."

Ida's recitation had been free of error and hesitation. A lifetime in the Lutheran church had left her ready for such a moment. Although it had seemed impossible before, she sat up straighter than ever.

"That was wonderful, Mrs. Claire. Could I ask what the word *trespass* means to you?"

Ida could not respond immediately. She tried to understand what David was getting at.

"*Trespass* was a word you just used in the prayer," he offered patiently.

"I realize that," Ida insisted. In reality, she had never noticed that particular word and its significance had escaped her for many years. As she thought it over, an image of a trespasser did come to mind; it was an image of a hunter who was often caught on her Uncle's land. The thought left her unable to reconcile the image with the prayer.

"As an alternative," David suggested, "the prayer is often said with the word *sinned* substituted for *trespass*. That may clear it up for you."

"Captain," Vale's voice rose in an obligatory objection. "What is all of this?"

"Mr. Wayne?" Captain Sloe forwarded the question to David.

"Captain, I'm trying to establish the basic tenets of our society. The Lord's Prayer is a foundational stone for those purporting to be Christian. To be plain spoken on the matter, Mrs. Claire has said she is a Christian woman. As such, she surely must recognize that according to the *Lord's* Prayer, we regularly ask God for the ability to forgive those who have sinned against us."

Ida Claire's piercing look gave no indication of her knowledge of any such charitable requests.

"Thank you, Mrs. Claire." David held out a hand to help her stand up. She ignored him and stood without assistance.

"Mr. Odston, would you please take the chair?" David asked.

Wavel did not hold back, but neither did he jump at the opportunity to be in the chair. He settled into it and gave David a half-curious look.

"Mr. Odston, do you believe our society has the right to forgive anyone? Does it ever happen?"

"Objection, Captain." Vale waved a hand. "Odston is hardly an expert on society. He's an accountant; just a guy off the street. No offence, Odston. But you're hardly one to expound on what society can and can't do."

"I don't agree, Captain." David was ready for Vale on this one. "A guy off the street is what society is made of. If Wavel Odston is not a voice for society, then no one is. And in addition, the fact that Mr. Odston will be a voting member of the jury means he is certainly worth listening to."

"That's hard to argue against," Captain Sloe conceded. "Continue."

"I don't think society does have that right, Mr. Wayne." Wavel spoke before the question was asked a second time. "The very fact that forgiveness is never doled out to the public proves my point."

"Are you saying that if I could prove forgiveness was given out to the public, it would prove the opposite? Would that convince you that society has the right to forgive?"

"You haven't proven it yet, so I'm not convinced of anything yet. But I would be interested to see you try and prove it. As far as I'm aware, people are punished for their crimes. The system of law would break down if they weren't. It just wouldn't work any other way."

"You're speaking of our criminal justice system?"

"Of course."

"I was only speaking of society as a whole, not within the courts. Does society ever forgive? Do people sincerely forgive each other?"

"On a limited basis, yes. For certain acts, and for certain people; yes. But in a broader sense? It doesn't happen often. People hold grudges far more than they forgive."

"I would argue with you on that point," said David. "But for now, I'll just say that I disagree. But you do agree that society can and does forgive?"

Vale interrupted again. He was clearly getting angrier by the minute. "This is silly, Captain. We're wasting time on things that are so simple a child would be bored. 'The Lord's Prayer says we should forgive', 'people forgive each other'. This is hardly illuminating."

"I'm glad you think so, Mr. Vale. Are you saying you agree with what I'm trying to establish?" David asked.

"Yes, fine, whatever you like. None of this is very novel."

"My point exactly, Mr. Vale. Thank you, Mr. Odston, you can sit back down with the others." He smiled at Wavel and was surprised to get a smile in return. He returned his attention to Vale. "I think you have made a valid point, Mr. Vale.

These are basic principles that a child knows. It's why children never hold grudges for long. They may pout and cry when they've been wronged, but before long they forget about it. It's only when they grow older that they learn how to withhold forgiveness."

"Young man," Vale leaned forward in his chair and looked up at David, "you're right. And we are none of us children. You cannot expect these people to think like children."

"I'm afraid you may be right about that." David turned to the jury. "Mr. Sherman, would you mind coming to the chair?"

Mr. George Sherman took the chair completely relaxed. He was smiling, as if he had just been told an inside joke. Crossing one leg over the other, he leaned an elbow on Captain Sloe's desk.

"Do you ever make mistakes?" David asked him as soon as he was seated.

"I haven't met the man who doesn't."

"Thank you for your honesty, Mr. Sherman. I knew you would not be a man too proud to admit his own mistakes. But don't worry, I'm not going to ask you to list them."

George nodded at David in gratitude.

"Do you like the mistakes you make, Mr. Sherman? Are you proud of them?"

"I don't like to be wrong," George admitted.

"Would you say you have a favorable impression of yourself? Or is there a great dislike for yourself? You know what I mean? When you look at yourself in the mirror, do you like what you see?"

"I like what I see; enough anyway."

"And yet, you do things you don't like. You make mistakes; maybe even troubling mistakes?"

"Doesn't everyone?"

"I would think so. I certainly do." David tried not to think of Elise. He did not want to lose track of what he was trying to say. "You know, I've made painful mistakes, embarrassing mistakes, and just plain stupid mistakes. So many, in fact, that it's amazing that I don't hate myself. I would guess everyone is like that. And I wonder, how is it we all don't hate ourselves? Mr. Sherman, any ideas why?"

"I'll let you answer that, Mr. Wayne. I'm sure you already have an answer in mind."

"Yes, I think I do. It's not very brilliant. But it might just be right. As far as I can tell, I think people have just learned to forgive themselves. Oh, they struggle with regret, and carry guilt around, maybe even hate themselves for a time. But the majority of us give that up very quickly. The majority of us just drop that painful part of our memory and move on. It's a survival instinct. It's a part of us that knows that without letting go, we'll eat ourselves up with worry, or regret, or even embarrassment. And those of us who can't forgive and forget are chained to depression and some of them eventually end their own lives.

"But not you and I, Mr. Sherman. We're still here, we haven't stuck our heads in a gas oven. That tells me we're a lot alike. You've learned, just as I have, that at some point we just have to say 'forget about it'. And most importantly; that's what we do. The same holds true for those who offend us. It's easy to spot someone who holds onto every offense. They tend to be bitter, dark people. But again, most of us aren't like that. Why not? We forgive on a daily basis. We have to. Without this ability, we would all end up isolated, unable to have even the most basic of relationships."

"That's all very nice, Mr. Wayne." George Sherman shook his head. He was irritated by David's simplistic approach to the subject. "But you cannot move from your interpretation of self-forgiveness to forgiving a criminal of Montane's reputation. There is, obviously, a greater degree of culpability—"

"Why? Why does that have to be?"

"You're speaking of personal mistakes as if they compare to serious crime. There's no real comparison that can be made."

"Why not? I think that if a man steals a ballpoint pen from his employer, he is far guiltier of stealing than a man who pilfers hundreds of thousands of dollars worth of merchandise. Think of the difference in what he is tempted to do. The pen means nothing. It is worthless. But what a temptation it is to have a chance to change your entire financial outlook. A chance to change your entire life. Which is the more difficult temptation to fight? Which action can be more easily understood? Yet the man who steals the pen is overlooked by society—he's forgiven every time because no one cares about the pen. No one gives it any thought."

"That's a rather naïve viewpoint," Mr. Sherman pronounced with a condescending smile. Vale's audible snort let everyone know he agreed.

"And yours is the more realistic? To believe in degrees of offense? To believe that taking a man's life is so much more unforgivable than taking a man's wife?"

George Sherman's smile vanished in an unguarded moment.

"What of the difference between a husband's physical abuse of his wife and a wife's persistent verbal and emotional abuse of her husband?" David found himself angered by George Sherman's smugness and could not resist going on the offensive. "Does the fact that the law prohibits the former make it any more damaging—any more reprehensible—than the latter? I mean, if a man beats another man in order to force him to reveal the whereabouts of valuables," a glance at Montane, "is he any more guilty than a woman who verbally abuses her husband—a man she has vowed to love and honor—every day for thirty years?

"I'm expected to press charges on Robert Montane for forcing me at gunpoint to join him on this cruise. Kidnapped! But what about someone who holds their own family member hostage through mental and emotional manipulation for decades. Or a husband who abandons his wife to alcohol for the sake of his business?"

"You worthless dog!" Vale jumped up with a fury. "You've no right to put any of us on trial!"

"To answer your question, Mr. Wayne," George spoke loud enough to edge Martin Vale back out of the conversation, "I say yes, there is a difference in every one of your examples. There is a great difference. You might say there is an *unforgivable* difference."

George Sherman was unshakable. He continued to lounge in the chair, secure in the belief he was right. David knew he would never change this man's heart. But what of the others? Had he made an impression on any of them? He was not sure he dared find out.

Chapter Twenty-Eight

A Voice in the Whirlwind

Captain Sloe was a fine seaman. He had traveled the waves in command of a ship for over twenty years. His skills as a weatherman and a navigator were well known amongst his peers. But his skills had finally come up short. The calculations he had made to avoid the storm had been perfect. The only factor he had not counted on was a storm with a sentient ability to seek them out and run them down. For that is what the clouds were doing. They had shifted in sync with *The Jenny*. And to Melvin and Macbeth in the wheelhouse, it seemed that *sinking* them was the storm's goal. It was closing in on them like a mad bull. Melvin had seen such storms before and knew what was coming. Macbeth had never seen one of this magnitude, but he was well acquainted with death, and recognized when it was about to strike.

"You get down and tell my captain that Hell is headed this way." Melvin spit on the teakwood deck of the wheelhouse and kept a hand on the engine's throttle. He was watching the growing wave action with a practiced eye. "If fact, you'd better tell your captain as well. That monster wants to catch us, and I got an odd feeling it's going to get what it wants."

Macbeth knew the old pilot was right. He did not need to worry about leaving the man he was supposed to be watching. As soon as he opened the door and felt the cold, hard wind hit him, he knew the old pilot had no place to go. Macbeth was not even sure if he should go on deck, but he knew it had to be done. He pushed his way out the door and with the aid of the wind, slammed it shut.

The deck was beginning to pitch. Macbeth looked at the

outer bands of the storm and estimated they were still a good five miles away. But the swells had already grown. Fleeing the storm, *The Jenny* rode the crest of a wind-driven wave. The engines drove it over the crest and she dropped into the trough. It was only a drop of five feet, but that was enough angle to pull at Macbeth as he made his way to the stairs. He reached out a hand and grabbed a rail. Over the rising wind he heard the sound of something heavy hitting something solid. For all the world, it sounded like someone cried out, followed by the wail of the wind.

Macbeth looked astern and could barely make out the dark form of the *Prowler* as it rose upon the crest the *Jenny* had just topped. The sub had dropped back away from the yacht in order to keep from ramming her in the low visibility. Although it was only a few hours after noon, the sky was a heavy gray with a low veil of white enshrouding the surface of the water and the decks of the two boats. Macbeth had begun to feel a drop or two of rain mix with the sea spray already soaking his coat.

After getting the door to the stairs open, Macbeth felt a hand grab him and pull him out of the wind. The hand that pulled him in let go and another hand yanked the door closed. The hands belonged to the Old Man.

"Getting funny out there, eh?" The Old Man cursed profusely in French.

Macbeth said nothing, but went in search of Montane. He found Matvie instead.

Matvie had been standing near the aft stairs, but came forward when he heard someone on the main stairs. He looked at Macbeth with suspicion. Macbeth watched Matvie. He was unprepared to challenge the Captain's bodyguard at that moment. He took a step back, deferring to Matvie's authority.

"The pilot says we will not stay ahead of the storm."

"I will tell Montane. Go back to the wheelhouse." Matvie turned and headed to the dining room, never looking back to see Macbeth's response. If he had, he would have seen that Macbeth had turned his back as well. Both men were proving they were not afraid to turn their backs on each other. It was not a gesture made among friends. It was a signal sent to an enemy. Defiance crackled like electricity in the passageway.

Matvie's large form filled the doorway of the dining-room-turned-courtroom. David Wayne stood in front of the jury. Matvie's size was too much to ignore. David raised his head and looked questioningly at the hulking pirate.

Montane followed David's gaze and knew something was wrong as soon as he saw Matvie. Throwing off the mantle of discouragement that had covered him since David had spoken of the girl, he once again transformed himself into the leader of his crew. He jumped to his feet and met Matvie at the door.

"Captain Sloe," Montane motioned for the Captain to join him, "I think we had better call a recess."

When Montane and Captain Sloe opened the door at the top of the stairs they were greeted by a cold wind that quickly wet them down. It was not raining yet but there was plenty of sea spray and mist in the air to signal what was to come. Captain Sloe pulled up the collar of his double breasted jacket in an attempt to keep reasonably dry. Montane ignored the water running down his hair and soaking into his turtleneck sweater. He was more concerned with the wind and the approaching storm.

"How bad does it look?" Montane's experience was on submarines. His skill was in the line of cat and mouse, not solid seamanship. For him, storms of any magnitude were easily avoided by dropping under the waves.

"To be quite frank," Captain Sloe had to speak forcefully to be heard, "it looks very bad. We could be in for a lot of trouble. I should think we're committed to it. It's too wide and moving too fast for us to escape it."

Montane looked Captain Sloe in the eye and studied him. He tried to gauge the captain's attitude and appearance. Factoring what he could see of the surrounding sea and sky, he could not determine what the immediate future would bring. Montane was not the greatest sea captain; he would never have suggested he was. But he knew how to handle a crisis. He could think on his feet with great efficiency. He did not hesitate to rely on Captain Sloe since he did not have enough knowledge of the present situation to make the decision on his own.

"What chance is there that *The Jenny* will make it?" One thing Montane did know was that *The Jenny* was not designed for heavy seas and storms. She was made for cruising up and down the coast. She was meant to be run into port at the first sign of a serious storm.

"Too difficult to say." Captain Sloe said apologetically. "If I had to answer, I would say 'fifty-fifty', but that's only if I had to answer. If I had the option, I would not give an answer."

"Well, you have to answer, man!" Montane's stoic façade cracked. He had already lost two passengers on this gamble. He felt now as if the whole business would end in complete disaster. He did not care if his own life ended, but he was beginning to fear he would die with everyone's death on his head. "It's time you quit being so passive, Captain! If I have to, I could get everyone onto the *Prowler*. It wouldn't be easy; I don't even know if there's time left to do it. But if you think this boat won't survive the storm, then the risk is worth it. Now give me an answer I can use!"

They approached the wheelhouse as they spoke. Captain Sloe stepped into the leeward side of it to gain a momentary shelter from the wind and spray. He pulled Montane close to him.

"I can't give you absolutes, Montane. My instincts tell me that *The Jenny* is a well-built little darling that will make it through just fine. But who can tell? I certainly don't think the situation is dire enough to risk transporting everyone over to your sub."

The deck pitched forward as *The Jenny* crested a swell and dropped into another trough. Both men fell forward and had to catch themselves from toppling over. Over the sound of the bow cutting through the sea, and the wind blowing all about them, they heard a high wail. As if the voice of a specter raced across the deck, the cry rose above the wind and carried out to sea.

"What the devil was that?" Captain Sloe looked at Montane. Montane said nothing. "Sounds as if *The Jenny* were unsure of her own survival. That can't be a good omen."

The Jenny continued to run into the trough until the bow scraped bottom, sending a great spray of salt water over the two men on deck. The wash pushed them against the wheelhouse, draining off even as it pulled them towards the rising sea.

"Get inside," Montane yanked open the door of the wheelhouse and tugged at Captain Sloe. Before the boat began to climb the next swell, it momentarily leveled out and the two captains shut themselves in.

"Well aren't you a couple of wet hens?" Melvin scowled at the dripping wet newcomers. "Do you's two know what kinda trouble we're in? If you don't have any fancy objections, Captain Sloe, I'm gonna turn her into the wind. We can't get away from it, so we may as well face it and get it over with as soon as possible."

Montane looked at Captain Sloe, indicating he was giving *The Jenny's* Captain free reign.

"Hold off a little longer, Melvin. We need a few minutes to secure things on deck. You," Captain Sloe pointed at Macbeth, "come with me. Montane, go below and send Never up on deck. I will also need the assistance of that big fellow."

"Othello? I'll give you him as well as Matvie. They should be able to do anything you ask. Do you need me also?"

"No. Just make sure everyone else shuts themselves up in their rooms. I'm afraid they're all in for a very long night. In a short time, we'll be making a turn into the storm. What about that sub of yours? I don't want to hit it."

"I'll take care of them." Montane opened the door and turned his head to avoid the wind. "Good luck, Captain Sloe."

"You might want to get that young priest of yours to say a

prayer."

Montane made his way to the stairs. Captain Sloe led Macbeth out onto the main deck. There was a great deal of work to be done in a very short time.

As soon as Montane and Captain Sloe left the dining room, Martin Vale seized what he saw as a golden opportunity.

"I think we've all heard enough of this foolishness. I say we get this over with."

"That makes sense to me," Ida Claire announced.

"Now hold on—" David objected.

"You keep out of this." Vale stood toe to toe with David, appearing for all the world as if he were going to swing a fist at the young man. "You've had your little say. You made your three-point sermon. Now stand down and let us bring this to an end. The man goes to jail; there's no other option. You tell the captain when they come back that you're done. Tell him it's up to the jury now. And then they can tell him that they refuse his demands. Right?" He turned back to the jury for a strong affirmation.

"Oh, I'm not so sure." Wavel Odston spoke quickly. "I think we should discuss it. I don't believe for a minute that everyone agrees with you, Vale."

"Whatever are you talking about?! This is my ship! I will not allow a pirate to walk out of here scot free!"

"Oh, quit sniveling, Marty." Cora waved him away as if he were a pesky fly. "It's not gonna hurt for us to talk this out. That's our job. We are a jury."

"You—are—a—ha!" He nearly choked on his laughter. "And I thought it was only the liquor that made you stupid. I guess I'd forgotten what you were like before you became a lush. Montane didn't do us any favors keeping you sober."

"No Marty, the liquor didn't change me; all it ever did was console me."

Cora closed her eyes and dropped her head. She was losing her will to keep fighting her husband. When she did open her eyes again, she stared at the ring on her finger. Her right hand folded over her left hand and hid the diamond from view.

Vale's attack on his wife silenced the room. All eyes fell on the owner of *The Jenny*. For that moment, even Fanny Odston and Ida Claire felt empathy for someone other than themselves. George Sherman eyed Vale with hatred. He decided he would stay quiet no longer. He stood and opened his mouth to speak.

At that very moment, the wail of the specter heard by Montane and Captain Sloe rose and died above the dining room.

"What is it?" asked a pale and frightened Mrs. Kaufman.

"Some sort of wicked ghost—" Fanny Odston shuddered.

"Merely the wind, my dear heart," Wavel said reassuringly.

"Sounds like something I'm familiar with," muttered Cora Vale. "It sounds like pain. It sounds like a poor soul in great pain."

Chapter Twenty-Nine

On the Doorstep of Fate

Hamlet watched *The Jenny* from the conning tower, his beard and pea coat soaked with rain. In fact, most of him and his clothes were soaked with rain. He accepted this, and stood with his feet wide to steady himself as he kept the pleasure yacht in view with his binoculars. The boat was driving steadily at close to twelve knots, he guessed. Slower as she climbed out of the troughs, and faster, of course, as she raced down from each crest.

The *Prowler* kept up with her for now, but the turbulent wind was beginning to break more waves over their bow, slowing them. Before long, Hamlet knew he would have to watch *The Jenny* continue to skim lightly over the surface while he would have to fight to keep the sub moving at all. The *Prowler* would wallow in the rolling sea unless he allowed it to drop below the surface. He needed to speak with Montane. He reached for the intercom phone.

"Radio room—" he shouted.

"Yes, Mr. Hamlet?" The voice was hard to hear on the old handset.

"Try to raise the other boat."

"You're too late," came the abrupt reply.

Too late? Hamlet wondered at the meaning of that.

"Captain Montane has already signaled us. I was just about to respond."

Even as the voice was overpowered by wind and sea, Hamlet was sure he could detect a laugh in the radioman's voice. That was Eugene; a smart-mouthed chain smoker who could never take life seriously.

"Always a step behind him, aren't we?" Hamlet admitted

freely. "Put him through to me. Better yet, just tell him to hold on, I'll take it in the radio room." He did not like the idea of Eugene listening in on their conversation. He dropped inside the conning tower and peeled off his coat before clambering down into the sub.

"This captain here wants to turn her into the storm." Montane's voice came over the small speaker screwed to the radio room's wall. "I'm going to let him do it. I don't see any alternatives. You'd better take the *Prowler* down. Will you be able to?"

"Yes, Captain. Castle says everything is in working order. We should be able to track you on radar. I only hope we don't fall behind. You're running too strong for us right now."

"I really don't think you'll have trouble keeping up once we turn nose into this thing." Montane hesitated before continuing. "Hamlet, is everything—secure over there?"

"Just a minute," Hamlet answered. He flipped a switch that routed the receiver to a set of earphones and held one of them to his left ear. "If you mean *him*, don't worry. I've enlisted an ally with Castle and his department. They are watching him." Static cut them off for a moment. Hamlet had dismissed Eugene in order to speak in private. He held the earphone with a tighter grip while he toggled a switch in an effort to regain the connection. "Did you get that?"

"Don't be over—"a hiss and pop, "—end up with your throat cut."

"You worry about staying afloat." Hamlet was not sure Montane had heard that last suggestion. He could not recover the connection and decided there was no need to keep trying.

He jammed a switch above his head and the lights in the sub turned from yellow to red. Taking a short walk from the radio room, he stepped into the control room and raised his chin, looking over the crew with cool eyes. His gaze came to a stop when he saw Lear. Without making eye contact, he nodded at the lunatic.

"We're going to take her down. Helmsman, dive planes at

fifteen degrees. Let's get in out of the weather."

"Are those the captain's orders?" asked Lear. The crew hesitated. Castle poked his head in from the battery room and waited for Hamlet to respond.

"They are my orders, Mr. Lear."

The crew began to move as soon as he spoke. Lear had only tested the waters. He had no support and he knew it.

Castle raised his brows at Hamlet then backed out of the control room.

The *Prowler* slid under the growing waves. Water closed over her and hungrily swallowed the iron coffin.

"Where's the captain?" Vale demanded of Montane as soon as he appeared in the dining room.

"He's topside. Never, he wants you to join him. Othello, you go as well. And do whatever he asks." Once the black pirate and the nervous steward exited the room, Montane faced the others. They were staring back at him suspiciously. "What seems to be the problem?"

"We want to see the captain. Or has he disappeared as well?" The others were content to let Vale speak for them.

"No, he has not disappeared. He is at this moment laboring to prepare *The Jenny* for a heavy storm that will quickly be upon us. He asked that I make sure you all go to your staterooms and stay there."

"That's nonsense!" Vale shook his fist, like a child defying its nanny. "I won't go! We'll stay right here!"

"Whatever you say, Vale. I don't care either way. I think his intent was that you ride out the storm in a room where you can't roll around so much. But I don't care. Enjoy yourself. But I would really suggest you stay below deck."

There was no need for Montane to stress the importance of that. The room was beginning to pitch with a greater degree. As he spoke, the dining room dipped down towards the galley door. Ida Claire fell forward and grabbed at Martin Vale for support. Everyone else did something similar. Fanny Odston actually fell down, though she fortuitously fell backward into a chair. Wavel reached out to catch her a little late.

"Maybe it would be best, Mr. Vale, if we all went to our rooms." David Wayne helped Mrs. Kaufman remain upright as he spoke.

"I told you to stay out of this," Vale sneered.

"If we're going to stay here, why don't we talk this trial over and make our decision?" George Sherman's ashen smile indicated a tinge of seasickness.

"I think that's a good idea. We'll do it while we wait for the captain." Wavel reached out a hand to assist Fanny but she smacked it away.

"I really must insist that *he*—" Ida pointed a long thin finger at Montane, "—leave the room. In fact, his little priest ought to leave as well."

"That's sensible," Fanny Odston readily agreed.

"Then I say Marty ought to go too," Cora threw in.

"That would be appropriate," George said, cutting off Vale's protest. "Just the jury can deliberate."

Montane and David headed for the door. Vale stalked out behind them, fuming. The three men walked into the day room. Vale considered heading to his own room but could not bring himself to be alone. He sat off in one corner in a straight-backed chair. Montane and David sat down on the couch.

It was an uncomfortable trio. Montane sat forward, hands at his knees, wanting to get up and find out what was happening on deck. David leaned back on the arm of the couch and cradled his head in one hand. His eyes were closed and he was thinking of all that he had said during the trial. There was so much more he had wanted to say. Had he said enough? Had he used the right words? He rubbed his temples and wished he could think of something else.

Vale was angry, but the more he thought about why he was angry, the less angry he became. What, after all, was he upset about? The sham trial had been interrupted, and he saw nothing to suggest that Montane would get what he wanted. The interruption would most likely end up being a great advantage for him. The thought warmed his heart. He thrilled at the thought of beating Montane. Yes, he anticipated great satisfaction there.

On deck, Captain Sloe had given orders efficiently, and Never, Othello, Macbeth, and Matvie were quick to follow them. Rain had begun to fall.

Macbeth was closing the port side hatches. He secured them just as Captain Sloe had specified. He was wet from head to toe, though this meant nothing to him. He kept his attention on Matvie. The big man was securing extra cables to the smoke stack. Macbeth watched him from the corner of his eye.

The man really was an ape, Macbeth thought. But like an ape, he was stupid and heavy-handed. Macbeth still firmly believed what he had told his brother. He could kill Matvie. He would kill Matvie.

Never was struggling with lounge chairs. He had one under each arm. Stumbling down the steps, he dropped them, picked them back up, staggered down the hall to the day room, and burst through its door. He dropped one of the chairs again upon seeing Montane, David Wayne, and his employer Mr. Vale.

"Excuse me, Mr. Vale. I was told to bring these down here." A second chair clattered to the floor.

"Aren't there any empty staterooms?" Vale whined. "Get those things out of here. We can't fill this room up with deck chairs. Can't you see we're in here?"

"Yes, certainly. I never—I mean—I didn't mean to interrupt. Take them away. To the empty rooms." Never stopped stammering as a thought overtook him. He cocked his head to one side and asked "would Mr. Alum's room be considered empty now?"

"Never!" Vale pointed to the door. "Out!"

"Yes, exactly, sir. Just like you said. Empty." At some point as he continued to agree with his employer, Never left the room.

The three continued to sit in silence. The steward's awkward appearance had given them all a common thread to ponder. But no one spoke. Vale poured his frustrations into a few harsh and vile names for the hapless Never. Montane thought back to his brief conversation with the nervous kid. Did Never really fear and despise him as much as he let on? All things considered, Never seemed to be just as afraid of Vale. Montane decided the boy must have emotional problems that went beyond a fear of pirates. David Wayne was the only one of the three men who genuinely liked Never Gamble. He could see the young boy (only a few years younger than himself!) was always trying his hardest to do the right thing. David found him refreshing.

A half hour had nearly passed when the door to the day room opened again. Captain Sloe stuck his head in and looked around.

"Oh yes, you are here. They told me you might be here. I just thought you should know that we've done all we could. I'm going to go up now and turn her into the storm. I'll be staying in the wheelhouse with Melvin. I hope you said that prayer, David."

Montane had not spoken to David directly since hearing about Elise. The news about the girl could not be ignored. Montane felt as if the laws of physics had been suspended, and that no matter the actual distance separating them, light bent at multiple angles to create vast stretches of immeasurable space between them. David could feel it too. If he tried to look at Montane, he felt, rather than saw, as if the pirate were at the far end of a spyglass held backwards.

"I was supposed to ask you to pray."

David heard the voice from the other end of the spyglass, filtered across the great expanse. He nodded in understanding, though did not really believe Montane could see the gesture from so far away. David wished he could tell Montane that he did not blame him for Elise's death. As improbable as it seemed, he really did forgive him. He wanted Montane to know he had only concealed the story to protect him. But how could Montane hear him? Would the words travel so far?

For Montane, he was glad of the distance, if only because he did not have to look David in the eye. He distinctly felt the burden of guilt. There could be no question about that. More importantly, it had highlighted the absurdity of Montane's quest for forgiveness. He felt like a child chasing after Santa Clause. Everyone else knew he was chasing a fantasy. And he was now only finding out for himself. Montane was now certain that even David knew it was a chimera. His assertions to the contrary must have been only to mollify his captor. That thought in particular was painful.

The rise and fall of *The Jenny* had become rhythmic; her movements predictable. But mere minutes after Captain Sloe announced his intentions, the men in the day room could feel her begin to heel over to the port side. It was a slow but recognizable shift. The rising swells attempted to overpower her as she precariously exposed her broadside to them. With dignified effort, *The Jenny* fought to keep upright as she turned to face the tempest.

Chapter Thirty

In the Balance

Three men and five women sat together around several tables that had been merged into one. There was no one else in the room. They were waiting for Never Gamble.

"I don't see why we need to wait for that little nitwit." That was Fanny, still waging her private war against the steward.

"There's no reason to hurry, love." That was Wavel, countering her every word. "What with this storm, no one's going anywhere soon. Let's wait for the little nitwit."

"You're not in charge, Wavel," Fanny pouted.

"Who is in charge?" asked Mrs. Kaufman.

The question silenced the room. Glances were thrown across the table. Great effort was made to avoid eye contact. Almost none of the jurors wanted to be put in charge. They were afraid eye contact might be misconstrued as a volunteering gesture. The few who wanted to be in charge wanted to appear reluctant. This left everybody looking at nobody.

The room pitched hard to port as Captain Sloe began his turn into the storm. No one mentioned it, merely grabbing at the tables for stability and waiting for *The Jenny* to right herself. The sound of the wind grew louder. All did their best to ignore it.

"Oh, criminy," Cora gave in and spoke her mind, "somebody ought to be in charge. I say put George in charge."

As she spoke, the door opened and Never Gamble stepped into the room.

"Hurrah," Fanny rolled her eyes, "the village idiot's arrived."

"Sit down, young man." Ida spoke with all the warmth of

a stepmother. "We were just about to appoint Mr. Sherman as our foreman."

"What about Mr. Odston?" Never froze before taking the indicated chair. "He really ought to be the foreman."

"Why is that, Never?" Wavel was as curious as everyone else as to why he should be the foreman.

Never could not bring himself to tell everyone about George's exit from Vale's stateroom. He very nearly said as much, but an intense look from the gentleman from Georgia sealed Never's lips.

"That's perfectly alright with me," George graciously acquiesced. Cora flashed him a look of admiration.

"Congratulations, Wavel," Fanny sighed. "So you really are in charge. What a major accomplishment."

"I can't say what your kind words mean to me, honey. No really, I can't."

"Oh, stop it, you two." Ida was sick of their verbal games. "Can we please get on with this? Mr. Odston, if you're going to be in charge, then do something."

"Well, frankly, Ida, there's nothing to do. We will simply tell the man he's forgiven and he'll leave, right? There's no point in doing anything else."

The jury stared in shocked silence. Wavel had said what no one else had dared. But once he had said it, no one could argue with him. It made more sense than anything they had been thinking.

The boat shuddered, as if it had run aground. Still, the jurors tried not to acknowledge the alarming storm.

"Did he say we are going to forgive him?" asked Mrs. Kaufman.

"Of course we aren't," Ida shushed her sister. "Not really."

"But why not?" asked Alice.

"What are you talking about?" Never said, alarmed. "Are you serious?"

"I just mean that despite the fact that we're going to let him go because we think we have to, on a different level, why couldn't we really forgive him?"

"He's as guilty as sin," Fanny blurted out, as if that were the only explanation needed.

"We know that," Alice pointed out, "he's already admitted to that. But isn't that the point of forgiveness? You have to be guilty of something before you can be forgiven."

"He's murdered Tom, Alice." Never converted the assumption to fact. "Poor Tom's dead because of him. You wouldn't really let him get away with it."

"We don't know Tom's dead," Alice nearly whispered.

"But if we know for sure, would you still forgive Montane?" asked George.

"Maybe she could," Wavel could see the conflict on the girl's face and tried to come to her rescue. "She wants to, anyway."

"While this is all rather academic, I must say that Montane's forgiveness would be a hard sell. He would have to prove he'd never pirate again," George said. "And that can't be proved. He hasn't even tried to convince us of that."

"Now you want to control him," Alice rarely had the courage to argue with anyone. She almost never had the courage to speak with anyone. Yet she felt a growing desire to see Montane forgiven. "You want conditions on your forgiveness. You want a guarantee."

"Something we'll never get," Fanny added, "so let's just lock him up."

"That's what he deserves," Ida pitched in.

"But don't you see? Mr. Wayne said this was a trick question. If we can't forgive him, without reservation, God can't forgive us. It's right there in that Bible."

They all looked at the little blue book that sat in the middle of the table. Suspicion clouded the faces of Ida, Fanny, and George. It was as if they had only now noticed the book Alice had given to Captain Sloe.

"Would you dare to suggest that I need to be forgiven?" Ida Claire turned and stared at Alice indignantly. "You don't know me well enough for that kind of talk."

"Oh, but she must," Fanny said mockingly. "She even knows who God won't forgive. That's very smart of her, don't you think? Do you think you could find out for us when this storm will be over?"

It was the first time someone had spoken of the storm. By then, it was impossible to ignore. *The Jenny* was no longer able to sail without first tilting her decks up, then down, then back up again. Added to the uneven movement was the trembling of the bow each time it rammed the cresting swells.

"You might rather ask the big guy if we're going to live through this," George corrected.

"It's hardly the time to be irreverent," Cora scolded them both. "If I have to go through this sober, I'd rather not listen to you two making jokes about God. Haven't you got any sense?"

They were all having trouble keeping their seats.

"Don't give Montane another thought," George instructed Alice. "You're worrying over nothing. He could never find forgiveness here. Not really. People don't do that sort of thing. At least not in polite society."

"But why not?" Alice persisted. "If you're going to let him go anyway, what harm would it do to forgive him? Would it be so bad?"

"And what good would it do him if we did?" George smiled condescendingly. "The man's guilty, right? So he'll have that on his conscience whether we forgive him or not. These semantics are really unnecessary."

"And a great waste of time!" added Ida. "Now let's stop all this rubbish about forgiving the man. And no more talk about us needing forgiveness, either, young lady. I don't need forgiveness; by God I'm sure of that!"

The Jenny seemed to drop into a hole. The deck fell away, and half of everyone at the table fell out of their chairs. Ida was the first to fall on her face. Those left in their seats only remained for a second or two before they too appeared to throw themselves to the floor. As a group, they all rolled forward, moving together like a poorly choreographed dance troupe.

"Sorry, Mrs. Odston," winced Never. "What's that stupid captain doing?" shouted Ida. "A bit like the days of our youth, don't you think, Wavel?" George chuckled with innuendo amidst the pile of arms and legs. "Wavel never had younger days like this," Fanny snapped. "No," Wavel intoned thoughtfully, "not since I met you, love." "I see what he means," Bob the cook laughed. "What's he mean?" asked Never.

This tangle of conversation went on until all legs, arms, and torsos had been returned to their rightful owners.

"Well, after all of that, I'm going to my bed," Cora announced.

"I think I'll do the same," George reached for a chair and pulled himself up.

Bob laughed again.

"Help me stand up, Wavel. We're gonna need seatbelts in bed tonight." Fanny had barely said the words when Bob started laughing even harder. She stared him down. "Cretin."

The room slowly emptied as each of the jurors tried to remain upright and move in their intended direction. Once in the hallway, they groped their way to their doors and fell into their staterooms in silence. The storm was beginning to overpower their thoughts. As each of them lay down in their berths, they lay listening to the screaming of the wind, the battering of the waves, and the whining of *The Jenny's* frame. There was no denying it would be a long night.

And once more, before anyone had drifted into their fitful sleep, a cry arose from the soul of the storm. It would be a long night indeed.

Chapter Thirty-One

Victims of the Departing Storm

The storm raged, though it had passed to the south. The seas were still disturbed, rising and falling with a froth that told of the long violent night. The gray dawn was bright against the dark waters. A stiff wind ran as if it were trying to catch up to the departed storm but lacked the desire and energy to do so.

The deck of *The Jenny* was clear. Its teakwood was soaked with saltwater, and only a fine mist coated the deck in a lack-luster effort to wash the brine away. A broken cable hung from the smokestack, sliding along the black metal in concert with the wind. The steel cable rang as it dragged along and popped when it snapped down hard.

Matvie stood on the rolling deck with his legs apart. He was watching the loose cable as a child might watch a passing car. He showed no curiosity; no interest. The cable twisted and swayed, and Matvie's eyes simply followed its movements. He might have stood in that manner for a long time had it not been for the voices. He could hear someone talking on the other side of the smoke stack.

"You heard it here?"

"Yes, I heard a voice cry out right here on deck, during the storm." Matvie recognized Othello's voice. The first voice sounded like Macbeth's.

"It must have come from here. Look, there is a door."

He heard a steel door grind open and a voice cry out.

"So here you are," Othello said with some surprise.

Matvie moved quietly around to the port side of the boat. He turned the corner just enough to see Macbeth and Othello standing on either side of the young man called Tom.

"They have been blaming my brother for this one's death. I'm sure it's why he was sent back to the sub. I thought you had killed him."

"No," Othello shook his head. "I only tried to catch him at your brother's command. I never did find him. It's good I heard him in the storm. Should I take him to Montane?"

"I don't think so." Macbeth gazed at Tom with empty eyes. "This one has caused us trouble. I think my brother would want me to take care of him."

Tom had listened to their exchange with a stoic face. His resolve crumbled as he understood Macbeth's intentions.

"I haven't caused trouble!" Tom argued. "I won't cause trouble. Let me go back to the others."

Othello drew back from Macbeth and the porter. "If you want to kill, that's your choice. I won't kill another one of them."

Tom caught the meaning of Othello's words and eyed him with dread. He turned his attention then to Macbeth.

"I can't think of any reason not to." Macbeth said simply.

"I can," Matvie said as he stepped into view.

Othello saw the square bulk of Matvie and knew they had made a grievous error in forgetting to watch for him. At the same time, he could see that Macbeth welcomed the interruption.

As if electrified by Matvie's word, Macbeth let go of Tom, giving the boy no more thought. The presence of another predator was too overpowering. He had wanted his chance, and he knew it had finally come. Circling away from Tom, he faced Matvie.

Matvie, too, was keenly aware that their sparring had come to an end, and their collision was no longer avoidable. He could not allow Macbeth to kill the boy. Montane had forbidden it. And Matvie had already allowed one of them to die. He had promised himself it would not happen again. He stood like a rock, no outward sign of the impending clash. He was not eager to fight. He did not desire to kill Macbeth. But he was resigned to the knowledge that he would never stop him unless he killed him.

Tom stepped slowly away from them, and then hastily ran for the stern. He was too concerned with his own survival to notice Othello had disappeared as well.

"I'm not afraid of you," Macbeth told Matvie.

"Good," said Matvie. "Then come here."

Macbeth was only too eager to comply.

The scene unfolded before the eyes of the man standing on the tower of the *Prowler.* Holding a pair of binoculars, he watched the two men collide with a jolt that rocked *The Jenny.* Riveted by the scene, he watched each and every move. The massive form of Matvie fused to the rock hard lethal frame of Macbeth. The spectator pressed the glasses more tightly to his face and whispered aloud.

"Come on, brother. Kill that gorilla." A trickle of sweat rolled down Lear's neck despite the cold morning wind. He feared for his brother, something he had never done before. He took a few quick breaths, lowered the binoculars, and grasped a radio mike.

"Control room, go ahead to two-thirds power, and make your bearing ten more degrees to starboard." Dropping the mike, Lear pulled the glasses back up and refocused on the fight.

It was not a fast and free swinging combat. The two men had locked themselves in a struggle that could only end when one of them lost his will to win. Lear cursed the engine room and waited impatiently for the sub to pick up speed. He was not sure his brother needed help, but he wanted to be close enough to lend a hand if it became necessary.

But he would never get that chance. His brightly lit eyes watched in fascinated horror as Matvie deliberately dragged Macbeth to the rail of *The Jenny* and pitched both himself and Macbeth over the rail and into the sea. Lear's heart burst with fury as he watched the black bulk of the two gladiators roll two separate times in the undulating sea before sinking out of sight.

For Matvie, once he had discovered he could not overpower Macbeth, it had been a logical decision. He had seen no alternative but to take his opponent to the bottom of the ocean.

Lear stood on the conning tower bridge with silent rage. He knew his brother would never rise from that ocean grave. And his brother would never stand by his side as Lear became captain of the *Prowler.* Lear watched the small shape of *The Jenny* grow closer and closer. Macbeth would be avenged. Lear shook with rage. There was no holding back any longer.

Hamlet lay in his bunk. He was on his side, his back to the wall of the submarine. Although his time asleep had been free of storm related noise and motion, he had been aware of it all the same. It had stayed in the back of his mind; always somewhere on the edge of his dreams. He was awake now. He lay with his eyes closed, thinking over the day to come. His first concern was *The Jenny* and her position. He would like to surface as soon as the weather permitted.

He vaguely recalled there was another item that demanded his attention. His eyes popped open at the answer—Lear. He could remember clearly that Lear had been in his dreams as well. Only he had not been on the edge of the dream like the storm. Lear had been the focus of his disturbed sleep.

Hamlet was too sensible to believe in portents and visions. But he was sensible enough to recognize that trouble was on the horizon. He sat up and felt dizzy, deciding he needed to eat. But as he stood up, it occurred to him that he wasn't dizzy. He was not suffering from lack of food. He could distinctly feel the *Prowler* roll as if it were on the surface. As impossible as it seemed to Hamlet, he knew he was not imagining the motion of the sub. The sub had surfaced.

He pulled his way through the narrow passage and stepped over the bulkhead which separated the control room from the forward quarters. A few crewmen were sitting quietly at their stations.

"We've surfaced, haven't we?" Hamlet demanded a response.

"Yes, sir." A tired sailor by the name of Reynolds answered promptly. "As you ordered, Mr. Hamlet."

"I ordered?" Hamlet leaned into Reynolds and expected to smell alcohol. "What are you talking about?"

"Mr. Lear gave us your orders a short time ago."

A coldness ran through Hamlet. He asked where Lear was located but could nearly have given the answer himself.

"He went up on the tower sir, to scout the weather. In fact, he just called down for a position change and speed adjustment, maybe five or ten minutes ago."

"Go get Castle, and tell him to meet me on the tower." Hamlet mashed a hat onto his head and reached out for the ladder. He feared he would be too late.

Once he raised the hatch, Hamlet pushed his head up and scanned the deck outside the conning tower. He did not see Lear. With a great effort, he hauled himself out of the hatchway and stood up. As expected, the sub was running alongside *The Jenny*. At that same moment, Hamlet sucked in a hoarse breath of air as a crippling pain charged through his back.

Lear had been standing behind the hatch. His knife thrust dug through Hamlet's back and into his lungs. Lear's eyes blazed brighter than ever.

Stumbling forward, Hamlet braced himself on the railing of the tower and moaned in defeat. He had been too careless. He had failed Montane. It was over. But he refused to go down without a fight. Even as strength ebbed from his body, Hamlet launched himself backwards and rammed Lear against the tower. He drove himself back with his legs, pinning Lear upright.

Below them, through the open hatch, Castle's face came into view. His red beard and large eyes stared up at the two men locked in their deadly struggle.

"Hamlet!" Castle called to him.

"Lock it down!" Hamlet hissed through his clenched teeth. "And dive! Dive, d'ya hear?" He released his pressure against Lear with one leg and kicked the hatch, slamming it shut.

Lear took advantage of the shift in weight and knocked

Hamlet to the deck. Hamlet spun as he fell and kicked Lear's legs out from under him. The two men sprawled together. Castle locked down the hatch, its wheel spinning and catching the sleeve of Lear's rain poncho. His arm twisted with the motion, and Hamlet grabbed his other arm, holding him down. Lear struggled but could not free himself.

"Don't worry, Lear," Hamlet hissed in his ear, "you wanted to see me die. If you can hold your breath long enough, you'll get to see it."

"I wouldn't bet the farm on it," said Lear. He had felt it. It had only been slight, but he had felt it. He knew Hamlet felt it as well. Hamlet's hold had weakened; the blood that ran from his back was stealing more and more of his energy.

Castle had not hesitated. As the *Prowler* began to sink below the surface, the cold foamy sea poured over the lip of the tower and filled the deck. Hamlet took a deep and explosively painful breath and tried desperately to clutch Lear ever tighter. He only wanted to save his Captain. His final thought was that he had failed.

Chapter Thirty-Two

Delivering the Verdict and Other Sporting Events

The assembly in the dining room was an ugly sight. Everyone had slept in their clothes. The storm had insured that their sleep had been brief and punctuated by many bouts of seasickness. All of the ladies looked the worse for wear. They had not had the chance to remove their previous day's makeup and had not applied a fresh coat either. Most everyone was unintentionally sporting a new and ridiculous hairstyle.

Despite this dishevelment, Ida Claire managed to hold herself with dignity. She sat ramrod straight in her chair and glanced haughtily at Cora and Fanny, both of whom she decided had failed to salvage any dignity from the storm.

"I don't see what the hurry is," Ida complained. "You ought to give us a few minutes to clean ourselves up. I'm sure a few of us need to, more than the rest of us."

"What you look like is neither here nor there," Montane sighed. "I just want this over with."

"At least let us finish eating," Fanny said peevishly.

"By all means," Montane waved a hand in mock courtesy. He knew that wouldn't take long. And there would be no niggling demand to wash the dishes afterwards. They were all eating apples and pieces of bread. There was not much more Bob had been able to make during the dying stages of the storm. "Old Man," Montane signaled for the Frenchman, "go and bring Matvie to me. I want to speak with him."

Maurice nodded and slipped from the room.

He met Kit in the passage and told him to follow. The pirates climbed the stairs and walked out on deck.

They made their way to the wheelhouse, expecting to see Matvie at any moment. When they did not see him, they entered the wheelhouse and were surprised to find Melvin all alone.

"Where is everyone, huh?" Maurice asked.

"I'd be sunk if I knew." Melvin was sitting in a chair with his feet propped on a bench. "As long as that storm keeps headin' the way it is, I don't really care where anyone is."

Maurice bowed his head in thanks and backed out of the wheelhouse. Scratching his head, he made his way towards the stern.

"What's that?" asked Kit.

"What are you pointing at? I don't see anything."

"There, on the deck, at the back of the boat."

They hurried aft and approached what appeared to be a bundle of wet clothes lying in a heap. The deck was wet from the stern rail to where the bundle lay in a puddle.

"Someone has climbed aboard." The Old Man knelt slowly, placed a hand on the man's shoulder, and gently shook it. "Hey, hey. What is the matter with you? Are you drowned?"

The body shook slightly, then twisted around with startling speed. The Old Man stared into a set of brightly shining eyes.

"*Mon Dieu*," Maurice said, his voice cracking. "Lear."

"*Bon jour*, Old Man." Lear pushed the Old Man away and rose unsteadily to his feet. His breathing was labored. He bent over and, after taking in a few deep draughts of fresh air, he vomited salt water.

Maurice backed away from Lear's violent spasms and made signs for Kit to do the same. As Lear fought to regain control of his stomach and lungs, the Frenchman silently sent Kit back downstairs. Straightening his back and standing as solidly as he could, Maurice casually ran his hand over the handle of the knife stuck in his belt.

Lear did not see him do it, but he did not have to.

"For a man who's lived this long, I don't see why you want to make a mistake like that." Lear was breathing more regularly. He too stood straight then, giving the Old Man a funny look. "You can relax. You act like something's wrong."

"There is blood on you." Maurice said matter-of-factly. He made a slight gesture to indicate the front of Lear's sweater.

"That doesn't concern you, Old Man."

"My name is Maurice," he said.

"Who cares?" Lear asked. The light in his eyes was fading. He felt as if his brother were standing there with him.

Maurice could sense the change in Lear. He almost began to believe he was talking to Macbeth instead of Lear.

"Stay out of this, do you understand?" Lear pushed the Old Man away and pulled out a gun that had been tucked into his belt.

Maurice watched Lear check the action on it to ensure it had not been damaged by the salt water. He knew he was incapable of stopping Lear. The truth pressed down on his soul with the bitter weight of failure. He knew without a doubt that he would not interfere. He knew he would not raise a hand to help the captain. He knew he was afraid.

"You just stay put, huh?" Lear tapped the Old Man's gut with the flat of the barrel.

Maurice watched Lear walk away and cursed his own fear and desire to live. It was Montane who would suffer, a fact which angered Maurice, though he stood rooted to the deck.

Several moments passed before he became aware of someone beside him. He turned to see Othello.

"You look troubled, Old Man."

"I am troubled, friend. Lear has just boarded the boat. I believe he has Hamlet's gun. I don't like to think how that could be. I should have taken him with my knife. I should have resisted him."

"He cannot be stopped." Othello put a hand on the Frenchman's shoulder. "You have done right. You are alive. We will stay that way. Alive."

"I don't like this kind of living," Maurice shook his head.

"Stay here, and live a little longer." Othello followed after

Lear.

Maurice stood brooding at the stern rail. He knew why he was unhappy. He was amazed as he considered what was really bothering him. He could not help thinking of that saucy Ida Claire. She would never have let Lear walk all over her the way that he had. Not without a fight. Maurice shook his head. No, she would never have accepted a life like this. His shame gave way to admiration and a smile creased his wrinkled face.

There was no more pomp and procedure. The tables were not neatly laid out as they had been the day before. Everyone was clustered around the room as if *The Jenny* had tossed them in every direction only moments before. They had, however, all managed to grab chairs and set them upright so that no one was standing.

"If you have no objections," Captain Sloe addressed Montane, "I was told the jury has already made their decision."

"David?" Montane looked at David for an answer.

"I don't see any reason to go on. There's not much more to be said if they've already made up their minds."

Montane nodded at Captain Sloe, who turned to Wavel Odston. "Well?" he asked.

"We have made a decision. Did you need it written down?"

"No," Captain Sloe answered hesitantly, "I wouldn't think so."

"In that case—" Wavel never finished his announcement.

"Just a moment," George Sherman stood up and held out a hand to stay Wavel. "I wonder if you might let me say a few words."

Captain Sloe made no objection, and all eyes turned towards George. The society gentleman was the only one of them who had donned fresh clothes. He wore a black sport jacket over a pale blue dress shirt. Casual khaki pants were accompanied by a pair of brown leather shoes.

"Mr. Odston was about to announce what we all agreed to last night. But I wanted you to know, Mr. Wayne, that our decision was everything I told you it would be. Do you remember?" George stood close to David and smiled. "There was a gun pointed at our heads, right? I told you the verdict would be 'forgiven' and 'good riddance.' Well, that was nearly the case last night."

"What's he doing?" Never panicked.

"Shut up, boy." George barked at the steward. "You see, there was one important piece of evidence left out. I would like to bring you all up to date on that now. To do so, I will need to tell you all a little story."

George unbuttoned his sport coat and reached into his jacket for a handkerchief. He carefully wiped at his forehead and then replaced the handkerchief in the jacket's left breast pocket.

"You were a little trivial in your confession regarding your former captain, Montane. I wish you hadn't been. You told us you were courageous enough to take this man on, but you were cowardly enough to force him overboard instead of killing him with your own hands. Did you think it mattered? Did you think it would be a gesture of humanity?

"The piece of evidence that has been left out is your true motive." George stood in front of Montane and grinned. "Black's behavior had nothing to do with your mutiny. You had every intention of taking command of that crew, long before that night. You always plan ahead. Just look at this little get-together here. You had been planning this too. You acted surprised to see Martin Vale, but you knew exactly who you were boarding. And the night you killed Black, you had planned it out as well."

"Now hold on," Never pushed his way into George's speech. "What do you know about this?"

"Only what my Uncle told me," George reached into his breast pocket again.

"Who's your Uncle?" asked Captain Sloe, trying to follow the new turn of events.

"My uncle was Captain Black." Instead of withdrawing his handkerchief, George held in his hand a chrome-finished revolver.

"Is that a gun?" asked Mrs. Kaufman.

"Yes, it is." George pointed the barrel at Montane. Montane did not respond, but sat in his chair as calmly as if George were only pointing a cigar in his direction. "My uncle was sure you would eventually make a move to kill him. He was also sure he would not be able to stop you. He had a high regard for you, Montane. It was why he sent me letters, informing me, educating me so that when the time came, you would not go unpunished."

"And you just happened to be on this boat?" Never could not keep his curiosity in check.

"I was more or less invited," George and Martin Vale exchanged a brief glance.

"And what now?" Montane finally spoke. His manner was soft; it was evident he was willing to accept his fate. "Prison? A bullet in the head?"

"Haven't you a shred of imagination?" George asked in disgust. "You're going overboard."

"You expect him to jump overboard instead of being shot? That hardly makes sense." Wavel tried to see the logic in George's plan.

"That's not justice, George." David urged George to reconsider.

"Not for an idealist, I agree."

"But a practical and pragmatic solution for the fatalist?"

"Surely you understand," George nodded at David. "But stay seated, Mr. Wayne. I would shoot you if I had to. Don't get any idealistic and romantic ideas in your head."

"Don't do it, George." David appealed to him. Montane touched him on the shoulder and shook his head.

"Thanks for everything, David. Don't worry. Maybe it is justice."

"Well," Ida Claire stood suddenly, clutching her large purse in both hands, "you can call it what you want, but I for one don't like it."

Ida stepped boldly across the room towards George. He turned, swinging the gun in her direction.

"Ida, you stupid old bat! Don't come a step nearer."

"I'm not afraid of you, George." Ida ignored the gun, raised the purse in her hand, and swung it with surprising speed, the purse's decorative sea shells cutting into George's face. Her attack was so direct, George failed to duck. His head snapped to one side and he stumbled in the same direction.

Wavel was the first to react. Leaping from his chair, he wrapped his hand around George's wrist and tried to shake the gun free. Ida swung the purse again, hitting George in nearly the same part of his jaw. George was dazed, but holding his own. He held fast to the gun and pushed at Wavel, knocking him off balance. Captain Sloe stepped into the struggle and pulled Ida away, fearing she might be shot. As Wavel began to fall, Fanny jumped up and rushed to help him.

"Wavel!" she screamed, "are you trying to get killed?"

"No, my love, I'm trying not to get killed," Wavel managed to say, his hand still clamped onto George's wrist like a vice.

"George!" Cora called out, "don't shoot him!"

George was trying to turn the gun on Wavel; Wavel was trying to stop him. George was winning the battle. The barrel of the gun slowly turned.

"Captain," Ida smacked at Captain Sloe, "leave me alone."

"I don't want you getting hit, Mrs. Claire."

"No one's going to get hit, Captain," Ida said with conviction.

George had said nothing since Ida hit him. He stood his ground, fighting to keep control of the revolver. He had very nearly lined the barrel up on Wavel when Fanny fell upon him and bit his hand. With a grunt, he jerked his hand back and let the revolver fly. It shot across the room and landed near the galley door.

George used his free hand to grab Fanny's hair, yanking her hard enough to make her release her teeth from his hand. She yelled in pain and stumbled back over a chair. Wavel let go of George's wrist and stepped back.

"That's my wife you're hurting," he said, cocking his arm

back to make a fist.

"I thought you'd thank me for the favor," George sneered.

Wavel punched George square on the sneer. George grabbed at Wavel as he fell backwards to the floor. He grabbed enough of Wavel's suit coat to pull him down with him. Wavel landed on top of George, who tried to roll out from under him. As George tried to scramble to his feet, he clawed at the lining of Wavel's jacket. A great ripping sound was heard and George broke free of his opponent. Several bright objects landed on the floor between them.

"It's them!" shouted Never, scooping them up and holding them out for all to see.

Fanny, only then getting back on her feet, looked up at Never's exclamation. She saw him holding her jewels.

"I knew it!" she howled. "You foul little thief! I was right!" She assaulted the steward with a fury. Never fell under her attack.

"Mrs. Odston!" Captain Sloe tried valiantly to save his steward, "he's not the thief. The jewels fell out of your husband's jacket."

Fanny, her hands around Never's throat, wore the face of an Amazon warrior. She continued to squeeze as she turned to look at the Captain. The face turned from hot fury to cold fury.

"What did you say?"

"He said," Never's constricted voice came out as a raspy whisper, "your husband stole them."

"Please, Mrs. Odston," Captain Sloe reached out and gently pried her fingers from Never's gullet, "the boy is innocent."

"I swear, Wavel," Fanny climbed off of Never and limped on one high heel towards her husband, "insurance money, huh? That was your stupid plan?"

"It was a very sound plan, dear heart." His clarification, capped with the usual endearment, was cut short as Fanny wrapped her hands around yet another throat.

George took advantage of the drama to look for the gun.

He had seen it land near the galley door, but it was no longer there. He dabbed at his bleeding face with his handkerchief; the shells had cut him in multiple locations. The missing gun bothered him more than the cuts.

"Did you get my gun back?" Martin Vale approached him and asked discreetly. "I recognized it right away. I thought Montane had taken it."

"Well I don't have it now," George said worriedly. "Where the devil did it go?"

"Were you really going to kill him?" Vale asked. "I'm not sure I could I have done it, to tell you the truth."

"That's why you hired me."

"Yes," Vale nodded with a wary eye, "but after hearing that bit about your uncle, I'm beginning to think you planned this instead of me."

"Does it matter either way? I need to find that gun!"

Chapter Thirty-Three

A Funny Thing Happened On the Way to Redemption

A melee is a distracting affair. The sight of a scrum of bodies on the floor is not only fascinating to watch, but nearly impossible to avert one's eyes from. Those not involved in Wavel and Fanny's wrestling match, sat silently as spectators. Even George Sherman and Martin Vale had given up the search for the gun and stood staring at the pile of inhumanity.

And so, no one saw two men enter the room. No one knew they were there until they heard the laughter; a cold, hard laughter.

"Am I invited to the party?"

The pile froze as if by magic. David Wayne tried to stand but Montane reached out a hand and stopped him.

"Hello, Lear." Montane stared at the 9mm gun held firmly in Lear's hand.

Lear had the gun trained on Montane. Othello loomed beside him brandishing his knife. Lear signaled to Othello, who walked across the room and put a hand on Alice's shoulder.

"Now let's remember who gets hurt, Montane. If you make any foolish moves, that girl dies. And what a waste that would be, eh?"

"You're the one with the foolish moves, Lear." Montane rose from his table.

"You need to catch up on current events. Your trained ape Matvie is dead. So's your lackey Hamlet." Lear looked down at his sweater and wiped at the stained material. "He sure did bleed a lot."

Montane's eyes narrowed as he tried to make sense of

what Lear was saying. He kept calm, but could see that his plans had fallen completely apart. He knew he was not the only one in danger. What he did at that moment would determine the fate of everyone on board.

"What do you want, Lear?"

"You, and the girl. I wouldn't give a dollar for these other idiots." He backed to the door and pulled it open. "Now, you come out here with me. And Othello, you take her with you out through the galley."

Othello was close to the galley door. Pulling Alice with him, he backed into the swinging door and pushed it open. As Montane stepped out the dining room entrance with Lear, Othello and Alice disappeared from view. The swinging door swayed slowly to a stop.

David jumped up from his chair and crossed to the door which Lear had pulled shut. David put his ear against it. He dared not open it. He could not risk Alice's life.

"We have to do something," Captain Sloe stood beside him.

"We can pray," David said. At that moment, he did not think the suggestion sounded very hopeful.

Othello still had his back to the galley as the door swung closed. He was completely unprepared to feel the barrel of a revolver press against his temple.

"Drop the knife, and let go of the lady."

Othello had no intention of killing the girl. He had only been following Lear's instructions. He readily complied and let the knife drop to the galley floor. Alice felt him release her and turned to look into the face of her deliverer.

She was shocked to see Tom standing bravely with revolver in hand.

"Get away from him, Alice." Tom said urgently. "He's a killer."

"Tom! You're alive!" She stood still with shock.

"Get away from him!" Tom pulled the hammer back on the revolver and nervously bit his lip. "Don't move, Pirate. I may only be a porter, but I won't hesitate to shoot you."

"Tom, don't." Alice spoke softly, "don't shoot him."

"Alice, get back. This man is dangerous. And why shouldn't I shoot him? I just heard him admit a few minutes ago that he killed one of us. It must have been Mr. Alum."

Alice turned her eyes on Othello, who stood silently with his hands at his side. She looked into his eyes and Othello felt as if her pure eyes pierced his very soul.

"It's true." Othello felt an unfamiliar rush of pain and fear. The moment of Barry Alum's death washed over him, overwhelming him with horror and regret. "I did kill him. I did not mean…"

"You see, Alice? Get back!" He too stepped back as he gripped the gun with both hands.

"No, Tom." Alice slipped between Tom and Othello and put a hand on the gun. Tom lowered it reluctantly. "You must not kill him."

Othello had never seen anything like that before. And he had never before felt so broken inside.

"But he might have murdered you, too." Tom felt his anger and fear melting in the presence of Alice's loveliness.

"But he didn't, thanks to you: my hero."

Tom realized he was still acting as her servant; this time he took pride in his role. He would always be there to serve her.

Lear did not wait for Othello. He followed Montane up the stairs and out onto the deck, keeping a few paces back from his captain. He could not risk allowing Montane to make a grab for the gun.

"You said that Matvie was dead?" Montane looked around the empty deck. "I wish you hadn't killed him. He was a loyal man. A good man."

"I didn't kill him. But he is dead. And I hope he rots in hell for killing my brother."

"We may all rot in hell, Lear." Montane made no attempt to grab the gun. He appeared to have given in to his fate, leaning back on the bulward rail and sinking his hands in his pockets. "Don't you get it?"

"I don't care about your soul, Montane. I just want to

take your crew and your sub. I don't hate you. I just want you out of the way."

"I was trying to get out of the way."

"But you weren't going to give me the reins. If only you had, Hamlet would be alive right now."

Montane looked up at Lear with hardness in his eyes. "Hamlet was a better man than you. He certainly would never have raped any young girls."

"So I raped a girl. What does it matter to you?" Lear shrugged at the accusation.

"Hamlet would have made a better captain than you could have ever dreamed of being. Now, why don't you put that gun to my head and pull the trigger?"

Montane leaned towards Lear. Lear was on his guard and stepped back as he raised the gun. Without warning, the bone handle of a knife crashed hard into Lear's temple and he crumpled to the deck.

"Thank you, my friend." Montane reached out a hand.

"No, no. It is nothing. I was only trying to impress that saucy Mrs. Claire." Maurice took Montane's hand and shook it. "You did a nice job of distracting him. Only, you should not use your head as a target, I think."

"Maybe not. Is Matvie really dead?"

"Did he tell you that?" Maurice kicked at Lear's body. "He may be speaking the truth. I have searched the boat and cannot find him."

"I have to try to keep that girl from harm." Montane bent down and picked up Lear's gun.

"I will take care of this one." Maurice stared at Lear with sad eyes. "He did not use to be so very bad. It is sad. Captain, is Mrs. Claire in danger?"

"No, the young girl. Othello has her."

"Othello? Do not worry about him. Tell him Lear is no longer a threat. He is no mutineer. He only wants to keep everyone alive."

"He's got a funny way of showing it."

"Yes," Maurice said as Montane walked away. "Yes, I suppose he does."

The ladies trembled when Othello walked back through the galley door. The men were surprised when Alice walked in behind him, and shocked when Tom came through the door clutching the revolver.

"Good lord, you're alive!" Captain Sloe beamed.

"Wasn't he dead?" asked Mrs. Kaufman.

"Tom! Where've you been?" Never, though happy to see his bunk mate, eyed him indignantly. "I searched this entire boat for you."

"I know you did. You nearly found me, too. You weren't too thorough checking out the storage in the smoke stack."

"You were in there all the time?"

"Yes. I'm surprised you all couldn't hear me howling my head off during that storm. I was flopping around in there like a fish in an empty bucket. I'll be bruised for six months."

"Whatever were you hiding for?" asked Captain Sloe.

"This one here," Tom indicated Othello, "was chasing me for that crazy pirate. I'd caught wind of their plan to harm Alice. My only hope was to stay out of sight. I didn't want to end up like Barry Alum. Not that I knew then what had happened to poor Mr. Alum."

"What did happen to him?" someone asked.

"Othello here confessed to killing him. He says it was an accident or something. I don't believe that part too much."

"I do," added Alice.

"At any rate, I've placed him under arrest. We can take him to the police."

"Yes, Tom," Captain Sloe pointed to the revolver, "but you had better uncock that hammer before you accidentally kill someone yourself."

"Oh, yeah, sorry about that."

"For pity's sake, he can't kill someone with that." Ida scoffed at the notion.

"Just what do you mean by that?" Never stared at her as if she had just announced she was the Queen of England.

"I mean this." She rummaged in her purse and pulled out a handful of bullets. "I took these out of Mr. Sherman's gun yesterday. It's perfectly harmless."

"Mrs. Claire!" Captain Sloe scolded her as he shot a wary look at Othello. George stared incredulously at the old woman.

"Did you have to say that out loud?" Tom complained. His hand shook as he continued to point the gun at the big pirate.

"There's nothing to worry about, is there, Othello?" Alice spoke softly to the contrite killer.

"No ma'am. I won't cause trouble. Not anymore."

"Now see here," Captain Sloe spoke to Ida, "what is this about removing bullets?"

"I knew he was up to no good. Maurice told me all about him. He was once a pirate like the rest of them."

"Who's Maurice?" asked Never.

"A friend of mine," she answered. "As I said, he warned me about this wolf in the fold. I kept an eye on him. Yesterday, he removed his jacket for breakfast. When he and the captain went in search of Tom, I happened to find the gun. It was a simple matter to remove the bullets. I tried to tell you captain that no one would be hurt."

Captain Sloe retrieved the revolver from Tom and opened his hand as Ida dropped the bullets. He methodically loaded the gun and looked over the room.

"Mr. Sherman, I'm afraid I will have to place you under arrest. If you'll just please move over next to Mr. Othello there."

"What about Mr. Odston?" Never suggested. "Shouldn't we arrest him, too?"

"Mr. Odston hasn't committed any crime, have you, Mr. Odston?" Captain Sloe smiled at Never's idea.

"Not committed a crime?" Never asked.

"A man can't steal his own property."

"It's not his property!" Fanny was sitting in a chair a good distance from her husband, where she had been forced by the captain and Never Gamble. "There're mine! He's a thief!"

As George followed the captain's orders to sit next to Othello, he passed Cora Vale. She looked up at him and he stopped to meet her gaze.

"Sorry, Cora."

"I am, too. It seems Marty has a talent for messing up my life."

"Maybe he does, but this one's my fault. I never lied to you. You are a wonderful and beautiful woman. Don't forget that." He wanted to say more, but he did not want to make matters worse for her. Martin had seen them talking and he came closer in order to hear what was being said.

"Goodbye, George." Cora lowered her head and said no more.

Captain Sloe handed the gun back to Tom.

"You've proven yourself, young man. Why don't you stay here with Never and keep an eye on these two. I'm going to go see if there is any way to help Captain Montane."

"Captain, do you think that's wise?" Wavel Odston cautioned him. "You shouldn't put yourself in danger like that."

"I doubt very much I'll be alone." Captain Sloe turned and looked at David Wayne.

"You won't be," David was still at the door. He pulled it open. "I'm going with you."

"I was sure you wouldn't let me leave you behind."

They ran into Montane as he came down the aft stairs.

"What are you two up to?" Montane asked.

"I'm afraid we're your rescue squad," Captain Sloe said apologetically. "But you don't seem to need one."

"I did, and one showed up. Where are Othello and the girl?"

"Alice is safe and sound," Captain Sloe reported happily. "Your man is under arrest."

"Tom arrested him," David said. Montane's questioning look prompted David to add "yes, Tom's the porter that you were sure Lear had killed."

"Wrong once again, huh?" Montane turned and led them out onto deck. He pulled a small radio from his pocket and squeezed the transmit button. "Come in, *Prowler*, are you receiving me?"

There was no answer.

"Old Man, where's the Kid? You don't think Lear—"

"If I know that Kid, I think I'll know right where to find him. He should be sound asleep right where I left him."

"Go get him," Montane ordered. "Captain? Should I be so bold as to ask you to allow me to leave without a fight?"

"I'm going to keep your man Othello. He's confessed to killing Barry Alum."

"Then keep this one, too." Montane looked down at Lear. He was still unconscious. "He's admitted to raping the girl. I don't know if you can make that stick or not in court. But I'm sure he'll give the police plenty to work with. He never could keep his mouth shut."

Again, Montane put the radio to his mouth and called the *Prowler*.

"I thought you told me all radio transmissions were being blocked?" Captain Sloe reminded him.

"Well, you know Captain, I kind of lied about that. I'm sorry. Do you think you could forgive me?"

"That's something I can do." Captain Sloe smiled. "I hope you find what you are looking for."

The two captains shook hands.

Montane, this is the Prowler. Is that you, Captain?

"Where are you guys?" Montane scanned the horizon, looking for his boat.

Right under you, sir. We'll surface off the port bow.

"I must get back to my passengers." Captain Sloe nodded at David Wayne and Montane and returned below deck.

"I don't guess you want to join me," Montane smiled at his joke.

"You couldn't drag me back on that sub. Well, I guess you could. You did once already."

"I thought you were real big into that forgive and forget thing. You gotta let that go."

"Look," David turned serious, "I've very sorry about—"

"You can't apologize, David. You haven't done anything wrong. I've been wrong from the very beginning of this thing. My pride was demanding something I couldn't get."

"Something you didn't need," David added.

"I'm the one who needs to say I'm sorry. This girl Elise, I had no idea—"

"That's okay. I forgave you for it. It wasn't important that you knew." David watched as the water began to stir off the port bow. He could think of nothing more to say as he watched the *Prowler* arise from the sea, its inky black form shedding the water from its tower and hull as if it were climbing out of a grave and letting the dirt fall back to the ground.

"I may have to call you one night. I still have your number."

"Great," David rolled his eyes. "As long as you don't kidnap me again."

"Let it go, David. Don't be bitter."

The two men laughed. It was only for a moment. But for that moment it was a chance to breathe deeply and share more than verbal forgiveness.

They stood together, watching the sub run alongside and the crew prepare to lay out the gangway. David could feel that the distance that had come between them was greatly diminished, though it would forever be there in some measure.

As the gangway was laid down, Maurice came up on deck with the Kid.

"Captain, I need to speak with you before you leave." The Frenchman wore a mischievous expression.

"Before *I* leave? That sounds suspiciously like you are contemplating desertion."

"Well," Maurice reached up and scratched the side of his wrinkled face and shuffled his feet, "I did not think you would allow me to kidnap the lovely Mrs. Claire. Yes?"

"Yes, I would not allow you to kidnap the lovely Mrs. Claire." Montane had trouble with the Frenchman's choice of adjectives.

"Yes, yes. I know this. And so, what am I to do? I am in love. *L'amour, l'amour,* what can one do, huh?"

"You can find out if she feels the same," Montane cocked his head to the side quizzically. "You really like her?"

"Ho Ho. *Oui,* she is – wonderful—well you see her. You

know what I mean."

"Not really, Old Man."

"Maurice. Call me Maurice. That is something she taught me." He stood up straight and assumed a dignified expression. "I am not just an old man. No, no. I am Maurice Baptiste! A man of great value and honor."

"She taught you that?" Montane winked at David. He stretched out his hand and shook Maurice's hand. "You'd better try to keep her then. Someone like that in your life is invaluable. Goodbye Maurice Baptiste. You keeping the Kid too?"

"He is no good as a pirate," Maurice shook his head and made a face. "Always sleeping. I'll take him and find him a good job where he can sleep and not get himself in trouble. Maybe cab driver or something, huh?"

"Goodbye David Wayne." Montane shook David's hand as well. "Maybe I'll show up in Cleveland and turn myself in to your fine police department."

"And maybe I'll never hear from you again."

"I hope not."

"Me too. Don't give up on your soul. Neither God nor I will. You don't need anyone's forgiveness but God's. But just for a bonus, you can count on mine."

Chapter Thirty-Four

The Jenny Gives Up Her Fools

"Wavel, you are such an idiot. All you had to do was tell me we were broke."

"And you would have understood, Pumpkin? Is that what you want me to think? You would have been happy with a bankrupt husband?"

"Of course not!" Fanny smacked Wavel with her gloved hand. "I would have quit making a fuss over the stolen jewelry and we could have collected the insurance money. Jeez, Wavel. You let a golden opportunity slip away. We were boarded by pirates, for Pete's sake. No one would have disputed our claim. We could have collected the insurance money and I still would have had mother's jewelry. You must be out of your mind."

"I think you might have something there, dearest one." Wavel watched their bags being unloaded from the yacht. "I may actually be out of my mind. At this very moment I'm wishing like mad that those pirates would have—"

"Would have what, Wavel?" Fanny stared him down.

"Would have kidnapped me and held me for ransom."

"You just said we were broke."

"I know. That's what I've been wishing."

"You really are out of your mind."

Not twenty feet away, another couple was communicating in much the same spirit.

"Marty," Cora Vale sat in the back seat of a luxury sedan, waiting while their driver loaded their bags into the trunk, "are you trying to tell me that you were certain pirates would attack this yacht and yet you allowed me to come on this cruise?"

"When have I ever been able to tell you when you can and can't go anywhere?"

"When have you ever tried to ask politely? Were you hoping I'd be murdered?"

"I certainly wasn't hoping you'd fall in love." Martin Vale was sure he had scored a point with that remark.

"I didn't fall in love, Marty. I was in love before this." Cora spoke without the usual edge in her voice.

"I knew it. Who is he? Or were you talking about the bottle?"

"I was talking about you."

Martin turned in the seat and looked at his wife.

Cora did not look at him. She stared out the window at the other passengers disembarking. She watched Ida Claire step off the gangway.

"I do not know what gave you this crazy idea, Maurice. I'm sure I never gave you reason to believe we would be anything more than friends. Now come along, Erma. Don't bother with Mr. Baptiste."

"Isn't he coming with us?" asked Mrs. Kaufman.

"He certainly is not," Ida adjusted the black felt hat on her head and straightened the lace veil. "Presumptuous French!"

"I can only admit," Maurice confessed, "that if I was presumptuous, it was from the wellspring of love that gushes out of me."

"There'll be no such gushing, do you hear me, Mr. Baptiste? Not if you plan to be around my sister and me for any length of time."

"Ho Ho, so you see? No more—shoo, shoo—yes? Now it is 'if I plan to be around', yes? Well, I can tell you, I plan to be around for a very long and pleasurable time."

"Really, Mr. Baptiste," Ida scowled. "You do insist on saying the most immoral and obscene things."

"I do, I do. I insist on it."

Never Gamble stood on the deck of *The Jenny* and watched the passengers as they made their way to their waiting cars. He had never completely relaxed until Othello, George Sherman, and the man called Lear were safely in police custody. Now, as the police drove out of sight, he sighed heavily. There was one last worry on his mind. He watched with impatience, making sure Fanny Odston and Ida Claire climbed into their cars and were indeed being driven away from the docks.

"What a pleasant end to a nightmare," he said softly.

"It has been rough," conceded Captain Sloe. "But for the regretful loss of Mr. Alum, we very nearly came through unscathed. I'm sure it could have been much worse. If not for the brave work of Tom. I shudder to think of what might have happened to young Alice."

"I shudder to think what could have happened to me," Never whimpered.

"Now, now, Mr. Gamble. You've come through it all safe enough. Don't let's dwell on unpleasantries. And here comes Miss Alice now. I hope you're not leaving us for good, young lady."

Alice came out on deck dressed in slacks and a soft blouse. She wore a red jacket over the blouse.

"I'll be back, Captain. I just have a short trip to take. Tom has agreed to give me a hand." She leaned forward and kissed the Captain on his beard. "Thank you for your extra attention, but really I'm fine. Keep Never out of trouble."

Like a brisk ocean breeze she left the yacht.

Tom came up on deck as she descended the gangway, carrying her bags.

"Still playing the butler for her," Never teased. "I told you you'll never get anywhere like that."

"I'm not so sure of that, Never." Captain Sloe nodded towards the red jacket draped over Alice's shoulders. "Isn't that your porter's jacket, Tom?"

"Yes, sir," Tom blushed. "She thought there was a chill this morning. I only offered because she had already packed hers. Sorry about that."

"Nothing to be sorry about. What was this she said about you agreeing to give her a hand?" asked Captain Sloe.

"Is that what she said?" Tom gave it some thought. "I guess you can put it that way. All I know is she wanted me to accompany her to her mom and dad's house. Said she wants me to meet them."

"You see, that's a step in the right direction, don't you think, Never?"

"Yes, Captain." Never sulked as he watched Tom catch up with Alice. "I've got things to do. I'll be below deck. Excuse me, Mr. Wayne."

David Wayne came on deck as Never slipped by him and headed down the stairs.

"All ready to get back to Cleveland?" Captain Sloe slapped him on the back.

"I guess so. There's no one there waiting for me or anything. But I'm ready to get home anyway."

"Your cab arrived a few minutes ago. Don't worry about the fare. Mr. Vale's picking that up for you."

"Tell him 'thank you' for me."

"No reason to do that. He'd have no idea what I was talking about. I'll walk you down."

The Captain allowed David to descend the gangway then followed close behind.

"I thought I should tell you, David, I admire what you tried to do."

"And what was that?" David asked.

"You tried to show these people who they really were. We've all got our sins that need forgiving. None of us are flawless."

"You might have held up under scrutiny," David said.

"Oh, you'd be surprised. I might not have after all. Prerogative of the court, you know. My secrets are safe behind my judge's robes."

"Mine aren't. They're right out where everyone could see them. I think I somehow became an accessory to piracy."

"No," Captain Sloe shook his head, "you're no pirate. You did do something very wrong, though."

"And that was?"

"You made a man believe that he could not only change, but that the people around him could change as well. You gave him hope that men would be honest with themselves and turn to him with mercy and compassion rather than self-righteousness. That's a grave mistake."

"I was a fool to believe it."

"And I hope you never stop believing it. Just be careful who you pass that hope on to. Hey, the verdict was 'forgiven'. You won."

"No, I don't think so. This was a mess from the beginning. Some kind of farce that got out of hand."

"That might be an appropriate way to describe life. For many of us, anyway." Captain Sloe opened the door of the cab and held out his hand.

"Thank you for everything, Captain." They shook hands.

"It's been refreshing to meet you, David Wayne. Godspeed."

The Captain watched as the cab pulled away from the docks. He stood staring at the diminishing yellow car until it turned out of sight. He was sorry to see the young man from Cleveland go.

But he was happy to get back to *The Jenny*. He stood inspecting her from the dock. She was a little battered, but all in all she had come through the storm magnificently. He smiled as he looked her over from bow to stern. She was a beauty. He climbed the short gangway and patted her rail as he stepped onto her deck. There was much to do to repair her and return her to her former glory. But he had plenty of time for that.

The End

About the Author:

Jason Phillip Reeser lives and writes in Louisiana. His short stories have appeared in such publications as *The Louisiana Review*, *Bewildering Stories*, and *Danse Macabre*. His novelette *The World that Slid Downhill* is available on Kindle. If you would like to contact him, you may do so at **rocketfirebooks.com**. He welcomes comments of any kind.

visit Rocket Fire Books at
rocketfirebooks.com

Turn the page for news on upcoming books.

www.ingramcontent.com/pod-product-compliance
Lightning Source LLC
Chambersburg PA
CBHW030913120626
46554CB00001B/132

* 9 7 8 0 6 1 5 5 9 3 2 8 9 *